NO PLACE LIKE HOME

JANE RENSHAW

INKUBATOR
BOOKS

PROLOGUE

They had wrapped nylon twine around his wrists and then around his ankles to hog-tie him, so he couldn't do anything, he couldn't use his arms or legs to brace himself as the van swerved, rolling him around like a pinball, flinging him against its metal sides. And every time he slid across the floor he slid, naked, through the rotting vegetables and pig shit they'd got from somewhere and piled in the middle of the otherwise empty space. There was shit on his face. In his eyes.

He could hear them in the cab, laughing.

And then one of them shouting: 'You okay back there, Owen?'

He tried to shout back through the gag, over the whine of the engine: '*Please! Please, let me out of here!*'

And maybe they'd heard him, maybe they thought they'd made their point, because suddenly the van braked and there was nothing he could do to stop himself flying forward and crashing into the divider panel between the cab and the back of the van, his head cracking off it.

The next thing he knew there was cool air on his bare skin and one of them was saying, 'Here we are. Out you come.'

He managed to open his eyes. He could see one of them, silhouetted against the bright white light of a torch moving in the dark beyond the open rear doors. He could see them as they jumped up into the van, hear them complain, raucously, about the stink. He tried to wriggle away, to slide himself around so his back was turned to them.

What the hell were they doing?

They were tying more twine around his ankles. More twine around his wrists. He could smell strong aftershave, cutting through the stench of pig shit. And then, in the gloom, there was the flash of a knife, and the original twine that had tied his wrists to his ankles had been sliced away so that now, thank Christ, he could straighten his body, but before the relief of it had transmitted from his muscles to his brain he was being hauled by rough hands, dragged across the floor, through the shit and out into the cold air and he was falling, his face was smacking on tarmac, and pain was screaming through his head.

His nose had bust.

There was blood in his nose, in his throat.

He was screaming, he was trying to scream but then he was just trying to breathe, *he couldn't breathe*, he was choking on the blood-soaked gag, trying to heave in just *one breath* –

'Oops-a-daisy.'

The gag was whipped away and he could breathe, but he didn't scream. All he could do was sob. All he could do was gasp. All he could do was repeat, over and over: '*Thank you. I'm sorry. I'm sorry. I'm sorry!*'

One of them grabbed his legs and one his shoulders

and they lifted him, and the torch went out but there was a bright harvest moon, and for the first time he could see where they were. In the wash of moonlight, he could see that they were parked up against the bollards that closed off the Old Bridge of Spey. The bridge was closed to traffic because a structure built in 1754 for carts and wagons and marching soldiers wasn't up to carrying modern traffic. He knew it was built in 1754 because he was into that stuff, he was into military history, he knew all about the network of military roads and bridges constructed to pacify the Highlands after the Jacobite Rebellion. Bonnie Prince Charlie and all that.

They carried him, quickly, half-running, through the bollards and up onto the hump of the old bridge.

'Aw, no!' he sobbed through the blood. '*Christ, please, no!*'

He had wet himself.

'*Up* we go,' said a cheerful voice. '*Up* and over!'

They dropped him.

And then his back exploded in pain, and *thank God*, they'd dropped him not over the edge but onto the stone parapet, and he was squirming away from them, he was begging: '*Please… Please!*'

They were laughing.

The bastards.

The absolute bastards.

But he was laughing too, weakly, hysterically. They weren't going to drop him over the bridge into the water below, into the River Spey, into that swift-flowing mass of water he could hear roaring under the bridge and away. They weren't going to kill him. All they were doing was putting the fear of God into him.

'I'm sorry,' he choked. 'I'll go. I'll go and I won't come back.'

'You've got that right.'

And now they were manhandling him again, flipping him onto his stomach, his head and shoulders out over the edge of the parapet so he could see the black water moving below, black touched with silver where the moonlight caught the churned-up surface as it roiled and swirled its way past the massive stone supports of the bridge. There had been rain. There had been a lot of rain in the last two days, and the river was swollen with it.

He tried to find a purchase with his hands, with his fingertips, on the rough wet stone of the parapet. He tried to cling on as his legs were hauled up over his head but he couldn't, he couldn't get a proper hold, and then his fingertips were ripped away and he was tipping right over and past the edge of the parapet until he was dangling, blood dripping off his face and down, down onto the roiling black water.

'*Don't let go! Don't let go!*' he shrieked.

As the hands holding his ankles released him and he fell, he heard her, up on the bridge, he heard her shout his name:

'*Owen!*'

1

'Nooooo! Dad, tell her she can't!' Max staggered back against the worktop, as if the shock of seeing the ingredients Phoebe had assembled on the table had sent him reeling. 'Please, you have to assert some sort of control here.'

'I'm *out of control*!' Phoebe shouted happily, dancing across the kitchen waving a wooden spoon in each hand, the oversized *Bake Off* apron impeding the execution of the moves she was attempting.

Bram saw it happen as if in slow motion: Phoebe's ill-conceived decision to go for a high kick; the long apron catching at her legs; the inevitable fall to the unforgiving Caithness slate floor, on which her nine-year-old skull would crack like an egg.

He shot across the kitchen, his dad-bod physique transformed into that of a superhero, leg muscles powering him into position, arms flying out with supernatural speed to catch her as she fell.

'Oof! Thanks, Dad!' She clutched at his shirt as he righted her, smiling up at him as if he really were her superhero.

He held on to her a moment before letting her go. 'Careful, Phoebs. It's a kitchen, not a dance floor. You shouldn't really be messing about in here.'

Maybe slate flooring hadn't been such a great choice for the kitchen after all.

'They mess about on *Bake Off* all the time,' Phoebe objected, the wooden spoons now drooping in her hands, her big blue eyes fixed on Bram reproachfully. Unless he was careful, they'd be streaming with tears in a second. Phoebe's moods were mercurial things, will-o'-the-wisps, giddy flames that flared and were gone.

Bram swept her up in his arms, making her squeal like a much younger child as he set her down on the table next to her chosen ingredients. Max had picked up the jar of jam.

Phoebe snatched it back. 'Peanut butter and jam is a classic combination.'

'Not in a quiche!'

'You're not the boss of me, Max.' Her brother may have been nine years older than Phoebe, but she had never let the age difference carry much weight. 'Each competitor gets to choose her or his own ingredients. Don't they, Dad?'

Bram grimaced a concession. 'Them's the rules, I guess.'

'But we can't make Grannie and Grandad and Uncle Fraser and Mum eat a *peanut butter and raspberry jam quiche*,' Max wailed, the wail turning into a chortle as the two of them gave themselves up to mirth.

Bram smiled as he opened the oven door. 'Okay, Phoebs, you have the time it takes to blind-bake the cases to ponder the wisdom of your choices.'

The three pastry cases were lined up ready to go into the oven. Phoebe's effort was already looking extremely unappetising, sweaty-looking and grey. Max's pastry, in contrast, was so perfect it looked like the bought stuff, neatly pressed into the wavy edge of the quiche tin and overlapping the edges just the right amount to allow for shrinkage.

When had this happened? When had Max become someone who made perfect pastry? Almost while Bram wasn't looking, their little boy had grown up. Up, up and away. After this last year of school he'd be off out into the world on his gap year – which absolutely terrified Bram, no matter how much Kirsty tried to reassure him that Max was a sensible boy and would be perfectly fine constructing a school with no proper training under the supervision of a load of randoms a hundred miles from the nearest hospital in the Rwandan bush, surrounded on all sides by Gaboon vipers, spitting cobras and black mambas, an encounter with any one of which could prove fatal. Kirsty had banned Bram from Googling snakes, but that only meant he'd moved on to spiders – and they were worse, if anything, being so much less visible.

He shoved the three pastry cases into the oven and threw an arm around Max's shoulders, trying and failing not to choke up. He'd really missed Max these last two months. After selling the flat in Islington, Bram, Kirsty and Phoebe had moved straight up to Scotland to live temporarily with Kirsty's parents until the new house was finished, but Max had stayed on with Bram's parents in London to finish the school year, with just the odd weekend trip up to Scotland.

'I'm relying on you to contain the force of nature that is your sister until I get back, okay? I'm going to the veg patch to harvest some onions.'

Bram had planted onions, leeks, carrots, lettuce and chard in late spring and tended them religiously on every visit to the new house. Today, hopefully, they could all enjoy the fruits of his labours.

'We'll try not to burn the place down in your absence,' said Max, pushing his floppy dark fringe to the side, the better to scrutinise the oven temperature. He was taller than Bram now, and fortunately blessed with Kirsty's looks rather than Bram's: her straight brows and soulful green eyes.

'That would be good.'

Phoebe laughed. 'Grandad wouldn't be happy if we burned the house down on our first day in the new kitchen!'

'I don't imagine he'd be best pleased, no.' Bram looked beyond the big antique pine table to the open-plan sitting area situated between the kitchen and the front door. Kirsty and her dad, David, who had built the house for them, had based this open-plan space on the Walton house – Kirsty had been obsessed with the TV show *The Waltons* as a child – with two windows either side of the door looking onto a verandah. There was a solid fuel-burning stove and even a radio cunningly disguised to look like an old-fashioned wireless.

In an hour's time David would be coming through that door, a compact, muscly bundle of contained energy, nose twitching, on the hunt for something to criticise. David and Linda, Kirsty's mum, lived in an 'executive bungalow' four miles away in Grantown-on-Spey. Bram had hoped that four miles out of town was far enough that David wouldn't be popping in all the time, but here they were, on their first day in residence, and David, Linda and Kirsty's brother, Fraser, were somehow coming to lunch.

How had that happened?

He ran a hand along the wooden worktop. David was an old-school builder who considered eco-friendly materials the work of the devil and had been appalled at the idea of using reclaimed wood in the kitchen, but had had to admit that the worktops looked great. 'You'd never know it was reclaimed crap, eh, Bram?' he'd said after his team had installed them.

'Is our house the best house in the world, Max, or what?' Phoebe demanded, whirling round on the spot. Phoebe had shown her brother around yesterday like an estate agent trying to sell the place to a potential purchaser. 'I'm never going to live anywhere else but here!'

Bram and Max exchanged indulgent looks. Phoebe, like Bram, was a real homebody, and had been desperate to move into *our house*, even though living at Grannie and Grandad's meant she could play with Lily, Rhona and Katie Miller whenever she liked. The Miller sisters, Phoebe's best friends, lived across the street from Linda and David, and Phoebe had got to know them well during all the holidays they'd spent up here. Back in London, Phoebe had somehow got off on the wrong foot with the girls in her class – Bram had never got to the bottom of the reason for this – and had had to deal with a certain amount of nastiness and bullying. When the decision to move up here had been made, Phoebe had immediately exclaimed: 'I can be in Rhona's class!' and burst into happy tears.

'Watch those quiche cases,' Bram instructed, heading across the kitchen to the door to the Room with a View, as David called it. He'd better check that everything was okay in there. David was bound to head straight for it.

He had to admit that David had been right to insist on an expanse of glass for the long end wall, the middle sections of which were sliding doors giving onto a terrace. Every room in the house had a lovely view – how could it not, in such an idyllic location? – but this was spectacular. Immediately behind the house was the paddock, where they hoped to keep goats, and beyond that another small field and, off to the left, the wood of pine and birch and beech trees that *actually belonged to them* – how amazing was it to actually own a wood? Was it deeply un-PC of him to be gloating about this? And just in front of the wood there was a stream, with a cute little footbridge carrying a Hansel and Gretel path across it, perfect for Phoebe's interminable games of Pooh sticks.

So much for his egalitarian principles. Dangle fourteen areas of idyllic Scottish countryside in front of Bram Hendriksen and it seemed his inner Tory would bite your hand off.

The ground beyond the field dipped down and then slowly rose, providing a panorama of forests and fields and farmhouses and, as a backdrop to it all, the hazy bulks of the Grampian Mountains. On this perfect midsummer day, it was a glorious, impossibly lush patchwork of greens and purples and blues.

Yeah.

Oh, yeah.

They'd done the right thing.

He missed his London friends like crazy, but this was a little piece of Scottish heaven. It was going to be amazing, living here with nature all around them – none of which, barring the very slim possibility of adders, had the potential to be fatal.

He straightened a picture, picked up some loose thread from the carpet and rearranged the fossils on the big fire surround made from old ship's timbers. He defied even David to find fault with this room. Their honey-coloured linen sofas, which had looked oversized in the Islington flat, were perfect here, and Bram had found vintage fabric online with which he'd made fresh covers for their collection of cushions. Which were looking a bit squashed from the four of them collapsing on the sofas last night at the end of the hectic moving-in day.

He picked up an orange and white cushion and plumped it, and set it back on the sofa in its proper place. But as he reached for a green and blue one, he stopped.

What was he doing?

Why was he pandering to the man? This was their home, not a show house, and if the cushions were flat, David would just have to suck it up. In a childish act of defiance, Bram grabbed the orange and white cushion and chucked it down on the sofa and sat on it, bouncing a couple of times to make sure it was completely de-plumped.

Starting as he meant to go on.

He stood without looking at the cushions again – because he wanted to plump those bloody cushions! – and opened the sliding doors. On the terrace, he took his phone from his pocket to capture the view. He'd do a blog post tonight about their first day in the new house, in Woodside, as they had called it.

The air was so clean, scented with pine resin, and as he walked round the side of the house and past the shed, he breathed it into his lungs. *Thanks, Bram*, his lungs were probably saying. *You've almost forty years of London pollution to make up for, but it's a start.* He chuckled, imagining what David would say if he knew Bram's lungs were talking to him.

His smile widened as he spotted Henrietta, the carved wooden goose from his childhood, positioned by Phoebe in a little drift of wildflowers – were they some kind of buttercup? He took a photo for the blog. He'd get a shot of the veg patch too. Or maybe a video of his hand picking the first onion? He switched to video function, angling the phone to get a long-range shot of the veg patch, and started walking again.

'So,' he narrated. 'First day in Woodside and it's time to pick some onions! Yep, Bram's much-derided self-sufficiency drive is finally paying off. Let's harvest those suckers! Let's–'

He stopped, looking from the screen of the phone to the actual ground.

'Oh, no! No no no!'

Where the veg patch should be there was just a rectangle of earth covered in shrivelled, dry, yellowing stalks and flopped-over leaves. Stupidly, he looked around for a moment, as if the real veg patch might be somewhere else, before dropping to his knees and examining the nearest plants, a row of Salad Bowl lettuces. They had been succulent lime green and deep purple last time he'd been here but were now a uniform gungy brown, the lower leaves stuck gummily to the soil, already half-decomposed.

Bloody Nora, as Kirsty's mum would say.

Everything was dead.

Okay so he'd not checked the veg for a few days – he'd been too distracted with the move – and they'd had a very sunny, dry spell. But this was Scotland. Surely it hadn't been hot enough to kill them? He touched the soil. The top layer was crumbly, powdery between his thumb and forefinger, but when he poked his finger down a few centimetres he hit dampish earth.

He stepped across the row of ex-lettuces to examine the other vegetables. The carrot shaws were withered and papery, but when he pulled up a carrot – a puny specimen at this time of year – it looked more or less okay. But if they'd been hit by some kind of blight, it probably wouldn't be a good idea to eat any of it.

The onions were just starting to fill out, too, the bulbs that were peeping up from the soil fattening nicely. It would have been satisfying to have a few home-grown onions, no matter how small, for their first lunch in the new house.

Oh, well. He supposed these things happened. He wasn't exactly an expert gardener, but he had grown chillies and peppers and courgettes in their tiny London garden, successfully enough to generate a surplus which he'd proudly offered to the neighbours.

He brushed the soil off his fingers and tapped his phone to start a new video, panning over the dead lettuces. 'The question I should probably be asking myself is: am I a fit person to have custody of vegetables? I feel like some sort of ban should be slapped on me.' He zoomed in on the pathetic carrot he'd left lying on the soil. 'Prohibiting the growing of vegetables for, say, five or ten years.'

He cut the video and pocketed his phone. At least the blog post tonight would be a bit more interesting than usual. A bit more entertaining. He lifted his face as the sun appeared from behind a fluffy white cloud.

And at the exact same moment, somebody screamed.

Phoebe!

He was off and running before the echo from the trees had died away, past the terrace, round the house, and then he could see them, Phoebe and Max, and *thank God, thank God*, neither of them was hurt, they didn't look hurt – Phoebe was running across the grass after Max, who was pelting towards the whirly drier, where something, a black cloth, was catching the breeze, flapping as the whirly turned –

It wasn't a black cloth.

It was a bird.

A crow. Tangled in the whirly, wings flapping.

But before Max reached it, Bram could see that the wings were only flapping because the whirly was spinning round, that the bird was dead, the wind catching its wings, seeming to reanimate it.

'*Daaaad!* He's caught his feet!' Phoebe wailed as he ran past her. 'You have to *help him!*'

Max had reached the whirly and stopped it with his hands. He stood staring at the bird, now hanging, obviously dead, wings spread in a cruel parody of flight.

'Okay, Max,' said Bram, gently pulling the boy away.

His face was white. 'I thought – I thought it was still alive. How did it get here?'

'I don't know. It must have become tangled–' But Bram could see, now, the blue nylon twine around the bird's legs, tying it to the cord.

'Oh God, Dad, did someone – did they tie it on, while it was still alive?'

'*What?*' sobbed Phoebe, suddenly there, suddenly reaching past Max –

'No no.' Bram pulled her away, hugged her to his chest. 'It must have already been dead.'

Phoebe wriggled away from him and reached out a hand to the crow, gently touching one of its wings. 'Are you *sure*?' she wailed. 'Are you *sure* he's dead?'

'Yes. Yes, I'm sure. Come on, *kleintje*. Let's go back inside.'

'What happened to him, Dad?'

He crouched in front of her, wiping the tears from her face. 'I don't know. I'm going to have a look at him and then bury him, okay?'

She gulped, wiping now at her own face. 'A kind of post mortem? Do you think he was – *murdered*?' She turned to look again at the crow, and of course that set her off again, her face collapsing on a sob.

Bram half-carried her back inside, and took her on

his knee for a while as she cried, sitting at the kitchen table while Max busied himself chopping up vegetables for his quiche. When Phoebe was calm again, she said, 'You have to do the post mortem now, Dad, and bury him,' and Max said, 'Come on then, Phoebs, what about this abomination of a quiche filling you're insisting on making?'

'Why would someone do it?' she whispered, looking at Bram as if he had the answers, as if he could explain it, as if he could tell her it was all a mistake and the crow was going to be fine.

But he could only shake his head.

Back out at the whirly, he shrinkingly studied the crow. Its eyes were filmed over and – ugh, yes, something was moving at its neck. Maggots. It must have been dead a while. Just as well he'd brought gloves. He held the dead bird around its middle as he gently untied the nylon twine, talking to it as he did so, ridiculously: 'I'm sorry, mate. I'm sorry.' There was dried blood on the feathers of its chest. It had been shot?

He couldn't get Phoebe's question out of his head:
Why would someone do it?

Not so much shoot the crow – Bram wasn't such a city slicker that he wasn't aware of the war on wildlife waged by many farmers – but bring it here and tie it to their whirly drier?

Why? Why would anyone do that?

2

D avid was manfully eating a large slice of Phoebe's quiche, washed down with frequent gulps of beer, as if it were a bush tucker trial. 'Are you a man or a mouse, Bram?' he chuckled when Bram declined to sample it. Fraser was also shovelling it in, but Linda had surreptitiously fed her portion, against her own *no feeding him at the table* rules, to her guide dog Bertie – who, being a Labrador, had inhaled it gratefully, hardly able to believe his luck.

Phoebe herself was sitting poking at the food on her plate, eyelids swollen and red from the bouts of crying she couldn't seem to stop.

'Aye,' said David, sitting back on his chair. 'Farmers hate crows. Shoot them on sight, and–'

'Do you want another beer?' Bram interrupted. He had told the other adults what had happened and explicitly asked them not to mention it in front of the kids.

'If you insist, Bram, if you insist.' David held out the empty bottle of Potholer as if Bram were a waiter. Bram took the bottle from him, dumped it by the sink and opened the fridge to get another.

'Farmers hate crows with a passion,' David continued. 'You see them strung up on fences all over the place out here – the theory is that crows flying by will think *Oh bloody hell, there's been a massacre down there* and move along to some other bastard's crop.'

'Dad,' murmured Kirsty.

'What?'

'He's right enough,' Fraser put his oar in.

Bram set the fresh bottle of beer at David's place firmly, giving first David and then Fraser a repressive frown. Fraser was bigger and even more muscle-bound than David, but their features were spookily alike, down to the squashed boxer's noses and shaved heads. They always reminded Bram of the Mitchell brothers in *East-Enders*, although he hadn't shared that little nugget with anyone.

Genetics had gone rogue in the McKechnie family – Fraser seemed to have received all David's genes and none of Linda's, and Kirsty vice versa, although Kirsty would probably tell him that wasn't possible.

Both the kids, thank God, also favoured Linda. Her greying hair had once been as dark as theirs and her features were delicate, her sightless eyes a striking green, her nose rather long and very elegant, if a nose could ever be described as such. Linda had been a premature baby, and the extra oxygen she'd received in the incubator had resulted in the retinal blood vessels growing abnormally. Retinopathy of prematurity, her type of blindness was called. Bram thought she was pretty amazing, the way she lived a normal life and had brought up two kids despite not being able to see a thing, not even light and dark, although he'd never come out and said so in case it came across as patronising.

'Phoebe and Max don't want to hear this,' Linda said now.

'Local farmer probably thought he was doing you a favour,' David continued regardless, pushing more quiche onto his fork. 'Keeping them off your vegetables – let's face it, you need all the help you can get.'

Bram had shown them the withered vegetables. A mistake, maybe, but it had been a distraction, he'd thought, from the dead crow. Typical of David to use it now in an attempt to deflect the women's ire. Attack was the best form of defence. But at least it was a change of topic.

'That sort of help we can do without,' said Kirsty, as Bram resumed his seat. 'Bram's green fingers are a bit rusty, that's all.'

Max smiled. 'That's some mixed metaphor, Mum.'

'Mixed metaphor!' David repeated in a silly high voice. 'Someone swallowed a dictionary? That a *metaphor* too, is it?'

It was pathetic, the way David made digs at Max for being a nerd, as if having a super-bright grandson was something to be ashamed of. Bram saw Kirsty tense, and Linda turned her head slightly towards her daughter in what Bram interpreted as a gesture of solidarity but also a plea for forbearance, as if to say *Never mind your father, we all know what he's like, just ignore the idiot*. David pushed everyone's buttons, but particularly Kirsty's, and two months of close proximity seemed not to have done their relationship much good.

Since Max had arrived last week, things had, inevitably, got worse, Max being something of a bone of contention between his parents and grandfather. Bram was only too well aware that David regarded him as a terrible role model for Max, and Bram returned the favour. He was fine with David teaching Max DIY skills and buying him weights for his birthday last month to improve his strength – ever since David had beaten his grandson in an arm-wrestling contest, he'd been going on about how Max had worse muscle tone than a pensioner. But he was less keen on David's other efforts to get Max to 'man up' – his attempts to teach him martial arts and boxing, and his gifts of books about the SAS and violent video games for Christmas, although, to Bram and Kirsty's satisfaction, Max hadn't even taken the shrink-wrap off *Call of Duty: Warzone*.

No wonder Kirsty had been so desperate to get them all moved out of her parents' house and into Woodside. David was, let's face it, a nightmare. Bram had made it crystal clear that they didn't want to talk about the dead crow over lunch, so what did David do?

Talk about the dead crow.

Kirsty met Bram's gaze with a grimace, and he gave her a reassuring smile. Kirsty was always apologising to him for David, as if David were a badly behaved child she'd failed to curb rather than her parent. Bram widened his smile, and did a mad eye-roll, and Kirsty's face finally relaxed as she smiled back.

KIRSTY MCKECHNIE HAD INTRIGUED Bram before he'd even set eyes on her. The name spoke to him, somehow, the very first time he stepped out of his room in the halls of residence to explore his new surroundings, after Ma and Pap had left in a flurry of tearful hugs. There it was, on the nameplate of the door of the room next to his.

'Kirsty McKechnie,' he murmured to himself, and smiled.

It was such a friendly name. 'Kirsty McKechnie,' he repeated, like a mantra, as he walked down that intimidat-

*ingly long corridor to the tiny common room-cum-kitchen.
Each corridor in the halls had one of these little communal
rooms, and it was full of chatter and laughter, full of other
students who all seemed to know each other already, although
he'd arrived only a couple of days late. Pap, Ma and Bram had
delayed their return from Amsterdam because his grandmother had sprained her ankle and Ma had wanted to stay
until she was mobile.*

*But the other students welcomed him like a long-lost
friend. 'Hi, Bram!' 'Bram Hendriksen – is that Dutch?' 'Your
English is amazing!'*

*Bram laughed. 'My parents are Dutch, but I was born and
bred in London. My mates from school insist I say some
words – like "bizarre" – with a Dutch accent, for some bizarre
reason.'*

'You do! I think you do say it with an accent! Bizarre!*'*

*They all introduced themselves, but none of the girls was
Kirsty McKechnie. When he asked about her, the girl called
Steph exchanged a look with the boy called Jake. 'Oh, right,
the Weird Girl.'*

*The Weird Girl who, Bram discovered over the next few
days, never socialised, scuttling along the corridor to and
from her room without making eye contact. When he said
hello, she said it back, but if he tried to expand the conversation she just aimed a smile somewhere over his left shoulder
and darted away, like a little wild animal he was unsuccess-
fully attempting to tame.*

*'She's just really, really shy,' he said one morning when
Steph started on again about her weirdness, as they were
eating breakfast in the big canteen that catered for all the
students in the halls.*

*'No, she's not.' Steph turned in her seat and regarded
Kirsty, who was eating toast at a table on her own, as usual.
'There's something* sinister *about her. I reckon she's a member
of a cult. Some sort of strange Highland religious sect,*

anyway. It's probably against her religion to eat with other people.'

'Don't stare at her like that,' Bram objected.

Gary immediately turned in his seat to stare too. 'She probably uses a mathematical formula to work out which table is furthest away from the other occupied ones.'

'She's doing maths?'

'Yeah. Course she is.'

The sun was streaming in through the big windows, striking chestnut highlights from Kirsty's long, glossy dark hair. As Bram watched, she put a hand through it in a languid, graceful gesture, and he found his gaze lingering on her face, on those high cheekbones and straight brows.

She had finished her toast and was looking out of the window.

It must be horrible to feel people staring at you. He averted his gaze, looking past her to the lawn that surrounded the canteen on three sides. There were two blackbirds out there, pecking at the grass, and some other smaller birds Bram didn't recognise. Siskins? As he idly watched them, one of the blackbirds decided to chase the other, which flew up onto a low wall topped with polished slate, slick after overnight rain. The first bird jumped up after it but misjudged his landing in the bird equivalent of a prat fall, slipping off the end of the wall and flapping onto the branch of a tree, as if that had been his intended perch all along.

Bram smiled, and glanced again at Kirsty.

She was looking out of the window and smiling too.

Somehow it seemed hugely significant that the two of them, amidst the hubbub of the canteen, amidst all those people chatting away to each other, intent on their own concerns, had been the only ones to see that happen. To see it, and find it funny.

.   .   .

ALMOST TWENTY-ONE YEARS LATER, here he was, sitting opposite the Weird Girl at their own kitchen table. It blew his mind whenever he thought about it.

'Crows are the farmer's traditional enemy,' David was ploughing on, talking around the quiche, bits of food visible in his mouth as he spoke. '*Bam bam bam*, problem solved!' He chuckled, forking in salad after the quiche.

Phoebe, sobbing, pushed herself up from her chair and bolted across the room to the stairs. Kirsty, flashing a black look at her father, dropped her napkin by her place and went after her.

David rolled his eyes at Fraser, who shrugged, grinning, and held out his empty glass to Bram for more Coke – Fraser was the designated driver. As he did so, his gaze fell on Max, who was sitting frowning down at the table. 'Hey, Max!' Fraser made his lower lip wobble. 'Don't *wuh*-way, the widdle cwow's gone up to *hea*-ven!'

But David, suddenly, was not amused. 'For Christ's sake, Max. You're not a nine-year-old girl.' But it was Bram he was looking at.

'Piss off, Fraser,' said Max, stabbing a piece of quiche crust.

Bram laid down his knife and fork. 'No one,' he said, slowly and clearly, 'no matter their age or gender, should ever feel ashamed of compassion for another living creature.' He ignored the empty glass Fraser was waving at him.

'Quite right,' said Linda.

When Kirsty and Phoebe eventually returned to the table, Phoebe subdued but at least not crying, Bram served the poached pears and yoghurt. When they'd all finished, the others moved with their coffee, or in Phoebe's case home-made lemonade, to the living area of the Walton Room, while Bram made a start on clearing up in the kitchen, making a point of donning his frilly apron.

'God almighty,' spluttered David. 'I hope you don't wear that in public.'

'You could hardly complain if I did, David. You gave it to me.'

'As a bloody joke!'

'I did once wear it to the shops. Forgot to take it off.'

Phoebe giggled as David put his head in his hands in mock despair. Well, *mock* mock despair. Then he looked up at Bram. 'I suppose in Islington no one turned a hair. Wear that to the shops in Grantown and see what happens.'

'Give it a rest, Dad,' said Kirsty. 'If Bram's confident enough in his masculinity to take on the traditionally female role, why should it bother you?'

'It doesn't bother me. As you say, if Bram's happy to be the little woman keeping house, spending your money on chai lattes and pointy shoes, and if *you're* happy to keep him in the style to which he has become accustomed, who am I to object?'

Kirsty opened and closed her mouth.

The problem was that David was a lot cleverer than he looked, and thrived, of course, on conflict, so it was rare that either of them got the better of him in these exchanges. He smiled, and leant back in the armchair he had selected, and closed his eyes.

He was soon snoring away, thank God, and Fraser followed suit, big booted feet stuck out in front of him on the rug. Max offered to take Linda and Bertie round the house so they could familiarise themselves with the layout of the furniture, and Phoebe went with them, chattering to her beloved Bertie and stroking his back, equanimity seemingly restored.

In the kitchen, Kirsty tugged at the front of Bram's

apron, pulling him towards her for a kiss. 'All together again in our new house.' She smiled. 'Thank you for today.'

Oh God, he loved her so much! He took her hand and led her through the Room with a View to the terrace, where he put his arms around her, holding her close as they looked across the field to the hills. How had he got to be so lucky? Little did nineteen-year-old Bram imagine, all those years ago, that the Weird Girl was going to turn out to be his whole world, that they would have this wonderful life together. That they would have two wonderful kids. Live happily ever after.

She had, he reflected with satisfaction, made much more of a success of her life than Gary or Jake or Steph who, last he heard, was attempting to raise cash to save her scuzzy beach bar in Goa. When he'd shown Kirsty the crowd-funding page, complete with photo of a leathery-skinned Steph standing in front of what was basically a falling-down shack, looking about ten years older than she was thanks to excessive sun exposure, Kirsty had just raised her eyebrows, her lips lifted in a little smile, and turned away.

Bram had kind of been hoping that Kirsty, a high-flying freelance forensic auditor, might suggest getting in touch with Steph and working on a rescue plan, but that had been unrealistic. Steph had been horrendous to Kirsty at uni – why should Kirsty help her now? It was nothing less than karma, although Kirsty, of course, wouldn't see it that way. In Kirsty's world view, if it couldn't be proved scientifically, it didn't exist.

'What did you do with the crow?' she asked him.

'Buried it. Over in the grass near the stream. I hope Bertie doesn't try to dig it up. Hopefully he's too much of a lazy sod to make the effort.'

Kirsty nodded. He could feel that she'd stiffened a

little in his arms. 'Do you think Dad's right, and it was just a farmer? The whirly was maybe a convenient place to put it, like a makeshift fence? Maybe he thought he was doing us a favour, like Dad said.'

'Yeah, maybe.'

Why would a farmer leave a dead crow there? Even if he thought he was doing them a favour, why wouldn't he just take the corpse away with him? But Bram wasn't about to voice his doubts to Kirsty. It wasn't as if he had a better explanation.

He kissed her hair. Maybe now was an appropriate time to broach the subject he'd been trying to talk to her about ever since they'd moved up here. 'It can't be easy. Being back home. Must be bringing back – memories?'

Kirsty turned in his arms and broke away, on the pretext of kicking a twig off the flagstones of the terrace. 'It's fine, Bram.' She looked at him, and grinned suddenly. 'But for God's sake take off that bloody apron.'

3

The sunlight was dancing on the shallow water of the stream where it widened and looped around a miniature sandy crescent Phoebe called The Beach. The water seemed to coat the pebbles and stones it ran over. They were all different colours, browns and yellows and whites and greys and pinks and blues. Some of them were clean as a whistle and some of them were covered in algae and weedy stuff that swayed and waved in the current.

It was incredibly soothing, watching the play of sun and water on the stones – right up until the moment Bertie launched himself into the middle of it, pushing his head into the stream to hoover up a stone before dropping it again, humphing, spluttering, as if indignant to find that the delicious-looking biscuit-sized object wasn't in fact edible.

'Mad dog.' Max laughed, picking up a stick. 'Bertie! Go get it!' He threw the stick across to the far bank.

Bertie ignored it.

This was their own stream.

Well, this stretch of it, through their wood and along

the edge of the rough grass that Bram and Max intended turning into a wildflower meadow. Downstream, it dog-legged away through Andrew and Sylvia Taylor's land to the bridge that carried the track leading to Woodside. The chimneys of the Taylors' house were just visible over the tops of the trees – Benlervie, it was called, a grand Georgian place that Bram found slightly intimidating. On the couple of occasions he'd been inside, he'd felt like a prole who should be using the back entrance.

This had once been Benlervie land, but the Taylors had decided to sell it as a plot because the whole kit and caboodle had been too much maintenance. The track and bridge still belonged to the Taylors, but the Woodside residents had right of access over them.

It was a perfect set-up – totally private and secluded, at the end of a track, but with neighbours near enough that you didn't feel isolated. When they'd been thinking of a name for the house, they had toyed with Àite Brèagha, meaning 'beautiful place' in Scottish Gaelic, but there had been pronunciation and spelling issues, and delivery drivers were going to have a hard enough time finding them as it was. When Linda had suggested simply Woodside, everyone had agreed it was perfect.

So Woodside it was.

Bertie splashed back through the stream and headed off across the grass towards the wood, probably reasoning that he was more likely to find something edible in there. Bram sat down on the grassy bank and let the sound of the stream and the dancing sunlight on the little ripples and eddies fill his senses.

It was three o'clock. Fraser had gone off back to McKechnie and Son's current building project, but David and Linda had decided to stay on for a bit and get Bram to run them home later. Surely they would only stay another hour at the most? He and Max could probably spin this 'walk' out for what, another forty minutes? Which would leave only twenty minutes more he'd have to spend in David's company, not counting the drive into Grantown.

Max flopped down next to Bram on the grass.

'Grandad's doing my head in,' he said, in that way he had sometimes of divining Bram's thoughts. 'I'd forgotten how full on he can be.'

'Mm,' said Bram. He tried not to bad-mouth David to the kids.

Max lay back to look at the sky. 'How do you stand it, Dad? It makes me hopping mad when he goes on about how you're living off Mum. You let her have her career at the expense of your own because I came along and–'

'No no no. I never wanted a "career", Max. Can you imagine me trotting into an office every day in a suit and tie, filling in spreadsheets and trying to talk corporate?'

Max grinned. 'But you could have done maybe social work, or something environment-focused.' Max had a conditional offer to study Ecology and Environmental Biology at Imperial College London. 'I'm not saying voluntary stuff isn't really worthwhile, but didn't you ever want more than that?'

In Islington, Bram had been a volunteer for various charities, primarily involved in befriending isolated pensioners and teaching disadvantaged children to swim in the local pool. It still gave him a warm glow to think of the weekend he'd taken some of the better swimmers to Wales for a wild swimming course. Watching their faces as they'd frolicked in that river had been one of the highlights of his life.

'Nope. Your mum loves her job, the cut and thrust of it, the challenge, but that's not me, is it?' They'd had Max while they were still at uni, and Bram had taken a break to look after him while Kirsty completed her education and started work as a forensic auditor for a top accountancy firm. Bram's intention had been to complete his history degree and pursue his own career when Max started school – but somehow that had never happened. Bram had loved being a parent too much, if that were possible.

And he really didn't envy Kirsty her career. In fact, during their last year in London, he'd become increasingly concerned about her. The job had been so pressured. One week, Bram had calculated that she'd spent less than four waking hours, total, with him and the kids.

He had suggested a radical change – why didn't she go freelance? They could move to the country, give the kids a better quality of life…

'We could live near Grannie and Grandad and Bertie!' Phoebe had enthused, and next time she'd Skyped them she'd come out with this suggestion. Bram had winced inwardly. This wasn't what he'd had in mind, but the idea had gained momentum. Both kids were really keen – once Max started university, he would have the perfect combo of London life during term time, when he could see his friends, and a country idyll in the holidays. And Phoebe had been desperate to leave her school and join Rhona at hers in Grantown. Bram had felt that the fly in the ointment – having to live near David – was an acceptable price to pay for a better life for all of them. Kirsty had been the one dragging her heels at first, but she'd come round to the idea. She missed home, particularly her mum, and felt guilty that she hadn't been around much.

He smiled. 'You know what, Max? It doesn't get much better than this.'

'It's so quiet here, isn't it?'

As if on cue, there was a sudden crack from off in the wood, like a branch of a tree had just whacked off another branch.

'What was that?' Max sat up.

Crack!

That wasn't a branch – it was a gunshot! And this time it was followed by a yelp. A howl.

'Bertie!' they both said at once.

Max was off and running before Bram had got to his feet.

'*No!* Max, *no*! Get back here!'

But Max kept going. Bram pounded after him, but before Max had reached the wood there was Bertie, limping out of the trees towards them, his yellow coat streaming blood.

'Okay, boy, okay.' Max dropped to his knees and took Bertie's head in his arms as Bram examined the wound. His shoulder was covered in blood.

There was a nasty gash where the bullet must have struck him and he was whimpering, whining, flinching away from Bram's fingers.

'Inside, *now!*' Bram gathered Bertie up in his arms, and the dog yelped again in pain. 'Go, Max. *Go!*'

'I'll help you carry–'

'No. I can manage. Run inside and call 999! Don't argue with me, Max. *Go!*'

4
———

'What the…?' David barrelled into the house, hammer in hand, as Bram and Kirsty were trying to get everyone out to the car – not an easy task with Bertie whining away in Bram's arms, bleeding all over the towel Kirsty was holding to his shoulder, while Linda insisted on keeping her hand on the dog's head at all times while simultaneously rubbing Kirsty's arm comfortingly, and Phoebe clung to Kirsty.

'Bertie's been shot!' Linda gasped.

'*What?*'

'Someone in the wood shot him,' Kirsty elaborated, her voice oddly flat. 'Can you get out of the way, Dad?'

The police had told them to stay inside, but they had to take Bertie to the vet, and Bram's instinct was to get everyone out. If there was a maniac running around with a gun, he didn't want to leave anyone behind in the house. The police said it might be half an hour at least until someone could 'attend the scene'. He'd got the Discovery and driven it right up to the bottom of the verandah steps and left it there with the engine running.

It wasn't likely that the shooter would actually take aim at people, but he wasn't taking any chances.

David bent over Bertie. 'Okay, boy. You're going to be okay.' Bertie's tail slapped weakly against Bram's leg. 'Looks like he's been grazed by an airgun pellet.' Then David was fixing Bram with steely blue eyes. 'Why aren't you out there going after the bastard?'

'Let me past, David – we have to get Bertie to the vet.'

David stood aside to let Bram out onto the verandah, and Bram heard him rap out: 'Where in the wood?'

'In our bit of it,' said Max. 'Near the stream.'

'Right.' David pushed past Bram, hefting the hammer in his hand – Bram recognised it now as his own red-handled one from the shed, presumably fetched for some snagging issue with the house – and barrelled off down the verandah steps.

'No! Dad!'

'David, don't be *stupid*!' Linda cried out.

But David had gone.

THAT JOURNEY to the vet was a nightmare. 'He's going to be all right,' Phoebe kept repeating between sobs. She, Max and Linda were on the back seat with Bertie lying across their laps, while Kirsty sat next to Bram in the passenger seat, dabbing a damp tissue at the blood on her top. Her expression had gone completely blank, in the way he remembered from uni, turning in on herself, turning away from the world.

'I'm texting Grandad,' said Max.

'He shouldn't have gone out there!' Phoebe wailed.

'No,' said Linda tightly. 'He shouldn't.'

It felt weird to be driving through this gorgeous scenery, the sun dappling the tarmac in front of them, canopies of big old beech trees stretching over the road to the right, and to the left a view over fields to the enticing wilderness of the Grampian Mountains, as if the beautiful summer's day was going on out there in another world in which nothing had happened, nothing was wrong, everything was fine.

'He'll be okay.' Bram made his voice firm and confident, and reached over to squeeze Kirsty's hand. 'No one messes with your grandad. And the police will be there by now.' Would they?

'But the psychopath's got a *guuuuun*!' Phoebe's wail filled the car.

'Grandad thinks it's just an airgun. And there isn't any *psychopath*.' Bram had to shout to make himself heard. *Bloody Nora.* Phoebe was meant to watch Linda and David's Netflix only under supervision, but he knew she sneaked a look at all kinds of inappropriate stuff that David and Max watched, the latest one featuring a serial killer who dismembered his victims and left various body parts in children's play areas. Phoebe hadn't been near a park since.

'There's Grandad texting back,' Max shouted. 'He's fine, Phoebs. For God's sake shut up – getting hysterical isn't helping Bertie, is it? We need to keep him calm.'

Phoebe's noise immediately stopped, like Max had flicked a switch. 'Sorry, Bertie,' she gulped. And then, in a small voice: 'That's good that Grandad's okay.'

'What does he say?' said Linda.

'Uh, he uses a pretty bad swear word. "No sign of the *blank*."'

'Thank God,' said Linda. 'You text him right back, Max, and tell him he's to get in the house and *stay there*. Tell him it's a message from me.'

Bloody Nora. This went to show just how rattled Linda was. She was usually as easy-going as Max, and rarely laid down the law to David or, indeed, anyone else. She let David get away with far too much, in Bram's opinion, although this was probably unfair of him. The only person responsible for David's actions was David himself.

Georgia the vet, reasonably enough, wasn't keen on all five of them accompanying Bertie into the treatment room, so Bram and the kids stayed in the waiting room while Linda and Kirsty went in with him.

When Phoebe wandered off to the shop area to choose a treat for Bertie, Max looked up from his phone. 'Grandad says he's searched the whole wood and there's no one there now. That *was* pretty foolhardy of him, wasn't it, going after them like that?'

Bram nodded. It was a source of secret delight to him and Kirsty, the way Max occasionally used old-fashioned words like *foolhardy*, but they never remarked on it in case he became self-conscious about it and stopped. Max was addicted to classic literature, particularly Dickens and George Elliot, as well as 1930s stuff like P. G. Wodehouse.

'They could have been really dangerous.' Max shook his head. 'What is Grandad like? It's as if he isn't scared of *anything*.'

Bram wanted to say that only an idiot wasn't scared of anything, but contented himself with, 'He's certainly not exactly risk-averse.'

Ten minutes later, a sorry-for-himself Bertie appeared sporting a large Perspex cone around his head.

'The vet thinks Dad was right and it was only an airgun pellet.' Kirsty caught Phoebe into a hug. 'It only grazed him. He was unlucky because it hit a couple of blood vessels.'

Thank God, Kirsty seemed to have come out of her fugue.

Bram put an arm round her shoulders. 'Well, big relief all round, eh?'

He gave Linda a hug for good measure, and Linda smiled at him and nodded, reaching out a hand to touch first Phoebe's head and then Bertie's flank.

They decided that it would be better, given the unwieldy nature of the cone, if Bertie travelled where he normally did, in the Discovery's boot, where he had a dog's-eye view out of the rear windscreen. Kirsty closed the boot on him gently. 'It was probably kids. Kids messing about.' She nodded, as if to reassure herself. 'Just kids with an airgun.'

Those were five words which, in Bram's opinion, did not belong together in the same sentence. He knew that people in rural communities had different social mores from those he was used to – Kirsty had told him so often enough – but *Just kids with an airgun*?

Really?

He didn't want to make a big thing of it, though, so 'Probably,' was all he said, as he looked through the tinted glass at Bertie, who had settled himself on the blankets with a huff.

'Thank goodness Dad didn't find them,' said Kirsty.

Max frowned. 'But they need to be told, Mum. They need to be told not to blast away with airguns in our wood. At crows or at dogs or at anything else.'

'And you think your grandfather would have restricted himself to giving them a bit of a telling off?' Linda suddenly put her hands up to her face, and Kirsty touched her arm.

'Mum? It's okay, he–'

'No, it's not *okay*, Kirsty!' Linda heaved in a big sigh,

and dropped her hands to reveal a face stiff with distress. 'Your father was convicted of assault last year and given a suspended sentence. If he gets into any more trouble – and I mean *any* more trouble – he's going to prison.'

Phoebe stared at her grandmother.

'Whooo,' said Max.

Kirsty said nothing, so it was left to Bram to ask: 'What did he do?'

'Another driver pulled out in front of him at the Carrbridge junction – you know how bad that junction is?' she appealed to Kirsty.

Kirsty looked blank, as if she hadn't heard.

'The man said the sun was in his eyes and he didn't see David approaching. David tailed him to his house and confronted him on his driveway, started shouting the odds, and ended up punching the poor man. Several times. Broke his nose and jaw.'

Kirsty briefly closed her eyes. She hated violence of any kind, and wouldn't even watch crime dramas on TV. Although she hardly ever talked about it, Bram knew how much she struggled with the bad memories of what she had been through as a teenager, and being back home must be churning it all up again. And now Bertie had been shot and she'd just discovered that her dad had been convicted of assault.

No wonder she was freaking out, in Kirsty's own particular, quiet way.

And Linda evidently sensed this, because she attempted a smile in Kirsty's direction. 'But it's all done and dusted – if he keeps out of trouble, there'll be no more repercussions. We didn't tell you because – well, there was no point in upsetting you.'

'He had to appear in court?' Kirsty asked at last. 'There was a trial?'

Linda nodded. 'He got a six-month suspended sentence.'

THE FIRST THING Bram saw as he drove over the little bridge and up the track to Woodside was the police car parked in front of the house, alongside a silver BMW he recognised as belonging to Scott Sinclair, Fraser's best mate, who was a Detective Inspector with Police Scotland and was based at Aviemore, a tourist hotspot about ten miles away. Presumably Fraser had called him. Bram parked in front of the verandah and hustled everyone up the steps and inside.

'Have the police caught him?' Phoebe asked.

'I don't know, *kleintje*. How about you see if Bertie wants some water?'

'I'm going out to see what's happening,' said Kirsty.

'I'll come with you. Kids, stay inside with Grannie and Bertie, okay?'

Phoebe immediately latched onto his arm. 'No, *please* don't go out there!'

'Whoever it was will be long gone. They're hardly going to hang around with the police all over the place, are they? Scott's a very important policeman in CID.' He pushed a stray strand of Phoebe's hair back into her ponytail. 'He's here to make sure the careless person with the airgun is caught. And remember what the vet said, Phoebs? It was only an airgun pellet, and those aren't really dangerous.'

'It hurt Bertie!'

'Yes, but it was only a graze, and he's going to be absolutely fine.'

Phoebe nodded, and then she smiled up first at Kirsty and then at Bram. 'Okay!' And she skipped happily off to the kitchen to show Linda where Bertie's water bowl was.

Their little will-o'-the-wisp. Bram smiled at Kirsty, and, to his relief, she gave him a little smile in return.

'Tell your father to come back to the house at once, please, Kirsty,' said Linda grimly.

They found David and Fraser standing at the edge of the wood talking to Scott. Scott Sinclair was one of those guys in whose presence Bram always found himself trying to stand tall and pull in his gut. Scott would definitely have a six-pack under that crisp white shirt and perfectly knotted grey tie. And he had a Paul Newman thing going on – bright blue eyes and chiselled features.

'Dad,' said Kirsty without preamble. 'Mum wants you back at the house *right now.*'

'Okay, princess.'

It bugged Bram when David called Kirsty that – there was an implicit sexism in it, not to mention classism. But Kirsty said she didn't mind it, that it was just the same as Bram calling Phoebe *kleintje*. '*Kleintje* means "little one",' Bram had objected, and Kirsty had countered: 'But you never used it for Max, did you?' Fair point.

Scott moved closer to Kirsty and leant in for a half-hug. 'You okay?'

Bram could feel his caveman instincts kicking in again. Scott and Kirsty had 'gone out together' when they were fourteen and thirteen, respectively. Scott was happily – as far as Bram knew – married with a kid, but still.

Kirsty nodded. 'What's happening? No sign of them?'

'Not a dickie-bird,' said David.

'Dad, you need to go in to Mum *right now!*' Kirsty

snapped. 'She's *fucking furious* with you and no wonder!'

Whoa.

Kirsty never swore.

'Okay, okay,' said David, backing off with his hands raised, as if placating a wild animal. 'I'm going, I'm going.'

'We know about the conviction,' Kirsty said to Scott and Fraser as they all stood watching David plod off across the grass towards the house.

Scott grimaced.

'Yeah,' said Fraser. 'I told Mum and Dad they should come clean – I mean, it was only a matter of time before you found out. But it was no big deal, Kirst. A road rage incident.'

'He *broke the man's nose and jaw*,' said Kirsty. 'He could have *killed* him!'

Fraser shrugged, looking as sheepish now as David had.

Tense silence, which Bram felt he should break. 'So, what's the story with this airgun enthusiast?' *Enthusiast?* That made it sound like the person responsible was enjoying a nice hobby, out in the fresh air shooting guide dogs. That was another thing about being around Scott – Bram often found himself coming out with a load of nonsense. 'Or psychopath, as Phoebe is calling him.' Oh yeah, that was so much better.

Scott raised his Paul Newman eyebrows. 'We've searched your wood, and a couple of PCs are giving the Taylors' land the once-over now – and I've been over there to alert the Taylors to what's happened. There's no sign of anyone hanging around, but there's evidence of a camp fire in the westernmost quadrant of your wood, the one furthest from the house. And some rubbish, cans of lager and crisp packets.' He shrugged. 'Kids.'

'This is a bit below your pay grade, Scott, isn't it?'
You ungrateful bastard, Bram. 'Thanks for coming out,' he
added weakly. And that made it sound like he was
talking to a tradesman.

More eyebrow action. 'Fraser called me.'

'Oh, ah, yes, right.'

It was a bit of a mystery why this ultra-sophisticated,
successful guy was friends with Fraser, but apparently
they'd been best mates since the first day of primary
school, when the two five-year-olds had bonded over a
shared obsession with football.

Bram became aware of the sound of a chugging
engine, and a massive four-by-four appeared over the
bridge.

'The Taylors,' said Kirsty.

Whenever the Taylors came over they drove,
although it was just a five-minute walk up the track
from their house. The lazy bastards.

Bram shook himself mentally. The Taylors were
lovely people. Where was this vitriol coming from?

Scott raised a hand and strode across the grass
towards the Taylors as they disembarked, twinkly Paul
Newman smile in place, as if he, and not Bram and
Kirsty, owned Woodside. Kirsty and Bram followed in
his wake.

The Taylors had brought their kids along for the ride,
Finn and Cara, nineteen and sixteen, respectively.
Andrew and Sylvia would probably be in their early
fifties, another generation, almost, from Kirsty and
Bram. Andrew was your archetypal middle-class,
middle-aged male, pink shirt and designer jeans,
polished brown shoes, living high on the hog and beginning to show it around the midriff and in the fleshy
ruddiness of his face. Sylvia was the archetypal mum,
plump and smiley and chatty, with a tip-tilted nose and

cat-like eyes that made her look like one of those 1950s actresses.

'What an awful, awful thing!' she exclaimed, bypassing Scott, Bram was pleased to note, and coming straight over to him and Kirsty. 'How's Bertie?'

'Oh, he's going to be fine,' Kirsty reassured her, smiling, almost visibly relaxing a little. Sylvia had that effect on you, somehow – she oozed empathetic sympathy.

Scott had engaged Andrew in conversation, and was now gesturing at the wood. The two kids were kicking their heels, in Finn's case literally. He was heeling a clump of grass and, as Bram watched, switched to kicking it with his toe. He was a tall, sporty boy who always seemed to be on the move, never sitting still for long, always fidgeting and jiggling about. His large brown eyes and strong jaw in combination with his mum's little tipped-up nose gave him a cartoonish look, like a teenage superhero in a comic, always on the lookout for action. His sister Cara, in contrast, looked half asleep and utterly, utterly bored. Her skinny frame was slumped against the four-by-four as if she couldn't wait for this to be over so she could get home and shut herself back in her room. Her hair was pink with green tips.

'Max is inside,' Bram called over to them.

'Why don't we all go in?' Kirsty suggested.

They found Linda in the armchair by the 'wireless' in the Walton Room, Bertie in his bed at her feet. David was slumped at the kitchen table. Bram got the impression that their arrival had interrupted a frosty silence.

Cara, touchingly, was transformed when she saw Bertie in his Perspex collar.

'Oh no, Bertie!' she crooned, dropping to her knees on the rug by his bed and gently stroking his head. 'Poor Bertie.'

'He's okay,' Phoebe assured her. 'It's just a flesh wound.'

Finn shook his head at Max, as if to say *Girls*.

The group separated into adults round the kitchen table and kids in the sitting area, and Bram bustled about getting everyone coffee and tea and biscuits.

'Probably just some idiot child,' said Andrew, stirring milk into his coffee. 'After rabbits.' He indicated Bertie with his teaspoon. 'Similar colouring.'

'Have you had any trouble before, with kids with airguns?' Bram asked.

'No, never.'

But Sylvia was looking at her husband. 'Local kids do hang out around here a bit. It seems the woods have been used by youngsters in the summer for years – just doing what teenagers do, hanging out and getting drunk. Loud music and high spirits. Litter. Some damage to trees…'

'Bloody Nora,' said David. 'And you didn't think you were in any way bound, in common decency, to let Kirsty and Bram know about this when you sold them the plot?'

Sylvia made a face. 'It was more of an issue when we first bought the place. Recently we've had hardly any trouble at all. So no, we didn't think to mention it. Sorry.'

'They're harmless,' said Andrew airily. 'Just kids letting off steam.'

'Do you know who they are?'

A shrug. 'No, sorry.'

'Finn? Cara?' Bram called over to the kids. 'Do you know who these kids with an airgun might be?'

Finn, who was standing with Max showing him something on his phone, shrugged. Cara ignored him. Bram waited for Andrew or Sylvia to tell them to answer when they were spoken to and stop being so rude, but nope.

Bram let it go. The teenage code of honour being such as it was, it was probably futile trying to get any information out of them. Maybe Max could go under-cover and try to find out what, if anything, they knew.

Scott was leaning back against the worktop, tie now slightly loosened, cup of coffee in one tanned hand. 'What I'd advise is putting up some notices in the wood. There are two paths through it, yes, that cross in the middle? Put the notices in prominent positions where each path enters and exits the wood itself, where they cross, and maybe where your track meets the public road.'

Kirsty nodded. 'Notices saying what?'

'Private property – please observe the Scottish Outdoor Access Code. Anyone caught lighting a fire, shooting or otherwise causing damage will be prose-cuted. Something like that.'

'Or,' said David, 'how about: "Enter at your own risk. The owner reserves the right to kick your arse"?'

'Which reminds me to add,' said Scott with a smile: 'Avoid inflammatory language.'

David snorted. 'They've got it coming. If I catch any of the wee toe-rags–'

'You'll what, Dad?' said Kirsty sharply.

David simpered at her. 'I'll give them a right earful. That's all I meant, princess. Read them the riot act.'

Kirsty got abruptly to her feet. 'I have some work to finish off. Excuse me.'

As she passed Bram's chair she shook her head at him, her expression saying *I'm fine, don't stress*, and strode away to the corridor that led to her study.

Awkward silence.

'What a thing to happen on your first day in your

beautiful new home!' said Sylvia brightly. 'It's gorgeous, Bram. This kitchen! Last time I saw it you were having the floor laid. I love the colour of the units.'

Bram leapt on this topic gratefully, describing his search for just the right shade of green. Sylvia enthused over everything in a rather gratifying way, and Bram found himself conducting a house tour for the Taylors plus Scott.

'Wow,' said Andrew in the Room with a View. 'This has really come together.'

Bram nodded smugly. Damn, he wished he'd plumped those cushions.

'The view's the star of the show, of course,' he said modestly, crossing to the doors to the terrace. He found himself pausing when he reached them, looking out across the paddock to the wood. He felt suddenly reluctant to open the doors.

And –

Bloody hell, yes, there was someone there!

Someone was coming out of the wood!

'There!' he said urgently, turning to Scott. 'There's someone–'

'Yes, Bram, that's one of the PCs.'

'Oh.' And now he saw that yes, it was a man in a police uniform, wading through the knee-high grass. Damn.

'I'd better go and see what they have to report.' Scott reached past Bram to open the sliding doors and strode away, over the terrace and along the path to the paddock, raising an imperious hand to summon the minions.

Sylvia was walking down the room to the reading area at the far end. 'It's so light and airy, but cosy at the same time.' She beamed at him. 'I love this bookcase, and the old leather chairs. Like a mini-library. You've got a designer's eye, Bram, you really have.'

'Oh well, I don't know about that. But thanks. Unfortunately, my efforts in the garden have been rather less successful. The vegetables I planted have all died.'

'Oh dear! What happened?'

'I've no idea. I think maybe I didn't water them enough.'

'But they were reasonably well established, weren't they? They shouldn't have needed much watering.'

'Or maybe they had some kind of blight.'

'They can't *all* have died?'

'Yep.'

'Hmm.'

Sylvia was a keen gardener. A few weeks ago she'd shown him and Kirsty round their garden with justifiable pride, and as they'd strolled down the gravel paths lined with clipped hedges and across well-tended lawns, Bram had picked her brains.

'Actually, Sylvia, would you mind taking a quick squizz?'

'Mind? *Mind?* I *love* a good problem area!'

Andrew groaned. 'There's no such thing as a *quick squizz* at a garden where Sylvia is concerned. We'll send out a search party if you're not back in an hour.'

As Bram and Sylvia headed out, he warned her: 'It's not so much a problem area as the scene of a natural disaster. Brace yourself. I don't imagine you've ever experienced quite this level of incompetence.'

When they returned to the house a speedy ten minutes later, Kirsty still hadn't reappeared, but Scott was standing on the rug with his back to the unlit stove in the Walton Room, like Poirot in the library smugly delivering his verdict.

'Nothing to report in the Taylors' wood either. As I

say, if you put up some notices, that'll hopefully discourage any more incursions.' As if they were talking about marauding hordes, Genghis Khan and his Mongol horsemen, thundering through the wood, battleaxes poised ready for action, but when they saw the notices, reining in their mounts to peer at them and wonder in what way they might be contravening the Scottish Outdoor Access Code.

'Right, thank you, Scott.' *Thank you and piss off.*

'Where have you *been*, Dad?' Phoebe launched herself at him. 'I was *really worried*.'

Damn. But he'd known her equanimity was too good to last, with Bertie lying there in his cone looking sorry for himself, a constant reminder of the 'psychopath'.

'Oh, well, no need to worry, Phoebs.' He kept his tone light. 'I just went out to look at the veg patch with Mrs Taylor.' He gently prised Phoebe away and looked over her head at Max. 'Why don't you and Max find paper and pens to make some notices with? You're the artist of the family, after all.'

'Come on, Picasso,' said Max, immediately divining Bram's intention. 'Let's see what you've got in your room.'

When they'd gone, Bram turned back to Scott. 'The vegetable plants have all been weedkilled.'

'*Weedkilled?*'

Sylvia nodded. 'That's my diagnosis. There's no other explanation for why every single plant would suddenly die. Someone's applied weedkiller to them.'

David burst out laughing. 'Before everyone jumps to conclusions and starts blaming the feral kids for that too, I think we may need to look closer to home on this one.' He slapped Bram's back. 'Eh, Bram?'

'I didn't weedkill my own vegetables!'

'Not deliberately, no – but the organic liquid feed

you've got in the shed comes in big red bottles, does it not? Been using that on the veg, yes?'

'Well, yes, but–'

'And the weedkiller I gave you a few weeks ago was also in a big red bottle?'

'The weedkiller's still there in the shed unopened.'

'No it's not, Bram. I know because I was in there after lunch and I thought maybe I'd have a go at the jungle you've got growing round the verandah, but no. Nada. The weedkiller has gone. I thought you'd maybe swallowed your eco-friendly organic principles and had a sneaky blitz. Little did I think you'd used it on your own bloody vegetables!'

The room erupted in laughter.

'No,' said Bram helplessly. 'I didn't.' But David just slapped him on the back again.

He had *not* used that weedkiller. He had noted the similarity between the containers and double-checked every time he used the liquid feed that he hadn't made a mistake, telling himself he needed to get David to take the weedkiller away. He knew he hadn't made a mistake. Someone had deliberately poured weedkiller all over the vegetable patch.

5

Phoebe was sitting at the kitchen table wielding the red felt-tip, head bent in concentration over her work. All around her were felt-tips, most with their tops off. It was another beautiful day, early morning sunshine slanting in through the side window and across the worktops.

Kirsty came into the room and looked over Phoebe's shoulder, and Bram braced himself for her reaction, but she smiled. 'Poor Bertie's leg has actually been shot off?'

Phoebe nodded. 'If I just showed the flesh wound it would look like it was no big deal.'

'And that's a *lot* of blood.'

'It has to attract people's attention, Mum.'

Phoebe's notice was quite something. At the top was a depiction of 'the psychopath', a heavy-browed figure, mouth wide open in glee as he pointed what looked like a machine-gun at the animal in the centre of the picture, a yellow dog with downturned mouth crying copious blue tears – and no wonder, given that one of his back legs was lying on the ground behind him and blood was pouring out of the stump to create a bright red lake.

Phoebe had drawn a huge black cross over this picture and under it written:

!!!NO!!!

It is WRONG to hurt animals. If you do, you will be COUGHT ON CAMERA and get in trouble with the POLICE. All dogs using this wood are PROTECTED BY PETCAM.

Underneath was a happy yellow dog with a massive camera around his neck, tongue lolling, mouth smiling, and the psychopath, this time, was prostrate in a second blood lake while a policeman stood pointing a gun down at him. A policeman with bright blue eyes.

Last night, Phoebe had refused to sleep in her own room. As dusk had fallen, the spectre of the psychopath had become all too real, and Phoebe kept insisting she had seen movement at first one window and then another, and became hysterical when Bram went out with a torch to investigate, which he'd thought would reassure her but had had the opposite effect.

They had taken her into their bed and she had snuggled in the warm space between them as Bram had shown her the motion-activated cameras with on-board storage that they had ordered and which were to be placed in the woods. Kirsty had had the brainwave of a petcam to be attached to Bertie's collar, and Phoebe solemnly participated in the selection of a suitable model from the website.

If there was anything guaranteed to bring Kirsty back from wherever she retreated to, it was one of the kids needing her.

They had printed off their own notices this morning and sealed them inside plastic wallets from one of

Kirsty's ring binders, ready to go up, side by side with Phoebe's one, in strategic positions around the wood:

PRIVATE PROPERTY

You are very welcome to use these woods, but please respect them and observe the Scottish Outdoor Access Code. NO SHOOTING OR FIRES, PLEASE. No littering.

Anyone shooting at wild or domestic animals or vandalising property will be prosecuted. CCTV is operating in these woods.

Bram joined Kirsty and Phoebe at the table. 'That's excellent, Phoebs, if a little bloodthirsty. Our notice is going to look very dull in comparison.'

A racket like a herd of wildebeest on the stairs heralded the arrival of Max, as usual an hour later for breakfast than the rest of them. He was dressed in a very short-sleeved T-shirt that exposed his upper arms, and Bram noticed that the weights were starting to have an effect. His biceps were definitely larger and more defined. David would be delighted.

Max grabbed a handful of nuts and raisins from the bowl on the table. 'I thought I might go out and – Oh, crikey.' He did a double-take at Phoebe's work. 'That's going to give them nightmares, all right.'

'Good,' said Phoebe, busily expanding the red lake around the psychopath. 'He's got it coming.' She'd heard David say that yesterday, presumably.

Max got himself a huge bowl of cornflakes, which he inhaled in two minutes flat, then disappeared off upstairs again, to return a minute later wearing his new trainers. 'I'm going over to Finn and Cara's – is that okay?'

'If Mr and Mrs Taylor don't mind, that's fine,' said Bram.

'No, Max!' Phoebe looked up at her brother with beseeching eyes. 'I don't think you should go out there.'

'You heard what the cops said,' Max attempted to reassure her. 'It's just kids messing about. It's not like we're going to be jumped by *him*' – he pointed at Phoebe's drawing – 'every time we set foot outside the house.'

'Now look, Phoebe.' Bram took a seat next to her. 'You know this boogie man doesn't actually exist, don't you? You heard what Scott said. What Mr and Mrs Taylor said. It's just a load of teenagers. They're not even bad people, probably, just thoughtless and silly.'

'Exactly,' said Kirsty. 'Most teenagers aren't as sensible as your brother. They often do silly things. It's nothing to get all worried and upset about, darling – it really isn't.' Was she trying to reassure Phoebe, or herself?

IT HADN'T QUITE BEEN Lord of the Flies, *but living in halls of residence had certainly been very different from being at home. Was it really a good idea, Bram wondered, to put a load of immature teenagers together in a building with hardly any adult supervision and let them get on with it? In those first few days, he really missed the cosy comfort of the little mews house, and the peace and quiet, and his parents' reassuring presence. Not to mention Ma's cooking.*

The little kitchen in the common room shared by the eight students on Bram's corridor was basic, to say the least: just a Formica table, six black, moulded plastic chairs, a sink and draining board, and a small area of worktop on which sat a microwave oven. A fridge in the corner. A cupboard with chipped plates and mugs. A stinky bin no one ever emptied. And that was it.

But they generally ended up there at the end of a night out, often with takeaways. On this particular night, Steph was more wasted than usual. She aimed the tomato ketchup at her chips, missed the plate and sent an arc of it whipping over the chair on which Bram was about to sit down.

'*It looks like the Weird Girl's been in here,*' *said Gary,* '*doing a spot of ritual killing.*'

The others found this hilarious. Steph crumpled onto the floor, eyes rolled back in her head.

'*Oh for God's sake,*' *muttered Bram, wiping the chair with a cloth.*

'*Weird loners do often end up going on a killing spree,*' *Steph pointed out, flopping over to look up at him.* '*You see it all the time in the media.*'

Bram sighed, and chucked the cloth in the direction of the sink. '*Kirsty McKechnie's the last person on this corridor I could imagine hurting anyone.*'

'*No, but you must admit she's creepy.*' *Liv shuddered, tucking into her own chips as Steph hauled herself back onto a chair.* '*The way she looks at you! It's like her soul has died.*'

'*It's like she's just the husk of what used to be Kirsty McKechnie,*' *Gary agreed.* '*Taken over by an alien life force.*'

There was a movement at the door, and Bram looked up, and met Kirsty McKechnie's clear green gaze. She had a mug in one hand and a plate in the other.

Awful, awful silence.

'*Hi,*' *said Bram.*

'*Hi.*' *Kirsty walked past them to the sink, where she used washing-up liquid and the brush to clean the mug and plate, wiped them with the tea towel, and put the plate away in the cupboard. Clutching the mug, which Bram saw had a picture of an owl on it, she walked back past them, head held high, and out into the corridor.*

'Oh-oh!' giggled Steph. 'Oh-oh, Gary! Guess who's just gone to the top of the list of potential victims!'

Bram stood. 'That's not cool. That's so not cool. How do you think she must have felt, hearing you saying all that crap? It's bullying, guys. That's what it is. You need to back off and leave her alone.' It was on the tip of his tongue to tell them what he had heard, through the thin wall separating his room from Kirsty's.

Crying.

Almost every night.

But knowing them, they were likely to find a way to use it against her. Gary and Steph exchanged mock-chastened looks, then burst out laughing again.

Bram raised his voice over them. 'Or better still, try to be her friends?'

'Uh, yeah,' cackled Steph. 'Let's all make friends with the poor little serial killer!'

That night, when Bram was woken by sobbing coming from Kirsty's room, he didn't just grimace in sympathy and turn over and go back to sleep. He padded out to the corridor in his bare feet and knocked on the door, standing shivering in the eery dim light of the night-time corridor.

'Kirsty?'

The noise stopped.

'It's Bram from next door. Are you all right?'

'I'm fine,' came a small, choked voice. 'Thanks.'

'Are you sure?' He put the palm of his hand flat against her door, as if he could somehow transmit comfort through it.

'Yes. But thanks.'

As he returned to his room and jumped back into bed, he made a decision. Kirsty was obviously horribly homesick, so far away from everyone and everything she knew in Scotland. This must all be so strange and frightening for her, on her own for probably the first time in her life, and instead of her fellow students rallying round and supporting her, they were *calling her names and laughing at her distress and joking about her being a potential serial killer.*

Oh my God. When he thought about it, he'd pretty much been complicit in that.

He needed to help her.

He needed to help Kirsty.

PHOEBE STOPPED dead in her tracks. 'What was *that*?'

Bram stopped too. 'I can't hear anything, Phoebe. Apart from a bird.'

They had stapled the first two notices to tree trunks where the path leading off the track entered the wood, and were now walking down that path deeper into the trees.

'It was a sort of *crunching* noise!'

Phoebe had bravely agreed, in the end, to accompany Bram and Max to put up the notices, but Bram was beginning to think that had been a mistake. When he'd slid open the glass doors onto the terrace, he'd had to fight a primitive instinct that had told him to shut them again, to keep doors and walls between his children and –

And what?

'There's nothing there,' he said firmly. 'Come on.'

They carried on through the trees, the path turning first one way and then another. In the stands of little birch trees, light dappled the mossy, hummocky ground, where brambles and other scrubby stuff grew, but as the path entered the beechwood, the huge canopies of the mature trees blocked the sun and they walked through a twilit world populated by giants, great grey giants with twisted trunks and roots that seemed to writhe their way out of the ground. Not much grew here. A russet carpet of previous years' dead leaves stretched away to a high bank to their right. Bram knew, because he'd googled it, that this carpet of beech leaves and husks suppressed the growth of most other plants.

'I guess you can appreciate why people in Medieval times thought woods were evil places,' Max mused. 'Dark and mysterious. Where robbers and outcasts hung out. Hence all the fairy tales warning children not to go into the woods because you never know what might happen, you might get stalked by wolves or kidnapped by a mad witch or–'

'Yes, okay, thank you, Max.'

'– a psychopath,' Phoebe finished for him in a small voice, her hand finding its way into Bram's as a sudden vortex of air whooshed through the branches over their heads.

Bram upped the pace. 'Max, I was thinking maybe you could sound out Finn and Cara, find out if they maybe do have an inkling about who might be using an airgun around here.'

'I already asked them, Dad. They don't have a clue. We've put out word on the social media grapevine, but so far nada.'

'Good thinking. Right. Let's put the rest of these notices up.'

They stapled the last two notices to a tree at the edge of the wood where it abutted the paddock. Bram looked from the mountains and woods and fields to the house, the cedar shingles glowing in the sunlight. A few days ago this view would have made him smile, but now he felt his stomach lurch a little. They were pretty isolated out here.

Phoebe ran ahead of them towards the house. But of course the sliding doors on the terrace were locked, and she had to stand there waiting for Bram and Max to catch up.

'Come *on*, Dad!'

For a moment, Bram couldn't find the small key that opened the sliding doors, and Phoebe pressed close against his side. He could see her small chest rising and falling under her blue sweatshirt as her breathing quickened.

'Here it is!'

Phoebe made sure he locked it again after them and even wanted to pull the curtains across the expanse of glass, but Bram was able to distract her with a text message from Kirsty, who was away for the day in Inverness meeting clients.

'Mum says well done for being so brave and helping put up the notices. See?'

Phoebe leant into him as she looked at the message on his phone, her head against his arm.

'You really did well, Phoebs. I'm proud of you. And now you've seen there's nothing to be frightened of out there, haven't you? Just a few noisy blackbirds and a deer or two!'

The deer had been pretty traumatic.

'Uh-huh.'

Maybe a sing-song would help. Bram had put the guitars at the library end of the Room with a View, and he fetched them now, slinging the strap of his own guitar over his neck and handing the other to Max, who perched on one of the sofas and started tuning the strings, while Phoebe skipped off to get her recorder.

'I've found a good song for our party piece,' said Bram. 'For the housewarming.' He fetched his tablet and brought up the bothy ballad he'd found on the internet. Bothy ballads were traditional Scottish songs, it seemed, sung by farm labourers in their bothies, basic accommodation that used to be provided on farms in Victorian times. They'd while away the evening hours after a long day's work by singing these ballads to each other, some tragic, some comical, some, it had to be said, offensively sexist and sometimes verging on the pornographic.

He'd found a nice one, though, about a 'kitchie deem' – a kitchen maid – in love with a ploughboy. He strummed his nails across the strings and began to sing.

> *'Doon yonder den there's a plooman lad,*
> *Some simmer's day he'll be aa my ain.*
> *And sing laddie-aye, and sing laddie-o,*
> *The plooman laddies are aa the go.'*

He paused. Was 'aa' a typo? No – he googled it, and found it meant 'all' in the Scots language.

'*Aa the go* means "all the rage",' he clarified for Max. 'What do you reckon?'

Max nodded. 'It's, uh, good to keep these traditional songs alive.'

'There are four more verses.'

He stumbled a bit over the unfamiliar words, but it really was a charming song, all about how the kitchie deem could have had the merchant or the miller, but no one else would do for her but her own humble ploughboy. Phoebe appeared for the last verse, piping away rhythmically but untunefully on her recorder. A musical interlude could generally be counted on to restore Phoebe's spirits.

'It's quite funny, really,' Bram said as he came to the end. 'These ballads were written by the farm labourers, and they often put themselves in the starring roles. The guy who wrote this one was probably a ploughman.'

Max was screwing up his face a little, in the way he did when he wanted to say something negative but wasn't sure how to phrase it in a non-hurtful way.

'It's a bit rough around the edges,' Bram conceded, 'but we've a few days to practise.'

'It's great, and the history behind it is really cool and everything, but they're not into that kind of stuff here, Dad. I'm not sure it's a good idea to sing that at the housewarming.'

'There's a long tradition of making your own entertainment in the north of Scotland,' Bram pointed out. 'At ceilidhs and get-togethers in the long winter evenings. People doing turns, singing a song or telling a story–'

'Yeah, maybe fifty years ago. Finn says they still have ceilidhs, but it's mainly just dancing now. And if there was any singing, I think it would be the locals doing it. That kind of stuff sounds... a bit peculiar, if you don't have the right accent.'

'*Och*, I've a few days to work on that too!'

Phoebe giggled, but Max rolled his eyes, setting his guitar aside on the sofa.

Max shared Bram's love of folk music from all corners of the world, and Bram had expected him to jump on this with his usual enthusiasm. He hardly thought Finn Taylor was representative of the tastes of the local population, but refrained from saying so. The Taylors were incomers too, having moved up here from Edinburgh a decade or so ago. Andrew had been in 'finance', whatever that meant, until he'd had a midlife crisis and decided to give up the rat race and open a restaurant in the Highlands. What did they know about the local culture?

'Don't do it, Dad,' Max muttered, getting up to replace his guitar in the corner by the bookcase.

'I thought it was good,' Phoebe asserted virtuously. 'You *kind* of sounded Scottish.'

'Och aye.' Bram stood, striking a pose. 'I'm a Hieland laddie now, you ken!'

WHEN EVERYONE else was in bed, Bram settled in the armchair next to the 'wireless' in the Walton Room, the 1930s vibe spoilt somewhat by the laptop open on his knee.

His blog, *Our Highland Home*, had gained a few followers – they now numbered two hundred and forty-nine, although most of them were friends and family. And there were twenty-six comments on this morning's post, which didn't surprise him given its content. There was no point doing a blog, in his opinion, unless it was warts and all, so he'd described the happenings of yesterday – the dead crow on the whirly, Bertie being shot at and the vegetable patch weedkilled.

He scrolled down the comments, pausing now and then to add quick replies: *Thanks, yes, we're all fine* or *The police are pretty sure it's just kids, which is borne out by what the neighbours have told us about hi-jinks going on in the woods a while back.*

The first comment from ManOnAMission was about halfway down.

Yeah. Okay. Your out-of-control animal rips its side on a barbed wire fence trying to get to a field of sheep (should sue the farmer – dear Bertie has every right to worry sheep if he so chooses). And, surprise surprise, you can't grow aubergines outdoors in Scotland. But no – someone 'shot Bertie' :-(:-(:-(and 'poured weedkiller on the vegetable patch.' :-(Sheesh.

There were a couple of replies from Jan and Freddie, two friends from London, telling ManOnAMission where to get off, and then a reply from someone called Red:

There ain't no cure for stupid, Man. Fucking wee hipster arsewipe.

Red had left his or her own comment further down. Just two words.

You people!

Bram snapped the laptop shut and sat for a moment, his fingers spread out on top of it, as if to contain what he'd just read safely inside. *You people...* What on earth was that about? *You people* as in what? Incomers? Londoners? Liberal-minded New Age lunatics? Had they got it all wrong? Had Bertie actually torn his shoulder on barbed wire trying to get into a field of sheep – had one of the locals seen it happen? Had the veg died from incompetence-stroke-overconfidence, from Bram's ignorance of the Scottish growing conditions? Were these trolls rightly indignant that the Hendriksens' default had been to blame local kids and call the police on them?

Well, even if that were the case, it was an honest mistake.

There was no excuse for trolling.

He'd warned Max and Phoebe often enough about cyber bullying. He'd never expected to be on the receiving end himself.

Just walk away, he always told them.

He stood, and set the laptop down on the chair, and literally walked away, across the room to the windows looking out onto the darkened verandah. The sky wasn't black, it still had a blue tint to it – the summer dusk this far north was late and slow – but it was dark enough to obliterate whatever was out there, the windows throwing back only his own reflection, an average Joe dressed in a vintage 1950s chocolate and beige polo shirt, navy M&S jeans and polished leather shoes, standing with arms dangling at his sides.

Fucking wee hipster arsewipe.

Bram wasn't 'wee'; he was five foot ten. And he wasn't a hipster. He was too old and he didn't even have a beard. Okay, the vintage polo shirt – but M&S jeans, for God's sake!

Before he quite knew what he was doing, he was twitching the curtains closed across all the windows and frowning at the four panes of glass in the upper section of the door, and asking himself why they hadn't thought to put up a door curtain.

6

If Bram was being honest, which he wasn't – 'Looks like a nice place,' he'd smiled as they'd parked up – the Inverluie Hotel was the kind of hostelry that showed to best advantage in the rear-view mirror. It had once, he supposed, been charming, a Victorian coaching inn by the side of the main road to Grantown, but uPVC window salesmen and lax planning regulations had done their worst. The bar was now housed in a hideous extension that resembled a public toilet.

'It used to be where all the cool kids hung out,' Kirsty told him, taking his arm as they walked from the car to the ramp at the door. 'The ones who had their own transport.'

Inside, the place smelt of spilt beer and stale cigarettes – how was that even possible when smoking in pubs had been banned in Scotland in 2006? The walls were covered in a shit-coloured atrocity that looked like laminate flooring gone wrong. There were garish plastic flowers in baskets on the windowsills, and 'Hi Ho Silver Lining' was blasting from speakers mounted on brackets near the ceiling.

Not surprisingly, only one table was occupied, but the far door, which seemed to be the fire exit, was propped open and there was smoke filtering through it from the unseen punters presumably standing just outside in order to have a fag, explaining the ash tray ambience of the place. At the occupied table sat an older woman and four young lads, all staring at the blank TV screen to one side of the bar.

The man behind the bar shook his head at Bram and Kirsty as they approached. 'TV's on the blink.'

The two men sitting on stools at the bar didn't look round.

'That's okay,' said Kirsty. 'We're here for the banter.'

The barman raised his eyebrows a millimetre. He was in his sixties, Bram guessed, a wiry little man with a head of thick wavy grey hair.

'Out on the razz,' Bram added.

'My brother's minding the kids and we're off the leash and running.' Kirsty's voice shook, just a little, with suppressed laughter. 'I'll have a white wine, please.'

'A bitter lemon for me.'

On the rare occasions they'd gone out for the evening in London, usually to friends' houses or the cinema, Max would babysit Phoebe. But when they'd suggested this arrangement for tonight, Phoebe hadn't been happy. 'Max won't be able to defend us,' she'd whispered to Bram. And so Fraser had been parachuted in. As far as Phoebe was concerned, Uncle Fraser was the ultimate tough guy, and he'd preened when she'd demanded to see his party trick of bending cutlery with his bare hands – not just teaspoons, but dinner knives and ladles and mashers. Bram had noticed Max surreptitiously trying and failing to bend a fork.

'I'm Kirsty and this is Bram.'

'Willie,' the barman reciprocated. 'You're the folk who've bought the Taylors' plot?'

Kirsty grinned. 'I'd forgotten how effective the bush telegraph is around here.'

'Oh aye,' said Willie, grimly pouring bitter lemon into a glass. 'No chance of keeping your private life private in this place.'

The two men on the barstools were shooting glances at Kirsty. She looked a million dollars in a stone-coloured linen dress, her hair loosely braided from the temples and pinned back behind her ears. With her cheekbones and tan and smoky eye make-up, and those striking green eyes, she was channelling Cleopatra, Hollywood-style. When he went out with Kirsty, he was well aware that people looking at the pair of them must be wondering what the hell she was doing with an ordinary bloke like him.

'Dog got shot,' one of the barflies muttered suddenly.

'Oh, um, yes.' Bram opened his wallet. 'Well, we think he was grazed by an airgun pellet. Or possibly he ripped his shoulder on barbed wire. Bit of a trauma, but he's going to be fine.'

Willie grimaced. 'Long as the wound doesn't get infected. Once sepsis sets in…'

'The vet gave him antibiotics, so he should be fine.'

'And what about the dead crow, eh, and the weed-killer? Someone's got it in for you folks and no mistake.'

'The police think it's just kids.'

Willie shook his head.

'Although…' Bram fished out his phone. Willie probably knew everyone within a ten-mile radius. Maybe he would be able to identify the trolls. 'We could have it all wrong. There could be a perfectly innocent explanation for it all. I've had some comments on my blog to that effect.'

'Trolls,' said Kirsty. 'Bram, I don't think Willie wants to see—'

Too late. 'Aye, go on, then.' Willie took the phone and narrowed his eyes at the screen. 'Jesus. Some right nutters out there, eh?'

'You don't recognise these names? ManOnAMission and Red?'

Willie shook his head. 'I don't do social media, and this is a good example of why not.' He sucked his teeth. 'The small-town mentality around here is shocking, let me tell you. And the xenophobia that comes with it. If I didn't have to work in this bloody bar I'd be off like a shot to Glasgow, or Edinburgh, or maybe London.'

'But why do you *have* to work in the bar?' Bram was genuinely interested.

Willie was counting out his change. 'Numpty of a brother owns the place.' As if this explained everything. 'What possessed you to leave London... for *this*?' He gestured around him.

Bram saw that the group at the table had transferred their stony gazes from the TV to him and Kirsty. He smiled at them. 'Hi.'

They continued to stare but remained mute, as if Bram were talking another language – or no, it was more as if he and Kirsty were animals in a zoo with which it wasn't even possible to communicate.

'Well, my family are here,' Kirsty told him. 'And it is home, when all's said and done.'

'And it's an absolutely gorgeous part of the world,' Bram enthused. 'You have to admit. London seems like a different planet. If I had to go back and live there now, I think I'd go crazy. I don't think I could cope with the hustle and bustle. It's amazing to wake up in the morning and hear birdsong drifting in at the window. And not another single sound.'

'Aye, granted.' Willie nodded. 'I like nature myself.'

Kirsty smiled. 'You say that as if you're confessing to some terrible addiction.'

'My name's Willie and I'm a forager,' he said, deadpan.

Bram practically jumped up and down. 'You forage for wild food? Oh, wow! That's exactly what I want to do once we're properly organised with the house. What kind of things do you forage for? Salady stuff? Mushrooms?'

'Aye, and pignuts, elderflowers, blaeberries… Best stay away from the mushrooms if you don't know what you're doing. Pick the wrong one and you could end up giving your whole family organ failure. Something like death cap, there's no antidote, right? Get that in your system and hello kidney dialysis for life, if you're lucky.' He swiped a cloth along the bar and gave a huge sigh. 'I *suppose* I *could* come over and show you the basics. Show you the safe ones you can't mistake for anything dangerous.'

'Well, that would be very kind of you, but I don't want to put you out.'

'It's no trouble.' Willie's tone was heavy with sarcasm.

'Right. Well, thank you very much.' Bram felt bad now, as if he'd badgered the man into agreeing to teach him how to forage for mushrooms. But playing the conversation back, he was pretty sure that wasn't how it had gone. He'd ask Kirsty later if she felt he'd been a bit pushy.

But Kirsty was no longer at his side. A new group of people had entered the bar, five or six women about their own age, and Kirsty was talking to them as they slung their bags over chairs and shrugged out of jackets. As Bram watched, Kirsty flung back her head and laughed, uninhibitedly, rather raucously.

Good. He'd hoped there might be people here she'd know.

They'd all been on edge since Bertie had been shot, and the revelation about David's conviction for assault had obviously hit Kirsty hard. She'd had a brittle quality to her these last couple of days, a closed-off look he knew all too well. He'd decided she needed to let off steam and she'd seemed keen on the idea of a night out, although when it had come to the point of leaving the house they had both hesitated, until Max had laughed: 'Go! What on earth do you think's going to happen with Uncle Fraser standing guard?'

The implication being that Fraser was a more effective 'guard' than Bram himself.

Fair point.

He joined the group of women at the table and tried to relax into it, nursing one soft drink after another as Kirsty knocked back the booze. The large, Marilyn Monroe-esque blonde called Isla keep trying to ply Bram with alcohol, no matter how often he repeated the mantra, 'I'm driving.'

'Oft, we're all taxiing. We can drop you two back. Go on, Bram, live a little!'

'Thanks, but no, we don't want to be too late. Kirsty's brother is babysitting.'

'Fraser? How is Fraser these days? Last I heard, he was at it with Graham Coull's missus.'

'Uh.' Bram realised that he had no idea about Fraser's love life. If he had thought about it at all, he supposed he had assumed just that sort of dubious arrangement. 'I suppose you all know each other from school?'

'Oh aye, thick as thieves!' Isla slapped her phone on the table in front of Bram as Kirsty, on the other side of the table, suddenly screamed with laughter, grabbing onto one of the other women, who was similarly red-faced with mirth. 'The gang.'

The image filling the screen was a throwback photo of a group of boys and girls in their early teens, the girls dressed rather inappropriately, Bram couldn't help thinking, in flimsy tops and very short skirts or cut-off jeans. They were in a park, against a backdrop of swings and a climbing frame, piling into the photo with wide-open mouths as they all shouted at whoever was taking the picture, obviously horrendously drunk. Some of them were holding cans, and there were bottles of cider and vodka visible on the grass behind them.

'Off out on the town!'

'You all look very young.'

'Thirteen, fourteen. There she is. There's Kirst.' She tapped a pink talon of a fingernail on the screen, on a face he only just recognised as Kirsty's. She was in the centre of the group, heavily made up, her babyish cheeks caked in foundation, her mouth shiny with bright pink lip gloss. Confident, happy, popular.

A different person entirely from the young woman he had known at uni.

'And that's Fraser.' The talon tapped at a muscly boy with his shirt off. Bram barely recognised Fraser with that mop of hair. 'And Scott was eye-candy even then.' Scott was, of course, playing it cool, in jeans and white T-shirt, smiling enigmatically, one arm round Kirsty.

'Andrew Taylor. *Andrew Taylor!*' the woman on the other side of Isla leant over to shout at Bram. Mhairi, he thought her name was. She had ruthlessly styled auburn hair and was very petite. Presumably the alcohol had affected her more quickly than the others.

'Uh, right?'

'Man who sold you the plot?'

'Yes, I–'

'*Tosser!*'

Bram's shock must have shown on his face, because Isla cackled: 'Not you, Bram, not you!'

'Andrew Taylor is a tosser,' Mhairi clarified.

'Ah. Okay. Is he? He seems a nice enough guy.'

Mhairi slumped over the table, the better to bring her face nearer to Bram's. 'Fully certified tosser. Decides what Grantown needs is a fancy-wanky "fine dining" experience – that's what he calls it on the website, a "fine dining experience"! These wee teuchters need educating about what food is, right, they need weaned off their nuggets and chips. Calls it *The Tappit Hen*. On the High Street?'

'Uh, yes, I've walked past the place.'

'Aye, you've walked past it, like everyone else!' laughed Isla.

Bram had in fact contemplated suggesting that the family go there for a meal, in the interests of good neighbourly relations. He'd stopped to examine the menu. There had been what looked like nice vegetarian options, and he had particularly fancied the 'supergreen soup with toasted almonds and artichoke toast', but then he'd seen that one of the other starters was 'pâté de foie gras with samphire and pain de campagne rondels'. He'd been meaning to talk to Andrew about that. Okay, to be honest, he'd been plucking up the courage.

'The place is going down the toilet,' said Mhairi with satisfaction.

He wasn't surprised. Whenever they passed, no matter the time of day, the restaurant was empty, or close to it.

'Aye, but what does he care?' said Isla. 'It's just a wee hobby for the man. They're rolling in it.'

Oh, well. If the restaurant was going under, maybe Bram shouldn't bring up the pâté de foie gras thing. Or should he? The place might limp on for months. Years, even, given that it seemed it was just a vanity project. Yes. He definitely needed to print out some stuff about how cruel the foie gras production process was, how they force-fed the poor birds, and give it to Andrew to peruse at his leisure.

'The Taylors seem like perfectly nice people,' he said stoutly.

The women blinked at him.

'Well of course they do,' said Mhairi at last. 'Of course they're all over you, rich bastards from London? No offence!'

Five minutes later and Bram was desperately thinking of excuses to leave. Maybe he could say Fraser had texted them and there was some sort of problem with the kids? Actually, it was possible Phoebe hadn't settled. He excused himself and went outside, past the smokers to a quiet corner of the car park to make the call.

'Aye, Bram, everything's hunky-dory, don't you worry, pal,' said Fraser. 'I've not even had a beer. Stone-cold sober, I am.'

'Right. Well, that's great. Thank you for doing this, Fraser. I just wondered how Phoebe was? She's not been settling at night, since Bertie…'

'The wee princess is off to the Land of Nod. Sleeping like a baby.'

'Really?'

'Nice cup of cocoa and a digestive, and she was out like a light. That's what Mum always gave us before we went to bed – cup of cocoa and a digestive. And yes, before you ask, she brushed her teeth afterwards.'

Wow. It seemed Fraser had hidden depths.

'Brilliant, fantastic. You're obviously a natural.'

'Aye, don't be hanging up the frilly apron just yet, Bram! Hey, you enjoy yourselves, right, and don't worry about us.'

He wasn't a bad guy, really.

'Thanks, Fraser. We really appreciate it.'

Back in the bar, Kirsty was lurching around with Mhairi and Isla, out on their own in the middle of the floor, trying to dance to 'Loch Lomond' by Runrig, a horrendous – in Bram's opinion – rock treatment of a lovely traditional Scottish air. Her hair had come out of her braids and she looked like a wild woman, swaying about barefoot, the two barflies hardly believing their luck, eyes out on stalks. Willie the barman, in contrast, was regarding the spectacle with a jaundiced expression.

She was just letting off steam.

She needed to let off steam.

Being back here, being home, would have been hard enough for Kirsty even without all the dramas of the last few days. It wasn't like this was going to be a regular thing. It wasn't like she was going to want to meet up with 'the gang' and get off-her-face drunk on a regular basis.

Was it?

7

B ram was an early riser, so at least he was up and about when the doorbell rang at 7:10 the next morning. At first he didn't recognise the diminutive man standing on the verandah dressed in a green knitted hat, red jacket and green trousers, a wicker basket tucked over his arm. He looked like a character in one of the fairy tales Bram used to read to Phoebe, and it took a moment before he recognised Willie the barman.

Willie raised an eyebrow a millimetre. 'Mushrooms.'

'Uh–'

'I thought you wanted some tips on foraging for mushrooms.'

'Yes! Yes, I did! Come in, Willie, come in. Good of you to call by.'

'I was coming this way anyway. I'll not come in.'

'Okay. Let me just leave a note for the slug-a-beds and get on my boots, and I'll be right with you.'

Bram wrote a note and left it on the kitchen table, adding 'Pick-me-up in fridge.' He didn't use the words 'hangover cure' in case the kids read it.

Kirsty was going to have one hell of a hangover when she eventually surfaced. Bram had zapped up his tried-and-tested cure and put it in the fridge to chill – apple juice, cranberry juice, prickly pear extract, ginger and Siberian ginseng. He couldn't remember the last time he'd had to make it.

Willie strode out in front, leading Bram across the paddock to the wood. At the tree to which two of the notices were stapled, Willie stopped, staring at Phoebe's.

'My daughter has quite an imagination,' Bram felt he should clarify.

Willie just nodded, striding off into the wood.

'Chanterelle,' he said, a couple of minutes later, pointing to a cluster of trumpet-shaped mushrooms by the side of the path, the colour of rich egg yolks.

'Wow, really?' Bram stooped to peer at them. 'I've only ever seen the dried variety. These look nothing like them.'

'Taste nothing like them. Slightly sweet, bit like a savoury apricot.' Willie cupped a hand gently under the largest one and twisted it out of the earth, brushing a couple of strands of moss off the ribs on its tapering sides. 'Smells of apricots too.' He held it to Bram's nose.

'Mm! It really does!'

'Of course, the false chanterelle, *Hygrophoropsis aurantiaca*, also has a fruity smell. Easy to confuse the two, but the gills of the true chanterelle are false gills, and the gills of the false chanterelle are true gills.'

Christ. 'Okay.'

'And the flesh of a true chanterelle is pale when you cut into it.' He picked another one and plunged a dirty fingernail into it, ripping it apart to show Bram the dense white flesh inside. 'But get them mixed up and…' He sucked his teeth.

'False chanterelle is poisonous?'

'Oh, aye. Wouldn't kill you, mind. Just cramps, diarrhoea, vomiting. Aye. The chanterelle is a good one for the amateur because it can't be confused with anything actually fatal.' Willie picked another half dozen chanterelles, and then straightened, but when Bram bent to do likewise, he said, 'Never take too many from the same clump. We want them to come back next year, don't we?'

So on they went, Bram's basket still empty. 'Maybe I could send you a photo of anything I forage, just until I get into the way of it, to confirm I haven't made a potentially dangerous error?'

Willie turned and looked at him. 'Aye, if you must, email me a photo.' He rummaged in his pocket for a pen and a scrap of paper on which to write his email address.

'Thanks very much.'

Bram imagined spooning unctuous chanterelle risotto onto Phoebe's plate, and telling her about gnome-like Willie who'd helped him find the chanterelle mushrooms in their own wood. It was important she realised that the wood wasn't a bad place – that good things could be found here.

After an hour's foraging, Willie announced that he was off, and when he'd gone, Bram started to relax into the whole thing. He was confident of being able to reliably identify the distinctive yellowy-orange trumpets, so he continued on into the wood, breathing in the earthy early-morning smells.

Foraging for food *from their own wood!*

Although of course he was more than happy for any of the locals, not just Willie, to do the same. Maybe he should put up notices to that effect next to the other ones, to soften the impact of what probably came across as rather aggressive territoriality.

Because he was intent on looking for the splashes of yellow on the forest floor, he didn't notice them until they were almost literally in his face: three crows, tied from the branches of a small birch tree by the legs, beaks swaying gently in the slight breeze.

Bram stopped, and slowly looked about him.

There were three more in another tree, this one further from the path. And another in a tree beyond that. The more he looked… It was like getting your eye in with the chanterelle. There was another. And two more, hanging from the gnarled branch of one of the old pine trees.

Jesus Christ!

He stood completely still, straining to listen, but all he could hear was the wind in the trees and a bird piping. Another answering. And then, suddenly, there were tiny birds all over the trees above his head, peeping and chirping and floating from one branch to the next. Tiny birds with long tails, moving in turn, it seemed, one past the other.

There was something obscene about it, this flock of living birds so busy about their business while on the branches under them hung the crows, silent and still.

As suddenly as they had appeared, the little birds were gone.

Maybe he'd scared them.

Or maybe something else had.

The problem with being in this part of the wood, the birchwood, was that you could only see a very limited distance in any direction. Bram started walking back down the path. And then he was running, the basket jiggling in his hand, the chanterelles jiggling out of it, and then he had dropped the basket and was sprinting along the path, feet hardly seeming to touch down he was flying along so fast, and –

'Vuuuuuw!' The wordless sound shot from his throat as he flew round a kink in the path and right into a man who grabbed him, whose strong hands tightened on Bram's upper arms, who –

Who said, '*Oofta*, Bram!'

Andrew Taylor, dressed head to toe in country gent wear, waxed jacket to the fore. He steadied Bram and released his arms.

'Crows,' Bram blurted, like a kid who'd run to an adult for help. 'There are crows, strung up in the branches. Dead crows.'

Andrew gave Bram's arm a dad pat. 'Ah.'

'Back there. I'd better get something to cut them down with before the kids see them. There must be – I don't know. At least a dozen.' And it struck him, suddenly. 'You don't seem surprised.'

'We can use this.' Andrew took a shiny penknife from a pocket of his jacket. Yup, Andrew would carry a penknife.

They started back along the path, and Bram retrieved his basket of chanterelles and the ones he'd dropped in his headlong flight, feeling a little sheepish that Andrew was obviously working out what had happened, that Bram had completely panicked.

How could he be so calm about this?

My God – could *Andrew* be responsible for the dead crows? But why would he want to shoot crows? Wild food for his restaurant? But surely not even Heston Blumenthal would serve up crow as a fine dining experience? And even if Andrew did have that in mind, he wouldn't just leave them hanging from the trees.

'There,' Bram said, needlessly, when they came to the place.

And there they were, the poor bloody crows, hanging like sick Hallowe'en decorations. As Andrew reached up to the first one, he said, 'They keep appearing in our wood too, which is why I carry the penknife. What I do is cut them down and put them in a pile, take the nylon string home, obviously, to be disposed of, and come back with a spade to bury them. I'll do that, if you like.' He dropped the first bird, *thwack*, to the ground, and turned to face Bram. 'I'm sorry. I – We haven't been entirely honest with you. Your father-in-law was right, we should have warned you that we've had… some trouble with local youths.'

Youths now, not *kids*, Bram noted. 'What kind of trouble?' he got out.

'Hanging around making a racket, bonfires, littering, graffiti – obscene graffiti. Cara was once followed through the woods by a couple of lads, which really shook her up, as you can imagine… But mainly it's dead animals. Crows, rabbits, hares, even a goose, a couple of cats… Strung up in the trees.'

'Oh my God.'

'Yobs. Yobs with airguns, or possibly shotguns, and nothing better to do.'

'But you told us you hadn't had issues with guns! For God's sake, Andrew! This is serious! Do the police know all this?'

'Not all of it, no. We decided it was best not to – antagonise the yobs further.'

'What do you mean, *further*?'

A sudden snap behind him had Bram jumping round, scanning the trees, the undergrowth, but he couldn't see anything. Anyone.

'We put notices up. *Private property – no right of way.* Which admittedly was a bit of a stretch. You know there's no law of trespass in Scotland? Only the area around one's house is sacrosanct. People have a "right to roam" through these woods, but we were hoping to discourage it. Had the opposite effect, unfortunately.'

'Great. So now the locals hate us.'

Andrew grimaced, reaching up to another bird.

'But this is extreme, surely? An extreme reaction to a few notices? It seems like the kind of thing seriously disturbed people do before – well, let's face it, before moving on to human targets.'

Andrew barked a laugh. 'This isn't the mean streets of London. You don't get many murderers to the square mile up here. I think we're safe enough.' He looked down at the small pile of dead crows at his feet, then back at Bram. 'Sorry. That was crass. I don't imagine Kirsty sees things that way. How is she holding up, after Bertie being shot?'

'Oh, she's okay, thanks.'

Of course, everyone up here would know about Kirsty's past, even relatively new arrivals like the Taylors. It was the kind of thing, he imagined, that was still talked about, still mulled over in the Inverluie Hotel bar, people putting forward their own pet theories, arguing, speculating.

'Dreadful thing, what happened – back in the nineties, wasn't it?' said Andrew, cutting down another bird and tossing it onto the pile.

Bram wasn't about to discuss this with Andrew. 'Well, I'd better get back. I left–'

It all happened in a heartbeat.

A crashing and a whooping, and a figure moving, at pace, in the trees to Bram's right.

Crack!

Thunk!

Crack thunk crack!

Something hit the tree right next to Bram.

'*Jesus, they're shooting at us!*' Andrew dropped to the

ground.

Bram just stood, frozen.

He could see him in glimpses through the trees, a figure in grey and black, running away. As Bram watched, he turned, just for a second, and *Oh God! Some kind of monster?* The contorted, hairy, grinning face of something not human –

A mask.

It was a mask.

And David's voice was in his head: *Are you a man or a mouse, Bram?*

He fumbled for his phone, taking a few stumbling steps into the wood, his fingertips stabbing at the screen. By the time he'd brought up the camera function the bastard was almost gone.

Almost, but not quite.

He pointed and tapped, pointed and tapped.

Andrew was lying on the ground with his arms over his head. Whimpering. Bram sank to the path next to him, his legs suddenly unequal to the task of holding him up. Had that really happened? Had someone really just tried to kill them?

Police.

He needed to call the police.

He stabbed 999.

'Police,' he squawked at the operator. And then, when he was put through: 'We've just been shot at. Someone in a mask with a gun. We're in the woods, we don't know if he's going to come back or–'

'Okay. What's your location?'

'Woodside. We're in the wood at Woodside, it's a new house, next to a house called Benlervie. Four miles outside Grantown-on-Spey. Postcode…' His mind went blank. 'Andrew, what's the postcode?'

He set a hand on Andrew's back.

Slowly, Andrew sat up. His hair was mussed and his expression fixed, confused, as if he'd just woken up. 'They shot at us.'

'What's the postcode?'

Andrew blinked. 'PH27 3TY.'

Bram repeated it into the phone.

'And what's your name?'

'What the hell does that matter? Bram Hendriksen and Andrew Taylor. Please. Just get here. *Someone's trying to kill us!'*

'Can you get inside your property and lock the doors?'

'No! We're in the woods! To the west of the house? Andrew?'

'North-west,' Andrew muttered.

'North-west of the house called Woodside!'

'All right, Bram. Can you get under cover and stay there, until the armed response unit arrives? Leave the phone on but keep quiet.'

Because the bastard might come back to finish the job. He might come back. Or –

What he if was *heading for the house?*

Bram was up and running before he had completed the thought process.

Kirsty. Max. Phoebe.

THE ARMED RESPONSE UNIT, from what Bram could see by peeking round the edge of the curtain in the TV room, consisted of four guys in bulky uniforms, presumably bulletproof vests. They trotted in single file across the grass to the wood and disappeared into it.

'I don't believe this,' Andrew kept saying. 'I don't believe it. And right after I'd said I thought we were safe from whoever's been shooting the animals. Do you think they heard me? Do you think they were listening to our conversation?'

Bram grimaced. 'Maybe.'

Andrew had called home and told Sylvia and the kids to stay inside. Now he was sitting slumped on the sofa, the mug of tea Bram had made him ignored on the side table. When Bram had taken off, Andrew must have run after him. When he'd reached Woodside, the first thing Bram had done, of course, was lock the door behind him, and Andrew had nearly given him a heart attack by pounding on it as Bram was heading upstairs to check on everyone.

They were all in the TV room now with the curtains closed. Kirsty was curled in one of the armchairs in her pyjamas, Phoebe squashed in beside her. Kirsty had hardly said a word when Bram had told her what had happened. She had just pulled him to her as if she never wanted to let him go.

They'd told Phoebe an edited version – that someone had been in the wood again, and some birds had been shot. But she was picking up on Kirsty's distress, latching onto her mother like a little limpet.

Max was pacing, staring at the screen of his phone.

That reminded Bram. He pulled out his own phone. 'I tried to get a photo, but… not much good for identification purposes.' He frowned at the blurry image.

'Can I see?' asked Andrew.

Bram held out the phone, which showed the trees and, if you looked very carefully, a blurry arm in some sort of grey garment and a leg in black. Useless. 'And that's the best one. I think he was wearing a mask.'

Bram rubbed his face. His face was tingling, as if the nerve endings had been primed by the bullets zinging past and were now on high alert.

The doorbell jangled, making them all jump.

'It might be Grandad,' said Max. 'I texted him. I thought – it might be good if he was here.'

'No, I'll go,' said Bram, pulling Max back. 'You all stay here.'

Thank God, thank God, it was more police officers. Two, three, four... Six in all. As they filed inside, a sturdy female officer, who introduced herself as DC Gemma something, rattled off a few quick questions about what had happened, finishing with, 'Your dog was recently shot with an airgun pellet, yes? Could this just have been an airgun too?'

'I don't know what kind of gun it was – all I know is he was shooting at us. Deliberately. Even if it was "just" an airgun, they can kill, can't they?'

'It has been known,' the DC conceded. She asked him to fetch Andrew so he could give his statement, and settled herself at the kitchen table with her notepad.

When Bram had ushered Andrew out of the TV room, he muttered, 'You'd better come clean about all the previous trouble you've had with youths in the woods.'

'All right, but – on reflection, I don't think this was kids. Someone *tried to kill us*, Bram!' Andrew looked at him. 'You don't think there could be a connection with – with what happened, back in the nineties?'

'What connection could there be?' Bram said weakly.

Andrew just continued to stare at him.

Bram headed across the Walton Room to the kitchen, awful thoughts chasing each other round his head.

'Okay, thanks, Mr Hendriksen,' said the DC. 'We'll take Mr Taylor's statement then someone will run him home.'

By that time Scott had arrived, and put on the kettle while Bram gave his statement to DC Gemma. Bram had just finished it when the door from the verandah crashed open and David stormed in.

'Is everyone okay?' David rapped out. 'Where's Kirsty? Where are the kids?'

Bram stood. 'In the TV room. David–'

'How did you get past the uniforms at the track entrance?' Scott wanted to know.

David waved this minor detail aside. 'There's a *bloody maniac* out there with a firearm *shooting at people!* Christ! He could shoot through the windows, he could–'

Scott got to his feet. 'Let's not panic here, okay?'

'I'm not *panicking*, I'm trying to *keep my family safe* because it seems no one else is bothering their arse!'

'They're in the TV room with the curtains closed,' said Bram, feeling himself bridle. 'And the windows are all toughened glass.' Even the ones that didn't need to be to comply with building regulations – David himself had persuaded them to go for that. Thank God. There was something to be said, it turned out, for David's jaundiced view of the world when it came to security.

'Aye, for general safety, not to stop a bullet! Are you a man or a mouse, Bram? You should be out there–'

'Sit down, David.' Scott gestured to a chair, indicating to Gemma with a tilt of the head that she should take herself off and give them some privacy.

The next couple of hours passed in a blur. After Scott had talked David down, David went off to 'protect' the family in the TV room. Scott downloaded the photographs of the gunman from Bram's phone, and then went outside, only to return to ask Bram to accompany him and the SOCO team to show them the spot where he and Andrew had been fired on.

Bram knew he was safe now – the gunman was hardly going to have stuck around with this massive police presence – but still he hesitated at the front door, reluctant to step out onto the verandah.

Scott looked back at him. 'Okay there?'

'Yes, right. Yes.'

Bram showed them the spot, and the tree the bullet had hit, and then Scott escorted him back to the house, where he sat with the others in the TV room watching cartoons until Scott appeared in the doorway and asked to speak to Bram, Kirsty and David in the kitchen. When they were all seated at the table, he smiled round at them.

'You'll be glad to hear that the "bullets" Bram described have been found by the SOCO team, and aren't in fact bullets at all. They're not even airgun pellets. They're airsoft BBs.'

Bram frowned. 'They're what?'

'BBs. Little plastic pellets kids use in BB guns for target practice and play battles? Same idea as paint-balling. If one of those hits you, it might sting a bit, but it won't penetrate the skin. You can relax.' The smile widened. 'I won't repeat what the leader of the armed response unit said when he was told.'

'But a BB gun is still a gun!' Kirsty exclaimed.

Scott shook his head. 'It's not classed as a firearm. BB guns carry a vanishingly small risk of serious injury at anything other than point-blank range – and this joker was keeping his distance. At that range, the worst that could have happened was an eye injury, or bruising from a pellet impact. It's nothing to worry about.'

'What about Bertie? What about the crows?'

'That must have been an airgun. Or in the case of the crows, maybe a shotgun.'

'Right.' David glared across the table at Scott. 'So the "joker" has access to a shotgun.'

'Obviously what's going on in that wood is cause for

concern.' Scott stood. 'Whoever shot at Bram and Andrew, even though it was just with a BB gun, was committing an offence by behaving in a such a way as to cause "fear or alarm", as the law puts it.'

Bram went with Scott to the door and out onto the verandah. It was another glorious day, the new gravel of the parking area and the roofs of all the police vehicles searingly bright in the sun.

'Scott,' said Bram, as the other man started down the steps. 'This wasn't just some kid messing with a BB gun who decided to have some innocent fun at our expense. There was… evil intent. He was wearing a mask, for God's sake.'

Scott came back up the steps. 'How sure are you about that? He was some distance away, you've said, and moving away from you at speed.'

'He turned – he looked back at one point, and I saw it. One of those Hallowe'en masks, a werewolf, I think…' He swallowed. 'This is all pretty disturbing stuff, Scott.'

'The chances are it's just the same kids who've been messing with the Taylors.'

Bram nodded. His face was still tingling; his senses super-alert for any movement on the track, in the grass, over by the trees. It was as if his brain knew he wasn't in danger any more, but the signals hadn't yet reached his body. He rubbed the skin under his eyes, his cheeks.

A radio in one of the cars crackled, and Bram saw there was someone in there, a female cop talking into the radio. Now she was getting out of the car and coming to the bottom of the verandah steps. 'Delivery driver at the track end,' she reported. 'Okay if one of the officers there signs for it, Mr Hendriksen? I can go down and get it?'

Bram froze. Was this someone trying to get past the police by pretending to be a delivery driver?

Then he remembered the cameras. They were due to be delivered today.

He nodded. 'Thanks. Thanks very much.'

WHEN THE LIGHT began to go, they pulled the curtains over all the windows, including the long expanse of glass in the Room with a View. There was something oppressive, he was beginning to think, about the emptiness of the landscape out there, the wild, uninhabited acres all around them.

'It's a room *without* a view now,' Max said, flopping down on a sofa.

Bram picked up the instruction booklet for the cameras and read the same paragraph for the third time, but he still couldn't make head nor tail of it. The arrival of the cameras had lifted his mood instantly. Finally, he felt they were doing something. When the little bastards were caught on camera, the police could take action.

Unless they were wearing masks.

He pushed the thought away.

Phoebe was curled up with Kirsty in the big armchair, already in her pyjamas. They were watching *Babe: Pig in the City* on the TV, Phoebe's eyelids heavy as she rested her head on Kirsty's chest.

Bram should probably ask Max to work out how to set up the cameras, but after the day they'd had, he felt the kids didn't need to see their dad at a loss when it came to the security measures they were installing. He was already feeling pretty chastened by the fact that, on learning that there could be a homicidal maniac out there, the first thing Max had done was summon David.

There was bound to be a YouTube video explaining it

all. Bram fetched his laptop, but instead of looking at YouTube, he couldn't help himself opening his blog. He'd added a post about the day's events, and the photo, in the vain hope that someone might recognise a blurry arm and leg.

Lots of comments from worried friends and family.

And another from ManOnAMission:

What actually happened was that you saw someone on the right of way through your wood and called the cops on them! That wood has been used by locals for centuries and now you're trying to exclude us? That's illegal.

God almighty! Bram knew it was probably a mistake to engage, but he couldn't let that go. He quickly typed:

We have no problem with people using the wood. What we have a problem with is being shot at, because that's what actually happened. My neighbour and I were shot at by a masked man. Excuse me for finding that unacceptable.

An hour later, there were eighteen replies to that, most of them from trolls – ManOnAMission and Red, but also some others.

You've had too many magic mushrooms, pal!

Oooh, a dangerous 'masked man' with a BB gun!!! :-)

What were you and your neighbour doing together in the woods in the first place?!! Oo-er!!

But it was Red's comment that made his blood run cold:

You're bringing this on yourself, Bram. Why don't you piss off back to London?

8

T he next morning, Bram, Kirsty and Max positioned the cameras in the wood, hiding them carefully in the trees. They were motion-activated, but only by large moving objects that gave off an infrared signal. Large creatures, basically. Anything from a fox up to a human. In daylight the pictures would be in the normal spectrum, but at night the cameras would switch to infrared imaging.

They removed all the notices, Kirsty agreeing with Bram that they could be seen as antagonistic, given the history the Taylors had with local youths. Then they gathered chanterelles for the risotto Bram was planning on making that night.

'It was just a BB gun,' Kirsty kept saying. 'If they'd really meant you harm, they wouldn't have used a *BB gun.*'

'No, of course they wouldn't.'

In the afternoon, David and Linda came over, and Max eagerly took David to check out the cameras. The two of them came back in high spirits, Max bounding onto the terrace where Kirsty and Bram were sitting. 'Grandad didn't spot a single one!'

He was obviously basking in the unaccustomed warmth of David's approval. David came onto the terrace behind him and turned to glare back at the wood with his feet apart, hands on hips, in the belligerent mode that always made Bram think of Henry VIII. Then he turned and smiled at Bram, and came over to literally pat him on the back. 'Good man. Good man. Now we'll get the bastards.'

'Yeah!' Max enthused.

Bram nodded, finding himself in complete sympathy, for once, with David.

But Kirsty looked from Max to her father and said, 'No one's *getting* anyone, Dad.'

'I'm sure David only means "get" as in "bring to book".'

Kirsty shot Bram a disappointed look.

'Those bloody Taylors, eh, Bram?' David muttered when Kirsty had gone back inside. 'Those bastards. They're to all intents and purposes at war with the local yobs, and they never saw fit to tell you?'

'I know. It was pretty unfair of them.'

'Unfair? *Unfair?*' David whistled. 'I know you like to try and see the good in everyone, Bram, but come on!'

'Yep, you're actually right, David.' And Sylvia had seemed so nice, too. But she'd lied to their faces, insisting that they hadn't had much trouble recently with yobs in the woods.

Max and Phoebe fitted Bertie with the petcam – not easy as he was still wearing the plastic cone – and they spent a hilarious hour or so watching the first bits of footage from it, Max and Phoebe describing to Linda what they were seeing as Bertie stuck his nose into every crevice in the kitchen that could conceivably harbour crumbs. The sound effects were particularly funny. 'You'd think the cone would stop him getting his head in there,' Max chuckled, 'but it seems not.'

David chuckled too. 'Oh aye, you'd have to put a hazmat suit on him to keep Bertie and crumbs apart.'

'Imagine Bertie in a hazmat suit!' Kirsty exclaimed. 'How cute would that be?' And father and daughter exchanged smiles.

Phoebe was delighted with Bertie-cam, and seemed to be reassured by the whole camera strategy in general. 'They can't do anything now, can they, Dad?'

'If they try, they'll soon be caught, *kleintje*.'

Then Kirsty had to leave for a meeting with a client, and Bram found himself pressing David and Linda to stay to dinner, but David wanted to 'swing by' a building site before dark on their way home.

So it was just Bram and the kids, but he was making a big pan of the risotto, as Kirsty would want some when she got back and Max would probably have at least two helpings. It smelt amazing, garlicky and savoury, and Bram's salivary glands were already going into overdrive. He'd carefully cleaned the chanterelle and left them to dry on tea towels, and sent a couple of photos to Willie to check that he wasn't about to give his family the gripes. Willie had been typically reassuring. *Not.*

Looks like you're good to go, but don't sue me if it all goes literally to shit.

But Bram had slit each mushroom to check that it was pale inside, which seemed to be a foolproof way of telling chanterelles from anything that would give you the runs. And at least there was nothing you could mistake for chanterelles that was really dangerous. He'd googled this just to confirm it.

So: chanterelle risotto with truffle oil and Parmigiano

Reggiano. *Mmmm!* He'd added half the chanterelles at the start of the cooking process, after he'd fried the onions and garlic and added the rice and the first splash of vegetable stock, to lend their flavour to the rice. The other half he'd add later, so those pieces would retain their texture better.

It had been a much better day, Bram reflected as he stood at the stove stirring the risotto. He had all the lamps on in the Walton Room and the halogens over the worktops, and it felt cosy and safe in here. He'd closed all the curtains and rigged up a makeshift cover for the panes in the door with a piece of cardboard and tacks, and he and Phoebe had drawn a mandala on the cardboard to match the one they'd painted on the wall of the downstairs loo, using a compass and her felt-tip pens.

It was very soothing, standing there stirring as the fat Carnaroli rice grains absorbed the liquid. He had Chilean cueca music playing on a loop on his iPod in the docking station, and found himself swaying in time and humming along.

'Da-aad?' called Phoebe from the Room with a View. 'Come and see this! It's so cute!'

'Okay, Phoebs.'

He turned down the heat under the risotto, added another splash of stock, and walked across the slate floor to the open door to the other room. Max and Phoebe were chilling on the sofas, one each, Max staring at his phone, Phoebe watching YouTube videos on the TV. The screen was filled by a freeze-frame image of an animal. Surprise, surprise.

'Hold on.' Phoebe frowned at the remote. 'I'll go back to the start.'

'Sixth time,' Max muttered.

'I'm going to watch it a *hundred* times!' Phoebe

gurgled. 'A *thousand*! Max is trying to pretend he doesn't think it's cute. He's trying to be cool. Keep trying, Max!'

'Ouch,' said Max, grinning.

Phoebe zapped the remote at the TV. A white rat was sitting on a fluffy pink blanket. Slowly, his eyes closed and his head dropped until his nose touched the blanket and he jerked awake again, only for the process to be repeated. The third time, when his nose hit the blanket it stayed there, little snuffling snoring sounds coming from the soundtrack.

'How cute is *that*?' Phoebe demanded.

'Super-cute, Phoebs.'

'Do you want to see it again?'

'In a bit. I'd better get back to the risotto. Hope you two are hungry – there's a tonne of it.'

Walking back out to the kitchen, he smiled to himself. Everything was getting back to normal. For maybe the first time, the house felt like a proper home. He shimmied across the kitchen in time to the cueca. Yep. It was –

Oh *Christ*!

Almost filling the pan of risotto was a big hunk of raw meat.

It was the shape of a massive strawberry, purplish-red with white fatty bits and stubby white tubes poking out of the top –

It was a heart.

A raw heart, oozing blood into the risotto.

And on the worktop next to the stove was scrawled in blood:

Your next

Someone was in the house!

His head snapped up as he scanned the open-plan

space between the kitchen and the door. He backed up, and then he turned and ran, he ran back into the Room with a View and slammed the door behind him, pressing his back against it.

'Max, call the police.'

Both kids looked up at him.

'Just do it! Now!'

'Why, what's happening? *Okay, okay.'* Max tapped at his phone and put it to his ear, then came to stand next to Bram. 'Police, please,' he said into the phone, and then: 'What do I tell them? What's happening?'

'There's someone in the house. Okay, okay, Phoebs, we're safe in here. I'm going to pull the sofa across the door. Max, stand here with your back against it while I – Phoebe, check that the sliding door is locked.'

Phoebe jumped off the sofa and ran over to the door, then stopped, her hand on the curtain. 'What if they're *right there?*' she said, her voice wobbling.

Bram hauled the sofa in front of the door and then went to Phoebe, pulling her into a quick hug and then putting her aside gently to twitch the curtain open and check that the door was locked. He removed the key and pocketed it.

'Who's in the house?' Phoebe said in a small voice, clinging to him.

He pulled the curtain back in place. 'I don't know. Probably just – just one of the naughty boys. The police will be here soon to sort it out.'

He hugged her close, watching Max as he talked to the 999 operator, marvelling that the boy was able to keep his voice steady. His kids. His precious, precious kids. Someone had come into their house, into their home, was out there now, maybe, standing on the other side of that door –

The fear, the terror for them seemed to expand until

it had nowhere to go, until, like a chemical reaction gone nuclear, it turned in on itself and changed, transmuted into pure, white-hot rage.

But he just stood, holding Phoebe, the rage coursing through him – useless, useless rage, because it wasn't enough, it wasn't enough to make him open that door and get out there and confront whoever was doing this.

'I wish Grandad was here,' muttered Max, and Bram couldn't help but agree.

Are you a man or a mouse, Bram?

Turned out he wasn't any sort of a man at all.

9

In the early morning light, Bram stood on the gravel area beyond the verandah, shaking his head. They were ranged in a semicircle in front of him – Kirsty, David, Fraser, Scott and Gemma the DC. Behind them, a man in a white suit was dusting the door for prints. It promised to be another beautiful day, already fragrant with pine resin and the dew evaporating off the grass.

'I locked the front door,' he said again. 'I know I did. After you left–' He turned to face Kirsty – 'I locked the door behind you and put the key on its hook in the key cabinet.'

David shook his head, staring off.

'You can't have done,' said Kirsty. 'The door wasn't locked when the police arrived.'

Bram couldn't explain that.

'Our working hypothesis,' said Scott, 'is that the intruder arrived with the intention of leaving the pig's heart on the doorstep. He tried the door just on the off chance and found it open, so decided to opportunistically leave the heart inside.'

'That message – "Your next" – surely that suggests

that this isn't just the kids the Taylors have been having issues with?' Bram stared at Scott, willing him to put two and two together so he wouldn't have to come out and say it in front of Kirsty.

That Andrew Taylor could be right.

That this wasn't just kids.

That it had something to do with what had happened all those years ago.

That this was about Kirsty.

THE BACK ROOM *of the Bull and Bell, a few blocks from the halls of residence, had been the venue for Zoë Fisher's twenty-first birthday party. Bram had arrived late on painfully blistered feet, tottering through the door in his size 9 burgundy court shoes. Was Kirsty McKechnie here? The party was in full swing and, with almost everyone having followed the fancy dress code and come as a character from* Father Ted, *it was difficult to recognise people.*

Zoë howled when she saw him. 'Oh my God! You're definitely the best Mrs Doyle!'

'Thanks,' Bram grinned, adjusting his hat, a blue felt 1950s number which kept threatening to fall off. 'And don't take this the wrong way, but you're a pretty good Tom.'

Zoë was dressed in a dirty T-shirt with 'I shot JR' on the front, jeans and filthy trainers, with her short hair mussed and mud on her face. She gave Bram a mad stare.

Bram shuddered. 'Almost too *good.'*

'I can't believe how much trouble everyone's gone to!' she enthused. 'And yes, before you ask, even Kirsty! She's here!'

'Ooh, really?' Bram had done his utmost to bring this miracle about, but he still hadn't expected her to come. He'd told Zoë, who was also doing history but in the year above him, all about Kirsty and how she needed to make friends, and got Zoë to ask Kirsty to the party. They'd set up an ambush to

enable this to happen. Zoë had lurked in Bram's room until they'd heard Kirsty leave hers and then pounced, engaging her in conversation and casually handing her an invitation. And then Bram had waged a campaign to persuade Kirsty to come, asking for advice on his costume and making suggestions for hers. She owned a fluffy white fleece, so he had suggested she accessorise it with a few well-chosen items and come as Chris the Sheep.

Now he could see her.

Standing by the far wall, with a glass in one hoof, was an adorable Chris the Sheep, wearing the fluffy fleece teamed with black leggings, black boots and black mitts. A sheep mask was pushed to the top of her head. Probably way too hot in this oven of a back room.

'Hey, Kirsty!' he tottered over to her. 'You look great!'

Her strained expression was transformed by a huge smile. 'Bram?!'

He attempted a pirouette to show off his costume. 'How the hell do women spend their lives dressed like this? It's a form of torture.'

'The shoes?'

'Yes, mainly the shoes.' He kicked them off. 'I'm going to ritually burn them tomorrow. But also the skirt. Draughty or what?'

'Now you know how it feels to be a real fashion victim.'

Bram indicated her glass. 'Want another?'

'Thanks.'

When he returned with a gin and tonic for Kirsty and a pint for himself, she asked him where he'd found all the components of his costume.

'Charity shops. Jake and I – Jake's also Mrs Doyle, although naturally an inferior version… he's here somewhere – Jake and I went on a mission on Friday, combing the charity shops for suitable attire. There's a surprisingly good selection, let me tell you, of size 9 court shoes.'

Kirsty spluttered. 'I can just imagine the scene!'

'Turns out I'm a size fourteen in tops, ten in a skirt.'

'It's the shoulders, I guess.'

He nodded happily. Wow, but this was great! She was talking to him normally, she was making eye contact – she was, unbelievably, bantering *with him! Kirsty! The Weird Girl!*

Although he mustn't think of her like that.

She was just shy.

Was she?

Now he wasn't so sure.

'The elderly women staffing the shops were not altogether on board with the whole cross-dressing thing. Are Jake and I the first people ever to be banned from the Sue Ryder on Tottenham Court Road for trying on a lilac Laura Ashley blouse and a lemon-yellow British Home Stores twinset?'

'I wish I'd been there!'

So do I.

Oh. Where had that come from?

Kirsty sipped her drink. 'I hope Zoë appreciates the traumas involved in these costumes.' She pulled the mask down over her face, and gestured at herself. She really was so adorable in that costume. 'There was Chris the Sheep, minding his own business, trotting along the pavement trying to find the Bull and Bell, when this urban fox appears from an alleyway round the side of a shop. Couldn't believe his luck! A defenceless sheep wandering the streets of Fitzrovia… And the mad thing was that just for a millisecond I did find myself thinking Oh-oh *– a predator of sheep!'*

Bram chuckled. 'You've inhabited the role.'

'I am *Chris the Sheep!' she gurgled happily, striking a pose.*

The party rocked. Both Bram and Kirsty were much in demand for photographs, and Bram lost track of her for five minutes when Zoë insisted on getting together the 'best'

Father Ted, Father Jack, Father Dougal and Mrs Doyle for a group photoshoot. As Father Jack leant in for a snog and Bram took evasive action, he noticed a commotion going on across the room. Nothing unusual about that, when you combined students and alcohol, but then he saw Chris the Sheep stumbling backwards away from Mrs Doyle, aka Jake, and shouting:

'Get away from me!'

And then Bram was across the room, putting himself between them. 'What's going on?' he demanded of Jake.

'Nothing! I never touched her!'

It was all Bram could do not to lay hands on him. He'd never felt anything like it, the surge of rage flooding his brain at the thought of anyone hurting Kirsty.

Bram turned to her. 'What did he do?'

'Nothing. He didn't do anything. It's–' She looked past Bram at Jake with a little grimace of apology. 'I'm sorry. I'm sorry.'

And she turned and fled.

Bram ran after her, out of the pub, out onto the pavement, wincing as his feet, protected only by thin nylon tights, made contact with little stones and other debris he wasn't normally conscious of. 'Kirsty! I'm ripping my feet to shreds here!'

She slowed at that, and stopped, and turned. In the harsh light of the street lamps, her face was paler than ever, tearstreaked, stricken. Bram tiptoed up to her.

She wiped at her face. 'Go back in. I'm fine.'

'Oh yeah, you're fine. *I can see that. What did Jake do?'*

She sighed, and looked off. 'He really did nothing. He – actually, he asked me if I wanted to go for a pizza.'

'Riiight…?'

'He was – you know when someone gets that look, they're bending over you like they want to kiss you?'

'Not personally, no.'

'I couldn't deal with it. But it wasn't his fault. He did nothing wrong.'

And the answer came to Bram, all at once. Oh God, poor Kirsty! And the rage was back. 'You were — you were assaulted, weren't you? You were sexually assaulted.'

She looked at him for a long moment, sweet little Chris the Sheep, tears drying on her face. 'No.'

'But something happened to you.' Very gently, Bram touched her arm.

'Something happened,' she said. 'But not to me.'

He said nothing. He just waited. But she didn't say any more, and in the end Bram suggested they return to the halls of residence.

'You'd better get your shoes,' she said.

'I think I'm better off without them. If we go slowly.'

Back at the halls, Bram expected Kirsty to scuttle into her room and close the door on him, but on the threshold she turned. 'If there's no one in the kitchen, do you fancy just — sitting in there a while? I don't want to... I don't want to...' She gestured at her empty room, the bed, the prospect ahead of her, presumably, of the usual crying herself to sleep.

'Sure. Just let me de-Doyle and I'll meet you in there.'

Bram slung on joggers and a T-shirt and found Kirsty in the kitchen. She had changed into cosy pyjamas and slippers. He put the kettle on for hot chocolates and Kirsty sat at the table. As he spooned cocoa into mugs, she said:

'My boyfriend... At home. My boyfriend Owen. He was murdered.'

Bram carefully put the spoon down and turned to look at her. 'Oh no, Kirsty.'

'And I can't — I can't even contemplate... the idea of being in another relationship, even going for a pizza with a boy — I can't do it. It's bad enough trying to hold it together at the best of times, it's bad enough being around people and trying to act normal, when — when—'

'I'm so sorry.' He didn't know what to do. He wanted to hug her, but she probably wouldn't want that. So he just sat down next to her without making any sort of a move to touch her and without saying anything more. If she wanted to tell him about it, presumably she would. And in the end, she said:

'They found his body in the river. The River Spey. He'd been... he'd been tied up.'

'Oh Christ! That's...' What the hell could he say? Anything he said would be so inadequate. 'That's really awful,' was all he could come up with.

She nodded, and he got up, in the end, to finish making the drinks and bring them to the table. For a while they blew on them and sipped without speaking. Then:

'I can't be with anyone else,' she said, and looked away.

'Because it would be like a sort of... betrayal? Of Owen?'

At the time he didn't think anything of it, the tiny hesitation before she nodded.

Another long silence, and then Bram, for some reason, found himself telling Kirsty about his family in Amsterdam, his grandparents and uncles and aunts and cousins, the whole noisy, impossible, wonderful tribe of them, and at last Kirsty smiled, and then she was slumping, asleep on his shoulder, making little puffs as she breathed.

He sat in that scuzzy kitchen and breathed in time with Kirsty, feeling the warmth of her against him, wanting so much to be able to take her pain away, to wave a magic wand and take it away. At one point he dared to kiss the top of her head, her clean, shiny, girl-smelling hair, as if she were his sister.

But she wasn't his sister.

Oh, good merciful heaven, no.

Scott didn't help him out, so Bram was forced to say, 'You don't think... This might seem like a stretch, but you don't think this could in any way be connected to Owen Napier's murder?'

David snorted, and Kirsty shook her head.

'What if there's some nutter out there who...' He stared at Kirsty. He really didn't want to say this, not in front of her, but what choice did he have? 'Who's obsessed with Kirsty, who killed Owen... And now Kirsty's back and she's got another partner – me – and the nutter wants *me* gone too?'

Kirsty was still shaking her head.

Scott was smiling. The bastard was actually smiling. 'That's quite a stretch. No, Bram, I think I can say with some confidence that the two things are pretty unlikely to be connected. Owen's murder was a drugs killing, ninety-nine per cent. The theory was that he was either supplying drugs to an organised crime group and there was a falling out, or he was muscling in on someone else's patch and they took exception to that.'

'But whoever's doing this to us seems to be targeting me specifically. The weedkilling of the veg, shooting at me in the wood... and the comments on my blog. And now the pig's heart in my risotto, and *Your next...* That's similar to some of the trolls' messages. There's one calling themselves Red.' Bram got out his phone. 'Take a look. "You people". And "You're bringing this on yourself, Bram". I think Red could be the one. Someone obsessed with Kirsty who's targeting me.'

Scott examined the comments. 'Although in this case the "you're" is grammatically correct.'

'They could have made a deliberate mistake to throw us off the scent.'

'It's just wee yobs,' said David scornfully. 'This has got nothing to do with Owen.'

'How can we know that?'

Kirsty put a hand on his arm. 'Dad's right. Scott's

right. I'm sure this has nothing to do with Owen.' Like
Bram, she hadn't got much sleep, after arriving back last
night to find the place swarming with cops. There were
dark, sunken-looking semicircles under her eyes, which
were bloodshot. 'Can we go up to our bedroom?' she
asked Scott.

'Aye, but use the terrace doors.'

Bram followed Kirsty into their room and crossed to
the expanse of glass in the gable to look out at the
paddock, the field, the wood, the hills beyond, but he
wasn't seeing gorgeous scenery. All he was seeing was
potential hiding places. Was Red out there now,
crouched in that concealed dip in the field, or lying on
his stomach in that clump of bushes? Watching and
waiting?

Kirsty sat down on the bed. 'We have to try to keep
things in proportion and not jump to wild conclusions.
There's no way this could have anything to do with…
with Owen.'

'How can you know that? We're obviously being
targeted – *I'm* being targeted.'

Kirsty sighed. 'This sort of stuff has happened before
to the Taylors. The only reason we're being "targeted" is
that we live next door to them. You're being paranoid.'

'But don't you think it's a bit of a coincidence that as
soon as you move back home, some nutter is coming
after me? And I'm getting messages on my blog telling
me – *me*, specifically – to go back to London or else?'

'No one's *coming after you*. And they're just trolls.
You shouldn't take anything they say personally, Bram,
you know that.'

Was he being paranoid?

Those BB pellets had been aimed at him. He was
almost sure of it. Okay so maybe they weren't dangerous, but still.

'Did Owen… The same kind of thing didn't happen to Owen, did it? In the time leading up to his murder? He wasn't threatened? Someone didn't try to put the frighteners on him, to get him to leave town? To leave *you*?'

'No. Owen's death… It was nothing to do with me. Like Scott said, Owen was involved in supplying drugs to an organised crime gang.'

Bram nodded. She was probably right. 'I'm sorry. For bringing all the Owen stuff up again.' He sat down beside her and pulled her into his arms. 'I'm sorry.'

'It's okay. I agree that this is really worrying, someone actually coming inside the house… What are we going to do? Should we have the kids stay on with Mum and Dad for now, or should we go and get them? I really want to go and get them, Bram.'

Max and Phoebe had been bundled off to David and Linda's house last night, while Bram and Kristy had stayed here with the police. Linda had called earlier to say that Phoebe was in quite a state and was desperate to come home. And Max also wanted to come back. It had surprised Bram to hear that Phoebe wanted to come home. Despite all their reassurances that it was just naughty boys and the police would sort them out, he'd assumed she'd be glad to be far away from the 'psychopath' – but Phoebe had never really settled at David and Linda's in the two months they'd spent there, always wanting to know 'When will *our* house be ready?'

Of course she wanted to come home, but was it safe?

Bram could only lift his shoulders, helplessly.

He didn't know.

He didn't know what to do.

'Okay,' said Kirsty briskly, standing up. 'I'll ask Scott what he thinks.'

Bram trailed her back down the stairs and outside and round the house to where the others were still standing. He watched Kirsty walk up to them. He watched her speak to Scott, saw Scott's slight smile as he turned to her. His hand, momentarily, going to touch her back.

David was listening to their conversation, nodding along to what Scott was saying, looking from Scott to Kirsty and back. David obviously had a lot of respect for Scott. His dream scenario would probably be Bram high-tailing it back to Islington, Scott leaving his wife and getting together with Kirsty. He'd be a great stepfather for Phoebe and, particularly, Max. *A great role model for the lad.*

The thought that flashed across Bram's mind was so outrageous, so awful, that he dismissed it immediately: *that it was David.* That David had shot at him in the wood, that David had left the heart in the risotto pan. David had a key, after all, to the house. Bram was positive he'd locked the front door.

But David would never have hurt Bertie. He adored that dog.

Maybe he hadn't. Maybe it was just kids who'd shot the crows, who'd accidentally shot Bertie. And David had used what had happened to his own ends, to escalate it, to terrorise Bram into leaving. Even Kirsty as a single parent would presumably be preferable to Kirsty lumbered with Bram.

No. David would never terrorise his beloved grandkids. *Never.*

Bram crossed the gravel to join them. David had stopped nodding along, he noted, and was standing with his feet apart, Henry VIII style.

'Scott thinks it's okay for the kids to come back,' said Kirsty.

'I've arranged for a patrol car to come by every few hours through the night,' said Scott. 'Not that I think you're in any actual physical danger. This has *bored wee yobs* written all over it.'

'How can you be sure they're harmless?' Bram objected. 'They broke into the house!'

'The door was unlocked. If they'd intended to actually hurt you, they had a golden opportunity, which they didn't take. I'm not saying they're harmless, Bram. Of course I'm not. Intimidation like this is harm in itself. When we get them, they'll be charged with harassment, don't you worry. The courts will slap a restraining order on them.'

David shook his head. 'Bram's right.' Everyone looked at him, as if they thought they'd misheard. David grimaced, almost apologetically, but he went on: 'What use is a patrol car calling by a few times in a night? Will they be detaching their arses from the car seats at all? How do they expect to catch the toe-rags by driving up and down the track a few times?'

'It's more the deterrent value. When they see there's a police presence, they're not likely to come anywhere near the place. The patrol car will call by here, and also Benlervie.'

'Have you let the Taylors know what's happened?'

Scott nodded, as two of the techie guys came down the verandah steps, one carrying a box that presumably contained their kit.

'Okay folks, all done,' one of them said.

'So we can use the kitchen?' said Kirsty.

'Yeah, go ahead.'

'Let's have a cup of tea. And I don't know about you, Bram, but I'm starving.'

They hadn't been able to access the kitchen since it happened. Scott – who thought of bloody everything –

had appeared bright and early this morning with a thermos of coffee and a couple of vegetarian pasties. But that was hours ago.

In the kitchen, the blackened pan was sitting on the worktop. Presumably they'd taken away the heart and the burnt rice. Before he filled the kettle, Bram put the pan in the sink and skooshed Fairy Liquid into it. Not that he wanted to use that pan ever again. But maybe he could donate it to a charity shop.

He turned on the hot tap and water gushed through the mixer into the pan. Then he got the kettle, shut off the hot tap and turned on the cold one.

Nothing happened.

The mixer tap just shuddered.

The techs must have shut off the water for some reason. Bram opened the cupboard under the sink and found the stopcock. He tried to turn it anticlockwise, but it wouldn't budge. It was already turned on.

Oh, great. This was all they needed.

'Got a problem here, guys. There's no water.'

SYLVIA WAS PRACTICALLY WRINGING her hands, standing in the kitchen frowning at the taps as if she could will the water back. 'I'm *so sorry*. After everything else that's happened…'

'We've never had a dry spell like this, in all the years we've been here,' Andrew added defensively, arms crossed above his belly. 'Seems the spring just isn't adequate for two households in the summer. A summer like this, anyway. Climate change, I suppose…'

Woodside's water supply was shared with Benlervie's. It came from a spring, apparently, that filled an underground tank on Benlervie's ground. But the spring, Andrew had informed them, had dried to a trickle.

'It couldn't have been sabotaged, could it?' asked Bram.

Andrew looked at him blankly. 'Sabotaged?'

Scott shook his head. 'How would someone go about sabotaging a spring?'

Bram could only shrug.

'I'm afraid we're going to have to ask you to make other arrangements,' Andrew went on. 'There was a clause, you'll remember, in the contract, in the section about the water supply, stating that we can't be held responsible for failure of the supply.'

Oh, you bastard, Bram wanted to say. But he just nodded numbly.

'That's so helpful,' sneered David. 'Thanks a lot, pal.'

'Dad,' said Kirsty.

'You'll need to sink a borehole,' Andrew added. 'Which is a simple enough procedure. Cost a bit, mind you.'

'But what are we going to do in the meantime?' Kirsty was standing with her back to the worktop, also with her arms folded.

'Come and live with us,' said David.

'And we've got the housewarming on Saturday,' Kirsty continued, as if David hadn't spoken. She was making eye contact with Bram, looking at him in the way she did sometimes, as if she knew he would sort it, she knew he would make it all right.

'The stream,' he found himself saying. 'We can get water from the stream in buckets, for flushing the loos and washing the dishes. Bottled water to drink.' In glass bottles, though, not plastic.

'What about showering?' from David.

'We can survive on sponge baths for a while. Or a

dunk in the stream. With the odd visit to you for a hot shower. Just until the borehole can be dug. I'll get onto that today.'

Sylvia was staring at him, her eyes filmed with tears. 'I'm *so sorry*,' she repeated. 'Is it really a good idea to be going back and forth to the stream all the time, with whoever is doing this still out there…? It's so scary, the way everything's just *escalated* suddenly. And all that cruel trolling stuff on your blog.' She shook her head. 'It's like that awful case a couple of years ago, do you remember it, that poor couple who moved into a house in the country in Perthshire? The locals took a dislike to them for some reason, and they were victimised for *months* without the police taking any action, and one of their children ended up being killed?'

Bloody Nora.

IT MADE sense to relocate the cameras from the wood to the house. When everyone had gone, and Kirsty had taken the Discovery to pick up bottled water and get the kids, Bram psyched himself up to go back into the wood. It would only take half an hour to remove the six cameras. Scott was right – whoever was doing this, their intention seemed to be to freak them out, no more. The way to deal with it was *not* to freak out.

Once they saw that their scare tactics weren't working, they'd stop.

Would they?

Or would they step it up a gear?

But their best chance of putting a stop to it was definitely the cameras.

Bram had been on the point of asking Scott if a police officer could stay behind and help him relocate them, but then he'd remembered the conversation with Willie in the bar about the bush telegraph. As things stood, the only people who knew about the cameras were Bram, Kirsty, the kids, David and Linda. Best it stayed that way. He would check the SD cards to see if they'd picked anything up, and only if they had would he tell the police about the cameras.

Funnily enough, as he carried his toolbox along the path through the paddock, he found that not too much psyching himself up was required. He was still running on adrenaline, he supposed. That surge of anger he'd felt last night – he found he could still tap into it as he approached the wood. He had his phone at the ready, with the camera function primed. He hoped he *did* see someone. This time he'd get a proper shot of the bastard.

The rage that had consumed him last night – and it had consumed him, as he stood there in the Room with a View with Max and Phoebe, with who knew what on the other side of that door – it had swept away all rational thought. He guessed it was primeval. Instinctive. There was probably a special neural pathway that lay dormant, that might lie dormant all your life, that was only activated if the lives of your children were threatened.

Okay, so with his rational mind, with the evolved, intelligent, logical part of it, he now accepted that the kids' lives had never actually been in danger. No one had tried to get into the room, to smash through that door, to burn the house down like the Big Bad Wolf coming after the Three Little Pigs. It was probably just some messed-up kid who'd never had the life chances Bram had been privileged to enjoy, who didn't have a loving family to set him on the right path. Someone to be pitied, not condemned.

But the primeval part of his brain wasn't rational.

And those neurons were still sparking off a signal whenever he thought about that bastard.

That complete and utter *bastard*.

Was that all that was happening, though? He was tapping into some primitive instinct? Wasn't it possible that the rational part of his brain was in agreement with the primitive bit? Was he having a Road to Damascus moment, only in reverse? Was this Bram Hendriksen reluctantly confronting the possibility that David McKechnie's repellent world view might be closer to reality than his own? He'd begun to worry about David's influence on Max, his gentle, sensitive boy who seemed to be starting to buy into David's mindset… But what if Max, clever Max, was weighing the two of them up and coming down on David's side because the evidence suggested that David was right?

David was always accusing Bram of being hopelessly naïve. Hopelessly liberal and gullible and in denial about the underlying dog-eat-dog nature of human interactions. And Bram, in his arrogance, hadn't even stopped for a second to consider the possibility that David could be in any way, shape or form right. He'd been completely dismissive of and dismayed by what he'd thought of as David's unreconstructed right-wing views.

But could David have a point, about this at least?

Bram had, after all, enjoyed a pretty charmed, sheltered existence, up till now. What did he know, really, about the darker side of life?

If he was going to defend his family, maybe it was time to lose the rose-tinted spectacles.

10

'Look,' said Kirsty. 'I know it's not ideal, but we
have to try to retain some sort of feeling of
normality, don't we? The kids have been
looking forward to the housewarming for weeks. The
Millers are coming, and you know how desperate
Phoebe is to see Lily, Rhona and Katie. It's not as if we
can have a sleepover at the moment – four little girls in
the house and no running water? And Phoebe's night
terrors would infect the lot of them. Can you imagine
the hysterics? They'd never get to sleep.'

Bram and Kirsty were sitting at the kitchen table,
sharing a bottle of water. It was weird how knowing
there was a limited supply of the stuff made you thirsty.
This was Bram's second bottle and it wasn't even eight
o'clock in the morning.

The morning of the bloody housewarming party,
which Kirsty was determined to go ahead with.

He grimaced. 'It's going to be a challenge, though,
isn't it, throwing a party with no water?'

'We've got plenty of bottled stuff, and lots of soft
drinks as well as the alcohol. We can fill up the cisterns

of each of the loos, and tell people not to flush unless strictly necessary. And we can line up buckets of water for refills, and for pouring into the sink for washing hands.'

'I guess. But with some nutter running around out there determined to terrorise us, does it really make sense to throw open our doors to all and sundry?'

There had been nothing on the cameras, which wasn't too surprising given that the intruder had probably approached the house via the track, not the woods. The camera sited where one of the paths through the wood met the track had been pointing the wrong way.

'I think it does.' Kirsty took a gulp from the bottle of water. 'It's not as if we're going to be in any danger, with a house full of people. And we need to try to get the locals onside. What better way than to welcome them into our home?'

Bram flashed on an image of the pig's heart, dumped in the middle of the risotto pan. 'I'm not sure how welcoming I'm going to manage to be. And as for the concept of a *housewarming*…' He grimaced. 'It just seems so inappropriate. The intruder – all the stuff that's been going on – it's like it's taken away the feeling of *home* altogether. He's taken it from us. Your home should be your sanctuary, where you feel safest.'

'Bram–'

'I'm starting to wonder if maybe your dad is right. The softly-softly approach with these people… How's that ever going to work? That notice we put up was pathetic – effectively *apologising* for asking the yobs to behave like decent human beings. We might as well have laid out the red carpet and asked them to trample all over us.'

'No, Bram. Dad isn't right. Of course he isn't!'

'Yeah, we look down our noses at him, don't we? We

think we're so much better than him? But if David had been there last night, he'd have been on that bastard like a Rottweiler.'

'Bram–'

'And I'm the better person?'

'Of course you are! Where do I even start?' She reached across the table and took his hand. 'And if it had come to it, you'd have done anything necessary to protect the kids.'

'Would I, though? Would I have been able to protect them? *In their own home?*' He shook his head. 'I'm sorry. I'm probably overreacting.'

She smiled. 'Of course you are. You've always wanted to… to wrap the people you love up in a safe place, haven't you?'

'What's wrong with that?'

'Oh, Bram, nothing, it's lovely!' The smile widened. 'Remember when we were deciding where to go on honeymoon, and I was suggesting all these exotic places, but I could tell you weren't keen, and then you said it might be nice to visit your grandparents in Amsterdam?'

Bram could feel himself blushing. 'Yeah. Sorry…'

That's what they had ended up doing, too, although Kirsty had seemed to enjoy herself, and Bram liked to think the success of the honeymoon had partly been down to the warmth with which his grandparents had welcomed them, the love in which they had been enveloped by all his Amsterdam relations during that wonderful week. Honeymoons were meant to be all about love, after all, weren't they?

Kirsty chuckled. 'It was so *Bram*! It was adorable! If you had your way you'd gather us all up together in a big castle, all our family and friends, and never let any of us out into the big bad world!'

He grinned. 'Yeah, that would be my dream scenario.'

'I know it was a horrible experience, but – it's still our home, Bram, and we still love it, don't we? Having a nice party will go some way to… to reclaiming it for ourselves, don't you think?'

'You're right. You're absolutely right.' She could always make him feel better. 'Let's do it.'

HE DIPPED the pail into the stream, trying not to think about all the microscopic creatures he was scooping up that were destined to be flushed down a loo. He'd already filled up the cisterns in the downstairs toilet, the family bathroom and his and Kirsty's en suite. Now he was doing the refills.

He lugged the full pails across the grass towards the house, trying not to slop the water out of them too much. When he reached Henrietta the goose, he set the pails down and rubbed his hands where the handles had dug into the flesh, and patted Henrietta's smooth white head.

'Well, Henny. What do you think of your new home?'

When Bram was eight years old, his walk to and from school had taken him past a beautiful wooden goose on the flagstone area outside a little house. He had worried that a bad person could steal her, so one day he had snatched the goose up in his arms and run. He'd told Ma and Pap that he'd found her thrown out with someone's rubbish, and made a nice safe home for her in their narrow back garden. But the next day, an elderly Ugandan lady, introduced by Ma as Mrs Nabirye, came to have coffee at their house, and Ma told him, 'This is the lady who owns the goose.'

Ma had, of course, known all along where he'd got the goose. Bram had broken down in tears and confessed that he'd taken her because he'd been so worried about her being stolen. Mrs Nabirye had explained that her late husband had made her, and her name was Henrietta. She said her husband would have been delighted to know that a young boy so loved Henrietta that he went to such lengths to protect her. She'd insisted that Bram keep her.

But Bram couldn't look Henrietta in the eye for a long time after that, he was so ashamed of what he'd done, thinking of poor Mrs Nabirye and her dead husband. Now, every time he looked at Henrietta, he remembered the lesson of empathy that Ma and Mrs Nabirye had taught him. He hadn't so much as stolen a grape from a supermarket since.

Mrs Nabirye had had a Ugandan proverb painted on a piece of driftwood in her conservatory: *A child does not grow up only in a single home.* He always smiled when he thought of that. He'd been so lucky, growing up in that wonderful little community in Primrose Hill where his parents still lived in their narrow little mews house which, they always said, reminded them of Amsterdam. Islington, too, had been a close-knit, almost village-like community. He really missed the support network they'd had there. He'd hoped to find another such 'village' here for Max and Phoebe, but that dream was fading fast.

Still, maybe this housewarming party would turn things around.

He took a moment to scan the house. He'd hidden some of the cameras under the eaves, quite successfully – he couldn't even see them himself, and he knew where they were. There was another under the gutter on the shed, one in a corner of the verandah, and another fixed to a tree covering the other gable. If anyone approached the house now, they'd be caught on camera.

He gave Henrietta's beak a pat and hefted the pails.

THE PARTY WOULD KICK off at five o'clock, so that people with kids could leave reasonably early, but Bram had all the catering side of things ready by four. Linda had been 'cooking for Scotland', as she put it, because it was problematic for Bram to prepare food with the limited water availability. The fridge was full of a range of vegetarian and meat-eater salads and quiches and tarts and sausage rolls, and David's supply of raw meat for the McKechnie Special barbecue. He'd set up the barbecue equipment this morning on the terrace.

Bram, against his expectations, found that he was actually looking forward to this shindig, and the kids were hyper, dashing about the house shouting at each other. Kirsty was stringing bunting around the walls of the Walton Room.

He headed up to the bedroom to change.

After he'd sponged himself with water from a bucket, he sat in his robe in the sun streaming through the big window and opened his laptop. Unbeknownst to Kirsty, he'd been googling Owen's murder. The articles he'd found so far had all been very repetitive – they must all have used the same source, or copied from each other. He did another search on 'Owen Napier Grantown-on-Spey' but instead of 'murder' he added the words 'body' and 'river'. This threw up some fresh results, and Bram copied and pasted the texts into the document he'd already created for all the material, which he was yet to read through properly. He'd go through it all when he had a bit of time to himself.

The first of the articles that his new search had

thrown up reported that the body found by a fisherman in the River Spey on Thursday had been identified as that of missing local man Owen Napier, age twenty-three, a pharmacy assistant. It seemed he'd been reported missing by his employer on 21 August, and the body had been found on 18 September. Most of this Bram already knew.

Another article described the finding of 'a man's body' by a fisherman near Cragganmore on the River Spey, caught in submerged branches. No mention, at this early stage, of a name. Another, much later article, published during the police investigation, added the information that Owen's ankles and wrists had been bound and added, needlessly, that the police were treating the death as 'suspicious'.

Sitting there in the hot sun, Bram shivered.

Bound hand and foot and thrown in the river to drown. Owen would have had no chance. The River Spey was the fastest flowing river in Scotland. Its catchment area was huge, and mountainous, so if there was a lot of rain it was guaranteed that the Spey would spate. They'd walked some of the Speyside Way, Bram and Kirsty and the kids, on one occasion after heavy rain, and it had been scary enough just standing on the path looking at that water, churning past in its headlong rush to the sea. Kirsty had soon turned away, suggesting an alternative path away from the river.

If whoever had tied Owen up and thrown him in that river was now after Bram –

But Scott and Kirsty and David and everyone else were no doubt right, and there was no connection at all between Owen's murder and what had been happening here at Woodside. Bram had no logical reason to think otherwise.

11

'Let's get this party started,' said David, heading past Bram to the kitchen, six-pack of lager dangling from one hand. 'No more bits of offal left lying around we could chuck on the barbecue?'

'That must have been really frightening,' said Amy, Scott's wife. She was beautiful, of course, with lots of wavy blonde hair and a model's figure.

'Yeah, it–'

'Hey, doc!' said Finn Taylor, grabbing a handful of crisps from the bowl Bram was holding. He looked Amy up and down appreciatively as he munched. 'Max has got this, uh, embarrassing problem?'

'Is it called Finn Taylor?' Amy came back at him, quick as a flash. She was a doctor who worked in A&E at the local hospital, and Bram could imagine her dealing with all the Saturday night drunks with just this sort of brisk no-nonsense attitude.

Finn flushed.

'Could you do me a favour and hand round some of these nibbles, Finn?' Bram said to cover his embarrassment – not that the boy deserved it.

Finn looked at the array of snacks as if Bram had asked him to handle nuclear waste, but reluctantly picked up a bowl of pretzels.

As Bram walked about topping up wine glasses, he was conscious of many pairs of eyes tracking his every move. Was that the silent family from the Inverluie Hotel, the ones who sat staring at the blank TV? Who the hell had invited them? And there were Isla and Mhairi and the rest of 'the gang', already well on the way to inebriation.

He couldn't help thinking: was one of these people the intruder who had left the heart and the threatening message? Kirsty was talking to a man whose name, Bram thought, was Craig – another old school friend. He was speaking to her earnestly, standing just a little too close. As Bram watched, he put a hand on Kirsty's shoulder, leaning in to make his point.

He had an intense look to him. Disturbingly intense?

Had Craig been obsessed with Kirsty at school? Had he and Owen maybe clashed? Was Craig a bit of a loner, a bit of a weirdo, the type who followed women around supermarkets and had to be ejected by security? He looked as if he might be. He looked as if he cut his own hair. Not that there was anything wrong with that, *per se*.

And there was bloody Scott, moving through the crowd, stopping to talk to people, working the room. He'd gone out with Kirsty at school, when they were young teenagers. Had it just been one of those early, experimental romances that was more like friendship, that had never really been going anywhere, or had Scott been serious about her?

Scott had been very quick to dismiss Bram's worries about an Owen connection. Suspiciously quick?

But all this speculation was pointless, and probably paranoid.

'Okay, folks, time for a song or two!' Bram called out. 'Who's up for a bit of *X Factor*? I'll be the first lamb to the slaughter!'

'Yessss!' exclaimed Phoebe, dancing up to him with the three Miller sisters in tow, all four girls flushed and overexcited. '*X Factor*! We can be the judges!'

'It's a *no* from me!' giggled Rhona Miller, the cheekiest of the three sisters and Phoebe's particular friend.

People started moving through to the Room with a View to find seats and places to stand, and Bram turned one of the leather library chairs to face outwards and sat down with his guitar. 'This is a bothy ballad.' He stroked the strings of the guitar. 'It's called *The Plooman Laddies* – about a kitchie deem's devotion to her man, a humble ploughman.' And he began to sing:

> *'Doon yonder den there's a plooman lad,*
> *Some simmer's day he'll be aa my ain.*
> *And sing laddie-aye, and sing laddie-o,*
> *The plooman laddies are aa the go.'*

He saw David, sitting on one of the sofas, shoot a horrified look at Fraser, who lowered his head to his hands. Finn Taylor was openly laughing, as were the other teenage boys standing with Max by the door. Max's face was slowly turning bright red.

Kirsty was perched on the arm of a chair, nodding along, a fixed smile on her face. A few of the other faces turned towards him were politely attentive, but most were stony or downright contemptuous. Only Phoebe and the three Miller sisters were grinning happily. The family from the Inverluie Hotel bar were clumped together by the sliding doors, silently staring. Willie was shaking his head, and as he met Bram's gaze, he swiped a hand across his neck to mime *cut*.

Linda's expression said it all:

Bloody Nora.

He fumbled his way through the verses about the merchant and the miller, tripping on the word 'stour' in the line 'The smell o' the stour wad hae done me ill' – was it pronounced *sto-ur* or *stoor*? – he went for *sto-ur* but that was evidently the wrong choice. He saw Kirsty and a few other people wince.

Finally he was through it, ending with a defiant flourish on 'The plooman laddies are *aa the go*', and there was a horrible, horrible silence before Linda and Kirsty started to clap, and others joined in politely but very briefly, Max, he noted, not among them; he was studying the carpet.

'Oh my God,' he heard Mhairi say in a low voice.

'Great, Bram, great!' Kirsty enthused, jumping up. 'Now, I think it's time to fire up the barbecue, eh Dad, and get some meat burnt for all you carnivores?'

Bram slunk out of the room and up the stairs to their bedroom, clutching the guitar to his chest, as if to comfort it. He slumped down with it on the bed.

This bloody housewarming had been a terrible idea.

And now Kirsty was coming in and sitting down next to him, hugging his arm. 'Never mind.'

'It was terrible, wasn't it?'

'It was pretty bad. But you tried, and that's the main thing.'

'Really?' He sighed. 'It was like they were… I don't know. Offended?'

'Oh, I don't think so.' Her tone was too bright.

'There was nothing dodgy in the song, was there?' He had a sudden, terrible thought. 'I know some of the bothy ballads are a bit… close to the bone. But I looked up the Scots words in *The Plooman Laddies* and none of them were obscene or anything, that I could see… But maybe there was a double meaning?'

'No no, it was fine.'

'So why –?'

'There's a bit of sensitivity, maybe, about English people… mocking the Scots language.'

'But I wasn't *mocking* it!' Bram gaped at her in consternation. 'No! *No!* I love it, I love all the different dialects and the history behind the Scots language and–'

'*I* know that, but they don't, necessarily.'

He jumped up. 'I have to explain.'

'No. Bram, just leave it–'

But this was terrible! He cannoned back down the stairs and made his way to the middle of the Walton Room, clapping his hands to silence the chatter, to get everyone's attention.

'People, I just have a few words to say.' God, what *was* he going to say? 'About that bothy ballad I just sang. Kirsty has pointed out to me that it might have been taken the wrong way? That maybe you might have thought I was having a go, having a laugh at it? At the Scots accent, the Scots language? Which I absolutely wasn't!'

'Dad, no,' groaned Max.

'I *love* the way you all talk!' Oh Christ. That had sounded so patronising.

'And waaee love the waaee yaaaooo tooook, Braayyyiiiim!' Fraser mimicked, and there was general laughter.

Not *with* him.

At him.

And he didn't know what to say. He just stood there

staring around him, and they all stared back, as if wondering what outrage he would perpetrate next.

'I know I messed it up,' he said lamely.

And he felt Kirsty's arms snake around his chest from behind. 'Oh, Bram, what are you like?' she said brightly. 'You're your own worst critic.'

Silence. A few perfunctory smiles.

'Absolutely,' said Amy stoutly.

'D'you want a bet?' David roared from the back of the room, which erupted in laughter.

Bram slunk off again, through the kitchen and through the Room with a View – he was coming to hate this room – and out onto the terrace, from which the smell of charring meat was drifting in through the sliding doors, drawing a bit of a crowd. Fraser was manning the barbecue, bottle of beer in hand. There seemed to be about a dozen of each item on the massive grill – burgers and chicken and kebabs and corn on the cob and sausages. Bram dropped onto one of the seats just outside the doors, bile rising as he thought of that huge raw heart, seeping blood into the risotto.

There was a group of teenagers on the other side of the terrace, some sitting on the low wall, some standing. Max approached them, holding a platter of the hors d'oeuvres he'd made – ricotta, avocado and pine nut toasts, tomato tartlets and crispy kale with a chilli yoghurt dip. As Bram watched, one of the girls picked up a piece of crispy kale and shoved it at a boy's mouth. The boy backed off, laughing, and the girl threw the kale at him.

'That's not food, that's what you'd scrape off the floor after a fire in a rabbit hutch,' she said. 'Did you make this crap?'

'Yep.'

'Man, you need to get a life,' said Finn Taylor.

'Although I guess you needed an excuse to get out of the room while your dad was practising his "singing"? He sometimes makes you do it, yeah?'

'He doesn't *make* me do it.'

'Can you imagine *two* of them giving it *fal-de-diddly-dee*?' giggled the girl.

'Actually,' said Max, 'a lot of folk songs are used in contemporary music. Modern-day songwriters derive inspiration from them.'

Finn whooped. '*Modern-day* songwriters *derive inspiration*? Oh, I say, old chap, how spiffing!'

'Such as who?' Cara Taylor spoke for the first time. 'What songwriters are you thinking of, Max?'

'Doja Cat,' laughed Finn.

'Kendrick Lamar,' suggested another boy. 'You reckon he'd *derive inspiration* from folk songs?'

Max shrugged.

'Name a Kendrick Lamar track, Max,' demanded Finn.

As Max looked blank, the others all laughed.

Apart from Cara. 'Shut up, idiots. I genuinely want to know. Which songwriters, Max?'

'The Beach Boys? Paul Simon?'

'Who?'

'As in Simon and Garfunkel.'

The teenagers looked at each other.

'Oh my God, you are my dad,' the loud girl cackled. 'Are you actually like fifty but you use a lot of moisturiser?'

Bram hadn't wanted to intervene and embarrass Max all the more, but this had gone far enough. He got up and walked over to the group, patting Max on the back. 'I think these particular delicacies are wasted on an immature palate.' He smiled round the group of kids.

'Yeah, you're right,' said Finn, looking Bram right in

the eye. 'I don't suppose you've got any chicken nuggets and chips, Mr Hendriksen?'

'We'll see what we can do. Max, could I have your assistance in the kitchen for a minute?'

The kitchen had emptied out a bit as people gravitated towards the barbecue. Max opened the freezer. 'The only battered stuff we've got is vegetable tempura, and I don't think that's going to cut it.'

'I think Finn was joking. And anyway, it's not as if there's any shortage of rubbish for them to eat, with Fraser manning the barbecue.'

Max shut the freezer door with a sigh. 'This party sucks.'

Bram spluttered a laugh. 'I couldn't have put it better myself.' He put a hand on Max's shoulder. 'You know, there's no shame in not wanting to buy into mainstream teenage culture. It's okay to have different interests; not to know about the rappers and so on. You're more into folk music and there's nothing wrong with that.'

Max, squirming in embarrassment, shrugged.

'It's a strength, Max, not a weakness, to be an individual rather than trying desperately to be like everyone else, like a silly sheep.'

'Maybe in London,' Max sighed. 'But we're not in Kansas anymore, Dad.'

12

When Bram had refilled another couple of pails from the stream, he sat down on the bank and took a moment. There was music booming from the house now, a high-energy dance track he was sure none of the Hendriksens possessed. One of those appalling kids must have brought an iPod and put it in the docking station.

He'd rather stay out here and be jumped by a psychopath than spend another minute in there. In their own house. But somehow it didn't feel like theirs any more. It didn't feel like home.

Kirsty was right – all Bram wanted was a nice safe place where the people he loved could be secure and happy. Was that too much to ask?

He had never understood people like Steph from uni, whose ultimate ambition was to travel the world, to live in exotic places among strangers. When Steph had enthused all about her latest trip to Italy or Turkey or Vietnam, Bram had always felt like enthusing about his own holiday spent in his parents' house in Primrose Hill, the wonderful, hilarious dinner parties with all their friends, the chats with neighbours, the casual popping in to people's houses to see what they'd done with the garden. It was *people* who imbued places with meaning, so how could anywhere populated by strangers possibly have more allure than the cities and towns and houses that contained the people you loved?

He hefted the pails and plodded back to the house. In the downstairs loo, he flicked on the light. The toilet hadn't been flushed in a while and it was pretty grim. As he reached for the toilet brush, he saw it.

The mandala that he and Phoebe had drawn on the wall above the loo roll holder, so laboriously, with a compass, had had the words '**STUPID HIPPY SHIT**' scrawled across it in black marker pen.

Bram reeled away.

It was like he was here; the intruder was here with him in this cramped space, shouting at him.

He *was* here.

In the house.

He was one of the people they'd invited into their house.

BRAM ROCKETED OUT of the loo and down the corridor to the Walton Room. David and Linda were sitting on the sofa with plates of food on their knees, and he found himself blurting out that the intruder was here, he'd vandalised the mandala –

'Come and see!'

David took one look at the mandala and nodded grimly. 'Okay. I'll sort this, Bram.' The look he gave Bram was dismissive, as if he was resigned to the fact that Bram wasn't going to step up.

'What is it?' said Linda, coming after them, her stick tapping the wall. They hadn't brought Bertie to the party as it had been felt he'd not cope well with the combination of all the food and attention.

'The bastard has defaced Phoebe's wee drawing, love. Right.' David squared his shoulders. 'None too bright, this joker. Probably has the marker pen still on him. And I know just where to start.'

'No, David,' said Linda. 'You can't go around accusing people with no evidence.'

'I'm not going to accuse anyone. All I'm going to do is ask those lads to turn out their pockets.'

'It amounts to the same thing.'

David marched past her and off down the corridor.

'Don't let him do anything stupid, Bram,' Linda begged.

Bram hurried after David, through the Walton Room, through the kitchen, through the Room with a View to the terrace, where the teenagers were still gathered.

'Right, you,' said David, pointing at Finn. 'And *you*, and *you*, and *you*.' He jabbed a finger at each of the boys. 'Pockets. Let's see what you've got in them. Turn them out. Contents on the table.'

Finn just looked at him, smiling slightly and shaking his head.

One of the men from the group by the barbecue had come over. 'What's the problem here?' One of the dads, presumably.

'Vandalism,' said David. 'One of these wee buggers has vandalised my nine-year-old granddaughter's artwork.'

'In the downstairs loo,' Bram elaborated. 'Someone's scrawled across it in black marker pen.'

And oh no, there was Phoebe, standing next to Fraser helping him with the burgers, along with her three friends. Phoebe had a roll in one hand and a buttery knife in the other, staring across at them. Bram hurried over to her.

'Okay, Phoebs, let's go inside and–'

'The mandala?' she whispered. 'Someone vandalised the mandala?'

Bram nodded. 'But we can paint over it and do another, can't we? An even better one.'

'Who did it?' She looked up at him. '*Why* did they do it?'

Bram cupped a hand over her head. 'I don't know, *kleintje.*'

'Let's be having you, lads,' said David. 'Contents of pockets on the table, *now.*'

One of the boys was complying, placing a wallet and keys on the picnic table, and pulling out the insides of his jeans pockets to show they were now empty. But Finn and the others hadn't moved.

'And what makes you think it was any of them?' the dad demanded.

'This is discriminatory,' Finn drawled. 'You're accusing us because of our age and sex. It could have been anyone. And what gives you stop and search powers anyway, Grandad?'

'That's right,' said the dad, squaring up to David. 'You've got a cheek, laying down the law to other folks' kids. It's usually you on the receiving end of the law, eh, McKechnie? What gives you the right to get in these lads' faces and–'

David, completely unperturbed, flicked a glance over at Bram.

The message was clear.

Are you a man or a mouse?

'This is our *home!*' Bram found himself suddenly shouting, striding across the terrace towards them.

'That's what gives him the *fucking right*! *Get out!* I want everyone out of this house and off our property *now*!'

IT TOOK an hour to get Phoebe into bed and off to sleep. On top of the traumas of the mandala being vandalised and watching her dad lose it, she was having to deal with the worry of what was going to happen with the Miller girls. Their parents had appeared on the terrace just as Bram was launching into his sweary diatribe, and had whisked their three young daughters away at once. 'Will they let us be friends now, Dad?' Phoebe kept asking.

He descended the stairs wearily. He found the family in the kitchen, Linda, Max and David sitting at the table and Kirsty and Fraser clearing up.

'Well, I've done it now, haven't I,' said Bram, collapsing onto a chair. 'And to think that this house-warming party was meant to help us integrate into the community. They're basically going to hate me forever.'

David chuckled. 'Na. People round here respect a man who stands up for himself. Who stands up for his family. Didn't know you had it in you, Bram.' He nodded. 'Nice one.'

Bram couldn't help himself smiling back, weakly. Having David's approbation was a new experience, and one that offset, just a little, the feeling of despair that was hanging over him. 'I *really* just threw all our guests out?'

'Yeah Dad,' grimaced Max. 'Way to go.'

Max was slouched over the table, his head resting on one arm, eyes closed.

'Hey,' said David, tapping the table in front of Max. 'Your dad was quite right. Some yob or yobs think they can get away with messing with this family, shooting

Bertie, shooting at Bram, breaking in and making threats, vandalising your wee sister's drawing, and who knows what all else. You think we should just let them get away with that?'

'Uh – no,' Max got out.

'You need to be ready to defend yourselves, because Fraser and I can't always be here, you know? You and your dad need to man up, lad.'

'No they don't,' said Kirsty. 'That's not the answer.'

'We have to let the police–' Linda began.

'Oh aye, the police are about as much use as a chocolate teapot when it comes to this kind of low-level stuff, as they call it – right up until it escalates and the bugger's coming at you with an axe. Oh aye, they'll maybe charge the bugger then.'

'I don't think that's a very likely scenario,' said Bram as Max's eyes suddenly came open and he lifted his head.

'You should come along to the boxing club,' David suggested to Max. David was a coach at a boxing club in the town, which took place in a grotty garage with punchbags strung from the rafters and an incongruously pristine boxing ring that they'd somehow wangled through lottery funding. 'It made a man of Fraser.'

Bram glanced round at Fraser, who was up on the stepladder, arms exposed in a short-sleeved T-shirt, huge biceps bunching as he ripped down the bunting. He turned and gave Bram a slow, rather menacing smile.

'I don't think boxing is really your thing, is it, Max?' said Bram.

Max shrugged. 'I'm willing to give it a go.'

·   ·   ·

TEN MINUTES LATER, Bram found Max slumped comatose on one of the sofas in the Room with a View, surrounded by the debris from the party – stained napkins and pulverised crisps and dirty plates and glasses.

'Max? *Max?*'

'Urgh?'

'Can't hold his drink,' said David at his elbow. 'That's what comes of having a father who's virtually teetotal. When Fraser was his age, he had it in his head that he liked wine.' David shook his head in amusement. 'Social suicide, Bram. As far as young lads are concerned, wine's a lassie's drink. I had to take him in hand.' He frowned at Max.

'Do you think he's okay?'

'Ach, he's fine.'

There was a string of drool from Max's open mouth to the cushion his head was pillowed on.

'Peer pressure,' said Bram.

'Aye, nothing like it to give a lad a kick up the backside. A good bit of healthy competition.'

Bram couldn't help chuckling at that. But: 'There's nothing *healthy* about this, David,' he said, taking a tissue from his pocket and wiping up the drool.

Max reluctantly opened his eyes. 'Wha'?'

'You need to drink some water, Max, to dilute the alcohol in your system.'

Bram sat with him and made sure he drank a whole bottle of water. He didn't like to come the heavy parent, but maybe in the morning he might suggest that Max stop spending quite so much time with Finn and his friends. Especially after what had happened tonight. David was probably right and one of those boys was responsible for vandalising the mandala. Maybe it was nothing to do with the other stuff, although he couldn't shake a nagging doubt. *Stupid hippy shit* was horribly reminiscent of *Fucking wee hipster arsewipe* in that troll's comment. He couldn't help thinking that both were directed at Bram specifically.

And the heart and *Your next.*

He stared at the bottle in Max's hand, at the water sloshing about as he lifted it to his lips.

Owen, bound hand and foot, struggling in a swollen river.

He sat down next to Max and ruffled his hair. 'You're a good lad, Max. I'm guessing you probably miss your old friends, am I right?'

'Yeah.'

Max's friends in London were a gentle, high-brow lot, into café culture and poetry and going to classical music concerts, and heavily involved in volunteering. Litter-picking. Fundraising for museums. Their idea of a wild night out was going to someone's house to watch four episodes of *University Challenge* back to back. A lot of them – like Max, until now – did not drink alcohol.

It was as if the four of them had landed in the midst of a primitive Pictish tribe and were being made to conform to their barbaric practices: first Kirsty and then Max getting off their faces, and Bram yelling at people to get out of his territory, basically, while preening in the glow of David's approval.

It was a disaster.

This whole move had been a complete disaster.

SOMETHING HAD WOKEN HIM.

Kirsty.

She was lying on her side, turned away from him, trying to muffle sobs.

He put his arms around her and she turned over

against him, and he held her close, and murmured nonsense to her, and she let him do it but she didn't hug him back, she just lay passive in his arms and he sensed, as he always did in these moments, a withdrawal, a holding back. There was still a part of her that he couldn't reach, this part that cried in the night, that had always cried in the night, for as long as he had known her, and passively resisted his comfort.

After the fancy dress party, Bram and Kirsty started having breakfast and dinner together in the canteen at the halls of residence, and, if Bram hadn't gone home to his parents, spending time in each other's company at the weekend. Then everyone disappeared off home for Christmas and New Year. When Bram got back for the new term, he realised, from something Kirsty said about fireworks keeping her awake, that she'd been back here for New Year. He didn't like to think of her all alone in the empty halls.

'I left it stupidly late to get my train ticket,' she explained. 'The only cheap return I could get was coming back on 28 December.'

Not only was she having to deal with the trauma of her boyfriend's murder, but she was so far away from her family that getting home and back was logistically difficult. He started inviting her to spend time at his own home, but she usually declined the offer.

Just before half term, Bram was standing in the lobby putting on his cycle helmet when he heard Kirsty's voice. 'Hi, Mum.'

She must be using the pay phone round the corner.

'I just thought I should let you know I can't come home after all – this girl who lives on a farm in Norfolk has asked a group of us to go and stay there. We're going to be sailing on the Broads and stuff... Yeah. That's what I thought... I'm

*sorry, but... Yes, they're a really nice bunch and it would to
be so much fun... And I'll see you at Easter, so...'*

What the...?

*Apart from Bram, Kirsty had no friends. Steph's folks
lived on a farm in Norfolk, but there was surely no way she
would invite Kirsty there?*

*And sure enough, at half term Steph disappeared off to
Paris and Kirsty went nowhere. She was obviously trying to
make out to her family that she was having a ball and had
invented a mythical social life. They would presumably be
really worried about her, given what had happened, so Kirsty
was pretending she was enjoying herself too much to go
running back home every holiday.*

That half term, Bram was determined that Kirsty would
*enjoy herself. He took her for a swim in his local pool in Prim-
rose Hill. He showed her London, the tourist stuff like the
museums and the galleries and the Tower of London – she
loved the ravens – but also lesser known points of interest.
Kirsty was particularly intrigued by the Victorian sewer lamp
behind the Savoy Hotel, which was still powered by methane
from the sewers.*

*It was the most delicious kind of agony: to spend so much
time with her, to talk with her for hours, to sit beside her in
the intimate gloom of the cinema and feel they were the only
people in the place, so conscious was he of her presence right
next to him, of her tiny giggle at a funny line, her caught
breath when the baddie suddenly loomed up from the dark, but
not even be able to take her hand.*

*And when he wasn't with her, he was thinking about her.
How to get her to open up to him? They chatted away like old
friends, but never about Kirsty herself, never about her past or
her home, although she talked about her family a bit, so he
knew that her dad was a builder and her mum was involved in
counselling people with sight loss, being blind herself from
birth. And there was one brother, Fraser, who was a year older*

than Kirsty. Because she had told him so little, his imagination was free to fill in the gaps, and he spent hours wondering about her, trying to picture her home and her life there.

His course work suffered a bit.

His director of studies asked to see him.

One bright April Saturday he took her to the Hampstead Pergola, a magical, romantically overgrown Edwardian folly where you could stroll along a grand elevated walkway, a bit like an avenue but with vine- and wisteria-covered stone pillars instead of trees, and the structure of the pergola overhead instead of branches; a long, high corridor that turned and turned again, went up and down steps, in and out of little pergola rooms, and all the while you were looking over beautiful gardens to the wooded Heath.

'Like something from a fairy tale!' she breathed, walking ahead of him, and then she was running like a child, hair flying, and he was running after her, laughing, slipping, almost falling as he skidded round a corner, desperate not to lose sight of her, his feet pounding on the criss-cross patterns thrown on the flagstones by the shadows of the pergola.

When she came to the end of it, to an open, circular space on top of a little tower, she twirled slowly, arms held out, face shining. And then, to his delight, she caught his hands in hers and twirled him with her, like they were dancing some wild Highland reel.

He pulled her to him and kissed her.

He couldn't help himself.

For two wonderful seconds, she kissed him back. And then she pulled away, all the laughter gone out of her eyes. 'I'm sorry, Bram. I'm so sorry. I can't. I just can't. I'm sorry.'

And he dropped her hands, and tried to smile. 'It's okay. It's fine. I'm sorry. I didn't mean to do that. Got a bit carried away there with the romance of it all.' And he grinned, and swept a hand at the pergola behind them, the gardens, the trees, while inwardly he was cursing himself, terrified, as he'd never been of anything in his life, that she would want to stop this, stop spending time with him. 'Can we just forget that happened?'

She smiled, and nodded, and he wanted to take her in his arms again and make it right, to take away that terrible pain that was never far beneath the surface, waiting to rise up and engulf her and sweep her away from him.

13

B ram was woken the next morning by a phone
call from Ma.
'Bram, whatever is happening on your blog?
And have you seen Max's Facebook page?'

His heart sank. He had a fair idea what would be on
there before he logged in. And sure enough, the trolls
were going wild in the comments section of the blog.
They had posted links to a Dropbox account on which a
video had appeared of Bram singing the bothy ballad.
And it had popped up on Max's Facebook page too.

Bram had deleted all the previous troll comments
from his blog and blocked those posters before his
parents had seen them. He hastily deleted all the new
ones, and then he woke Max, pulling the curtains open
and setting his laptop down on the covers.

'You need to take a look at these.'

Max half sat up in bed. His hair was sticking up
around his face in a mad punk look, and he seemed
unable to open his eyes. There was a sweaty, vinegary
stench in the room.

Bram opened the window. 'There are a whole lot of

troll comments on your Facebook timeline. We need to get them deleted. That's possible, isn't it? Ideally we should block them too. Is *that* possible?'

'Yeah, but they'll just pop up again with new profiles.'

'They'll soon get tired of it.' Bram sat down on the bed. 'You need to do this now, Max. Oma and Opa have seen the comments and are pretty upset.'

That had him screwing his eyes open. Max loved his Dutch grandparents. He sat up properly and Bram gave him the laptop.

'Look at this one,' Max said, frowning at the screen. 'Dad, look!'

Someone calling themselves William Wallace had posted a photo of Bram singing the bothy ballad to Max's timeline, with the text:

Talk about cultural appropriation.

Cara Taylor had waded in:

What, so unless you can trace your Scottish ancestry back five generations you're not allowed to sing a Scottish song? Talk about racism.

That had been a red rag to a bull, with half a dozen people commenting that it was fine as long as they did it respectfully, but Bram was just having a go. Bessie Brown – aka Red? – had posted:

The guy's out of control.

'Good of Cara to stick up for me,' Bram said weakly.

'I'll get on to it,' Max promised, his eyelids drooping again.

'Okay, but see that you do. Don't go back to sleep.'

Kirsty appeared an hour later, when Bram and Phoebe were sitting on the sofa together in the Room with a View designing a new mandala for the wall of the downstairs loo. Bram had photographed the writing 'Stupid hippy shit' and then painted over it, but it looked like it would need at least two more coats to obliterate that aggressive black marker pen.

Phoebe jumped up and ran at her. Kirsty stooped to her level, adjusting the collar of Phoebe's shirt. 'What are you two doing?'

'We have to make a new mandala. Because the psychopath – Okay, okay, Dad,' Phoebe pre-empted him. 'I know: *there is no psychopath.*'

'Well,' said Bram, going over to them and tweaking Phoebe's plait. 'Do you really think one of the people at the party last night was a psychopath?'

Phoebe nodded. Damn. 'I know Grandad thinks it was one of Max's friends, but I don't. It's someone older.'

'What makes you say that, *kleintje*?'

Phoebe frowned. 'I don't know. There's just… too many things, and too horrible, for it to be just a kid.' She grabbed Bram's hand. 'Don't go outside today!'

'We have to get water from the stream. But other than to do that, I won't.'

'What are the police doing to catch him?'

Good question. 'How about I call Scott right now and ask him?'

Phoebe nodded vigorously. 'Yes! Scott needs to make more of an effort, Dad.'

Scott didn't answer, but called Bram back half an hour later, when he was heating stream water on the stove in four pans for a bath he and Kirsty planned to share.

He checked he was alone in the room. 'Hi, Scott, thanks for calling back. I just wanted to let you know the latest. Trolls on Max's Facebook page and my blog are mouthing off and linking to a video of me at the party. One or more of them must have been here last night, or at least know someone who was.'

'You really think these trolls could be responsible for the incidents at Woodside?'

Bram sighed. 'Who knows, but it's a line of inquiry, isn't it?'

'Okay, I'll take a look at the blog and Max's Facebook. It might be possible to identify some of them with a bit of local knowledge, without going through the rigmarole of contacting Facebook's Law Enforcement Response Team.'

'Oh, uh, actually, we just deleted all the comments. And blocked the trolls.'

'Well, not to worry – I'm sure they'll be back. Let me know when more comments appear.'

When, Bram noted, not *if*. 'Okay. And we've got two writing samples now, the "Your next" written in blood on the worktop and "Stupid hippy shit" across the mandala. You could get everyone who was here last night to provide writing samples and see if they match up.'

'Scrawling in marker pen on a wall isn't exactly a crime, Bram. And there's nothing to suggest that whoever did that left the other message, and the heart in the risotto.'

'So it's just a coincidence?'

'There were a lot of drunk people in the house last night. Any one of them might have scrawled on the wall without meaning it to be in any way threatening.' Silence. Then: 'In these situations, it's very easy to become… not paranoid, but oversensitive. Having a go at those kids last night, when really you had no evidence that they'd done anything… Telling everyone to leave…'

'Oh God, I know,' said Bram. 'I know I overreacted. The thing is, Scott, I've got this feeling that it's all aimed at me. Not the family. Me personally. All the stuff online is about me. My suspicion is that it's not a dozen or so different people, it's one person with multiple online identities.'

'Right…?'

'"Fucking wee hipster arsewipe"… "Your next"… "Stupid hippy shit"… And I was the one who was fired at, in the wood. It was my vegetable patch that was weedkilled.'

'Bram, the Taylors were having issues with local youths before you even bought the plot.'

'But this is a level up from that, surely? I know you don't think it's possible that all this could be connected to Owen Napier's murder, but – could you at least consider it?'

'We're keeping an open mind, of course, but really, Bram, I think you're tilting at windmills.'

'Yes,' said Bram patiently, turning off the heat under the pans as the water began to bubble. 'I know that's what you think.'

But does he really? The little niggle of doubt wormed its way to the surface again. Was Scott too eager to dismiss the possibility of an Owen connection?

'What leads did the police have on Owen's murder?'

'It was long before my time on the force, but I know they didn't have much. A couple reported seeing him walking along the High Street in Grantown on the Friday night before he failed to turn up for work on the Saturday. He'd been drinking in his local, The Foresters pub. His drinking cronies said he seemed just as normal. Had a couple of pints and then left. He had a bedsit on Seafield Avenue, so this sighting of him on the High Street makes sense if that was him on his way back home from the pub.'

'So the thinking is that he was ambushed as he walked home?'

'It's one possibility, yes.'

'And then what? He was beaten up, tied up–'

'The length of time his body had been in that river, there wasn't a hell of a lot of forensic evidence of any use, although the pathologist did note that there seemed to be pre-mortem bruising to his body and face. So yes, probably he was beaten up, bundled into a vehicle. Taken to the river and dumped in there. Classic drugs gang stuff.'

'Did anyone ever look into the…' He checked again than there was no one within earshot, but lowered his voice anyway. 'The Kirsty angle? Maybe some guy carried a torch for Kirsty and wanted Owen out of the picture?'

'Bit of a drastic way to edge out a love rival.' An exhalation. 'All his friends were interviewed, and Kirsty, of course, but nothing came from that line of inquiry, other than the drugs stuff. He had a nice little scam going in which he filled out fake prescriptions, pocketed the drugs and sold them on. His pals came clean after his murder, otherwise no one would have been any the wiser. His employers at the pharmacy hadn't rumbled him.'

'God. How did Kirsty get mixed up with someone like that in the first place?'

'She said she didn't know about it. Owen was very plausible. Seemed like a fine upstanding young man, played five-a-side football at the weekend, did a bit of boxing at David's club, which is how he and Kirsty got to know each other.'

'So, before the drugs stuff came out, David probably thought he was ideal boyfriend material?'

'I wouldn't go that far, Bram. I don't imagine the paragon exists who qualifies as ideal partner material for David's princess. When I went out with her – we were just babies, remember, thirteen and fourteen, we're talking holding hands and sharing a banana milkshake in the ice cream parlour – I was subjected to the full interrogation, down to the marks I'd got in my last exams. You've no doubt been there.'

'Been there, done that, got the frilly apron.'

Scott laughed. 'You're a braver man than I am. Look, I'll keep it in mind, all right, that there's a slim – *slim* – possibility of a link with Owen, but I really wouldn't worry about it. I doubt we'll be fishing you out of the River Spey any time soon.'

Bram leant back against the worktop. 'Is that meant to be reassuring?'

'Ha, sorry! Cop's black humour.'

'Yeah, funny.'

After ending the call, Bram poured the hot water into buckets and lugged it upstairs. Thank God the bore-hole people were coming on Thursday to do a geological survey. If all went to plan, they could have a new water supply up and running, according to the guy Bram had spoken to, within two weeks.

AFTER A LATE LUNCH, all four of them rather subdued, Bram took his laptop up to the bedroom and sat in the armchair by the window to properly read through the stuff on Owen he'd gathered together. Scott had said it had happened before his time, which was obviously true. The dates on these contemporaneous articles were September, October and November 1996. Scott was the same age as Fraser and Bram – thirty-nine. Just a year older than Kirsty. And 1996 was twenty-three years ago. Thirty-nine minus twenty-three was sixteen.

That meant…

Kirsty had been born on 17 November 1980. In

September 1996, when Owen had gone missing, she hadn't yet turned sixteen. And Owen had been twenty-three.

Kirsty was in the home office, staring at a spread-sheet. She swivelled the chair round to face him as he came into the room. 'How are you holding up?'

He shrugged. 'I'm fine. How about you?'

'Fighting a losing battle with a deadline.'

He perched on the kick stool by her shelving unit. 'Okay, I'll leave you be, but first – can I ask you some-thing?' God. This was awkward. 'About Owen?'

'Oh, Bram, no. Forget Owen. What happened to him has nothing to do with any of this.'

'But how can you know that?' he asked gently.

'Like Scott said – Owen's death was drugs related.'

'That's just a best guess, no more. Kirsty – I hadn't realised how young you were. When you went out with Owen. You were only fifteen when he was killed.'

She sighed. 'What can I say? I was a bit of a wild child back then.'

'But he was twenty-three. If you were sleeping together…' There was no easy way to say this. 'That was statutory rape. Were you? Sleeping together?'

Another sigh. 'Yes.'

'And did David know you were in a relationship with a twenty-three-year-old man? How did he feel about that?'

'Of course he didn't know. I used to sneak out to see Owen. Easy enough, living in a bungalow. I used to get in and out through my bedroom window.'

'From what Scott said, I thought David knew. About you and Owen.'

'Well, he found out, obviously, after Owen went missing and the police started picking his life apart. He found out then.'

'I can imagine his reaction.'

She grimaced, and swivelled her chair back to face the screen. 'Sorry, but I need to get this done.'

'You don't want to talk about Owen. I get that. But if this is connected–'

'You're tilting at windmills, Bram.'

Exactly the words Scott had used. How likely was that to be a coincidence? They had known each other forever. Of course Scott would have got off the phone to Bram and immediately called Kirsty. And said what? That Bram seemed to be losing it? He wouldn't put it past him.

He gave Kirsty's shoulders a squeeze and dropped a kiss on the top of her head, but she didn't respond. He patted her shoulders and left the room.

The day before Kirsty's nineteenth birthday, Bram had turned up at the halls of residence in a rented car and told her to pack a bag – they were off for a birthday weekend extravaganza to a mystery destination.

Kirsty's face lit up, and she looked around her room, obviously wondering what to take, but then she sort of drooped. 'I don't know, Bram.'

'Hey, don't worry, I'm not going to get any ideas! Separate bedrooms!' He made his tone hearty and upbeat and cheery. Bram the best friend, not Bram the wannabe lover.

The smile crept back into Kirsty's face, and then it became a wide grin, and she was clapping her hands like a little kid. He wanted to take her in his arms right there and then. Poor Kirsty! Over the summer, she'd gone home for only a few days. She'd spent the rest of the holiday in the halls and got a job in a pub. She'd probably told her family she was off inter-railing with a group of friends. He was beginning to think that Kirsty staying in the halls over the holidays was about more than just pretending to her family that she was happy; it must be difficult for her, being home, with all those traumatic memories of Owen to face.

So she didn't get out of London much.

No wonder she was excited to be going away. It was nothing to do with Bram himself.

Smugglers' Cottage on the North Devon coast turned out to be as perfect as Bram had been hoping. He'd scrutinised the photos and made sure it was a suitably cute period property with beams and a real fire, and there was direct access to a beach along the coastal path that went right past the garden gate.

'I want to stay here forever!' Kirsty shouted when they'd dumped their bags in their separate rooms and gone straight down to the beach, wrapped up in coats and scarves against the wind coming off the sea.

They collected shells and stones and watched hermit crabs in a pool, and then they ate pizza and ice cream and watched crap on TV in front of a roaring fire, Kirsty lying on the sofa, Bram sitting on the rug by the fire, not saying much, just smiling at each other from time to time.

The next day, Kirsty's birthday, she had a long conversation with her mum, and Bram persuaded her to do a bit of early morning meditation, sitting in the cottage's tiny sunroom overlooking the sea. Then he took her fossil-hunting along the rocky shore, as he used to as a kid with Pap. Kirsty was thrilled when she found her first ammonite amongst the pebbles and hurried to show Bram, her palm extended proudly: a perfect bronze spiral, wetly glinting in the pale sunlight.

'What is it made of? I mean, the type of stone? It almost looks like metal!'

'Iron pyrites, I think. Fool's gold. If it was polished up it would look like actual gold, but I like them as they are.'

'Me too.'

They had lunch in a café in Ilfracombe, the ammonite sitting on the table between them. Kirsty tried to explain to Bram that the ammonite's shell was a perfect logarithmic spiral with self-similarity. 'See, this tiny central part has the same form as the whole thing.'

Bram pretended to get it.

In the afternoon they did a walk along the coastal path – an old smugglers' path, according to the guidebooks – and scrambled down to a cave that was apparently used by the smuggler 'Old Worm' Williams in the 1700s when he was on the run from the coastguard. They sat for a while in the gloom right at the back of the cave, where it was surprisingly dry and warmer than out on the beach. Kirsty explained that this was because of geothermal energy stored in the surrounding rock, which meant that caves maintained the same temperature all year round. 'Usually equal to the annual average temperature at the cave's entrance, so inside a cave is warmer than outside in winter.'

Back at the cottage, Bram cooked Kirsty's birthday meal, even though he was vegetarian: her favourite food, roast chicken with oatmeal stuffing, bread sauce, roast potatoes and sprouts. He drew the line at eating it, though, and made a nut roast for himself, although they shared the sprouts. Then there was apple crumble, and coffee and posh mint chocolates, and Bram presented her with her present, a colourful velvet and silk scarf made by a friend of his mother's who used recycled scraps in her creations.

'Oh, Bram, I love it!' Kirsty looped it round her neck and looked at herself in the mirror in the hall. 'The colours are amazing – like a stained-glass window. And it feels so luxurious! It's gorgeous!'

'Not as gorgeous as you,' Bram couldn't help himself mutter, as the thought came to him that she was like a girl in a Klimt painting, the rich colours of the scarf in all its sumptuousness surely something you would want to gaze at forever

but no, you barely noticed them, because all your attention was captured by the beautiful face, the shining green eyes, the glowing skin...

He winced at himself.

But she met his eyes in the mirror and smiled.

They sat together on the sofa that night, and Kirsty put her head on his shoulder and told him it had been the best birthday ever.

'I'm glad you're enjoying it,' he said. And after a while: 'I know you've had some really awful things happen to you, and no, I'm not going to ask you to talk about them. I know you don't want to. But – you have the rest of your life ahead of you, you know? I reckon it's going to be pretty good.'

She didn't say anything for a long time, and he cursed himself again for an insensitive idiot. Saying he knew she didn't want to talk about it was bringing it all back for her, wasn't it? She was probably thinking about it now. But then: 'I reckon maybe it is,' she said.

That night, Bram woke in the dark to a waft of air and an expanding triangle of light moving across the floorboards from the opening door. A figure flitted into the room and over to the bed, and then the mattress sank slightly as she slipped under the covers. There was a soft drift of hair across his face; a warm body against his.

'Hello,' she said.

His heart was pounding so hard he was sure she would feel it knocking against her.

He felt her fingers, exploring his face, trailing across his lips, and he reached up and touched the fall of her hair, slippery as silk. 'Are you sure?' he said.

'Yes,' she answered him at once. 'I love you.'

I love you I love you I love you. *The words seemed to chase themselves around in his head so he could hardly make sense of them, he could hardly comprehend what she was saying.*

'*Do you?*' *he said, stupidly.*

'*Of course.*' *He could hear the smile in her voice.*

Of course?!

He ran his fingers through her hair, pushing it back over her shoulder. 'And I love you,' he said. 'But neither of those things means that you have to do this.'

'*I know. I want to. I'm sure, Bram. I've never wanted anything in my life as much as I want to be with you.*' *She touched his lips again, as if to silence any objection. 'In every way there is. It's like you're already a part of me. An indivisible part.'*

How many times had he fantasised about this moment? But the reality – it was almost more than one human being could handle. There was the intense physical pleasure of what they were doing, the release of all the sexual tension that had been building up over the weeks and months, but this was magnified and at the same time dwarfed by the overwhelming, dizzying, unimaginable joy of what was now possible between them. Now they could have what no mere friends could have, the closeness that came with, but was so much more than, a physical relationship.

It was as if they had been sitting companionably together in a nice, warm, dark cave through a long winter, but now summer had come, and she was taking his hand and pulling him to his feet, and they were running together into the light.

14

The Inverluie Hotel bar was just as bad as Bram remembered, but Max was looking about him as if they'd just stepped into the Ritz. He'd jumped on David's suggestion that the two of them go to the Inverluie 'for a bit of grandad and grandson time', and Bram and Kirsty hadn't had the heart to say no.

'Don't get him drunk, Dad,' Kirsty had said sternly as they'd left.

David had waved a hand at her as they'd jogged down the verandah steps to Max's car. David was leaving his own car at Woodside and they'd leave Max's overnight at the hotel and get a taxi to drop them at their respective homes afterwards.

As Max's red VW Polo disappeared off down the track, Kirsty grabbed Bram's arm. 'I'm not happy about this. I'm not happy about the way Max has latched onto Dad. If Dad said *jump*, Max would ask *how high?* Could you go with them? Make sure nothing happens?'

So Bram followed them in the Discovery. He soon caught up with them on the single-track public road that wended its way through the trees. Max was a cautious newly qualified driver, thank God. But as Bram hung back to give him plenty space, the Polo accelerated and began to pull away.

Bram could just imagine David in the passenger seat, telling Max to put his foot down. Max's innate caution obviously won out, though, and when they hit the A road he slowed back down. Bram had caught up with them in the car park at the Inverluie.

Now, walking up to the bar with the blank TV screen looming over it, trying to summon a friendly smile for Willie, who was looking at them as if to say *What the hell would you want to come here for?*, Bram had a horrible feeling of déjà vu, as if he was fated to repeat this moment over and over again. And yes, there was the staring family at the nearest table, still watching the dead TV.

'Hello, Willie!' Bram put a hand on Max's shoulder. 'You met my son, Max, at the – um – at the party, didn't you? And you know my father-in-law, David?'

Willie tipped his chin at them and swiped at the bar with a dirty cloth. 'What a party that was.'

Bram could feel himself colouring. He was sure the starers were now staring at his back. Along with everyone else in the bar. 'Yes, sorry about the… the rather abrupt finish. I lost it, I freely admit. I owe everyone an apology.'

Willie's lips quirked. 'No need, Bram. No need. It was a blast.' A sound that might have been a chuckle left his throat. 'So what'll it be, gents?'

'Mineral water, please,' said Bram.

'Pint of Stella for me and the same for the lad,' said David.

Bram frowned. 'Maybe Max should just have a half.'

'*Dad!*' hissed Max.

'What an embarrassment, eh?' David laughed, but

the look he flashed at Bram was contemptuous. 'The lad can handle a pint. And are you wanting crisps? You got crisps, Willie? What flavour do you like, Max? Cheese and onion? Good old ready salted?'

'If this is us living life on the edge, Grandad, we should maybe be a bit more adventurous. What more exotic flavours have you got?'

Willie sighed and, as if with a huge effort, turned to contemplate the open boxes of crisps behind him. 'Salt and vinegar, prawn cocktail, pickled onion–'

'Pickled onion, please,' said Max.

Willie fished out a packet and dropped it onto the bar. 'You folks drowning your sorrows, then?'

'I wouldn't say that,' Bram objected.

As Willie got their drinks, he began to enumerate: 'First a crow gets shot and tied to your clothesline. Then your dog. Then more crows, and Bram here has a narrow escape. Then some bastard breaks in and–'

David held up a hand to stop him. 'They didn't break in. Bram left the door open.'

'Not open,' Max corrected.

'Unlocked.'

Willie flicked a look at Bram. 'Some bastard *gets* in and leaves a bloody great chunk of offal in the chanterelle risotto. Writes "Your next" in blood on the worktop.' He sucked air through his teeth. 'Classic escalation.'

How the hell did Willie know all this? Presumably some of the police officers who'd attended the incident were local, and it was all round Grantown and environs by now.

'And the mandala was vandalised at the party,' Max put in. 'They wrote "Stupid hippy shit" on it. Well, we don't know if it was the same person…'

Willie shook his head, setting the first pint on the

drip tray. 'And the water failing – that's surely no coincidence. Someone has got it in for you, no question. And I don't suppose the police are doing anything about it.'

'Got that right,' said David, and turned round to lean back against the bar and contemplate the room. He raised his voice: 'But if that toe-rag thinks the McKechnies are waiting around on their arses for the police to get their finger out, he can think again.'

Max was looking at David with his mouth open.

'Aye, that bastard needs to watch himself,' David boomed. 'We've got his number.'

'David,' Bram hissed. '*Please!* This isn't helping. Antagonising people–'

David turned back round and lifted the first pint, took a long gulp, and wiped his lips. 'Oh no, Bram. No. They're not the ones *antagonised* here. Not – at – *all*.'

'Remember your suspended sentence,' Bram said in his ear.

'Aye, I've previous convictions for assault,' David shouted. 'They call me Mad McKechnie for a reason, eh, Max? Mad McKechnie and Mad Max, that's us! Ha!'

Max was shaking his head, but he was laughing. 'Grandad, you're incorrigible.' He lifted his own pint and took a long swallow.

'Pace yourself, Max.' Bram opened the packet of crisps. 'Can we have some more crisps, Willie?' Hopefully they would soak up some of the alcohol.

'And what about Bram?' said David. 'Mad McKechnie, Mad Max and Bricking-It Bram? A-hahahahaha*haa*!'

'If you mean I'm going to let the police deal with the situation and not do anything stupid, then yes. Bricking-It Bram, if you like.'

David had sunk half his pint already. He leant over and hissed at Bram: 'No, Bram, in fact I *don't* like. You need to step up. You need to get your head down out of the clouds, son. My daughter and grandkids are depending on *you* to keep them safe. Right? As the man of the family, the most important job you have is to *keep them safe.'*

'I'm well aware of that, David, thank you.'

'So what are you proposing to do about this yob, eh? I'm talking reality here, not airy-fairy-skipping-through-the-daisies Bram world.'

'As I said, the police–'

'*Christ* almighty! What have the police done so far?'

Max, who'd been pretending not to listen, ate a handful of crisps, shooting furtive sideways looks at them.

'Scott's as anxious about all this as any of us. He's on top of it, I'm sure.'

'Aye, Scott's a good lad, but they don't have the resources to throw at it that we need. It's down to us to sort this.'

'No it's not. It's–'

'Heeeeey, Maximilian!' came a shout from the door.

Finn Taylor and his little gang. They loped over to the bar and Finn slung an arm across Max's shoulders. He was wearing a shiny blue football shirt with 'Taylor' across the back. 'Not going to have us thrown out, are you, Grandad? You can search us for marker pens if you want!'

'Ah, yes, Finn, um.' Bram needed to offer an olive branch here. 'We're sorry about that. We didn't mean to *accuse* any of you–'

'Oh, you know, I think that's just what you did, though, isn't it? My old man's thinking of suing you for slander. Reputational damage, you know what I'm saying? I can't walk down the street now without people whispering and pointing.' He jigged backwards.

'*There's the guy that writes on walls!*' He ran in slow-motion down the length of the bar and back.

The other lads whooped encouragement.

'Hey, Maximilian,' said Finn, coming back and draping his arm round Max again. 'You don't think I'm guilty of...' He gasped. '... *wall mutilation*, do you?'

Bram was in a quandary. Should he intervene? Tell Finn to go and sit down and leave them to have their drinks in peace? But after what had happened at the party, that would probably do more harm than good. He looked at David.

And found David staring back at him, a challenge in his eyes.

Oh, bloody Nora. David was leaving this situation to Bram to deal with, as a sort of test?

So what should he do?

'*Is* your full name Maximilian?' Finn asked.

'Of course not,' said Max, and shrugged him off.

'Maxine?'

'It's Maxwell. It's my grandmother's maiden name.'

Finn hooted. 'Ooh, classic! A *maiden* name for our fair maiden!'

'Okay, Max, let's get a table,' said Bram, and scooped up the crisp packets. 'How about that one by the wall over there?' A small table with only three seats.

'Mind if we join you?' said Finn.

'Oh, not at all, son,' said David heartily. 'It's my idea of a grand night out, babysitting a bunch of wee pricks with delusions of fucking adequacy.' And as he left them in his wake, David shot a look at Bram, as if to say *Watch and learn, Bram, watch and learn.*

The kids gravitated to the open smokers' door, and David started talking about his time on 'the rigs', when, as a young man, he'd worked on the North Sea oil rigs

and made a packet of money with which to start up his
building firm.

'Health and safety in those days wasn't the best, but
this guy Steve, he was all about health and safety, never
went anywhere without his hard hat, not even to the
toilet. It was a standing joke with the lads, and he used
to get ribbed about it all the time.'

Max was nodding along, smiling, knowing something good was coming.

'This one day, Steve's standing right under the
heavy-lift crane boom when out of nowhere, bang! It
drops to the platform – ten tonnes of steel falling from a
height of eighty metres. Metal fatigue. The lad never
stood a chance. When we got it off him he was strawberry jam with a yellow hard hat floating on top. Hard
hat was intact, like.' David chuckled.

Max's smile was frozen in place. Then he gave a
small chuckle just like David's.

'What a terrible thing to happen,' Bram managed.
'No wonder you're so health and safety conscious on
your building sites.'

As David launched into a much more acceptable but
excruciatingly dull discussion of building regs, Bram
excused himself to go to the toilet. He took his time,
looking at the row of old photographs in the corridor
showing the Inverluie as it used to be in the early 1900s,
totally charming, with some smart men in suits standing
outside and a couple of beautifully dressed women in
long Edwardian coats. The age of elegance. If they could
only see it now.

In the gloom of the dusty corridor, it was easy to
imagine the building itself in mourning for those better
times. Buildings, he was sure, absorbed happiness, were
imprinted with the memories of their previous inhabi-

tants. That was one of the reasons why he never wanted to go back and see his grandparents' house in Amsterdam. He had a feeling that something of them would still be there, that some lingering essence left behind would be aware of Bram walking along the street towards the house, only for him to walk on past. Kirsty thought this was mad, and he knew, objectively, that he was just projecting his own feelings onto the bricks and mortar. But still. He imagined Opa and Oma, waiting behind the door to welcome him, and Bram walking on past.

He hoped the people in these photos weren't still lingering here. He patted the wall in sympathy and made his way back down the corridor, aware, now, of an increase in noise level.

He opened the door to the bar.

A cluster of young men were standing in a circle. Willie, coming out from behind the bar, shouted something at him, but the noise level was so high, with all the lads whooping and yelling, that Bram couldn't make out the words.

And then he saw that in the middle of the circle were Finn and Max.

Max had his shirt pulled up almost over his head, and as he twisted and pushed Finn away, Bram saw that his face was bleeding. That the flesh around his left eye was starting to swell up.

'No! No, no, no!' Bram shouted, pushing his way through the whooping crowd.

David was standing inside the circle, shouting instructions: 'Are you a man or a mouse, Max? Get in after him! Right on the nose, lad, right on the nose!'

Max, breathing hard, launched himself at Finn, fists flailing wildly. Finn's head snapped back and he staggered, and David shouted, '*Yesss!*'

And Bram couldn't help himself, internally, echo the sentiment: *Yesss!*

Two of the other youths caught Finn, as Bram and Willie forced their way into the circle between the two boys.

'Out!' Willie growled. 'Anyone under the age of twenty, *out now!*' He pointed at Finn, now hunched over dabbing at his nose, and shouted at his friends: 'Get that wee animal out of here! He's barred!'

Bram wanted to take Max's face in his hands and scrutinise it – he needed to know what damage that little bastard had done – but David already had an arm around his grandson and was guiding him out of the bar. Bram followed, in time to hear Max say, 'I got him, Grandad! I think his nose is *bleeding*!' He turned, trying to look back into the bar.

'Aye, that was a cracker, son,' said David, slapping Max's back, all proud grandfather.

And the worst of it was, Bram felt his own lips move in a smile. Proud father? Surely not? But he couldn't pretend to himself that he wasn't feeling a little warm glow of satisfaction at how pleased David was with Max. David wasn't exactly big on positive grandparent-ing, and Max was lapping it up.

In the car park, Bram found himself checking over his shoulder, almost expecting a baying mob to come pounding after them. 'Come on, let's go,' he said, fishing out his car key and zapping the doors open.

'Did you see, Dad?' Max's battered face was alight.

Bram could only nod. Once they were in the car with the doors locked, he twisted in his seat to look at Max. 'Maybe we'd better take you to get checked out at A&E.'

Max laughed. 'I'm fine. Just a few bruises.'

'The lad's a natural,' enthused David, reaching back between the front seats to slap Max's arm. 'That wee toe-rag can dish it out but he can't take it, eh? I've a feeling we've seen the last of your boogie man, folks.'

'I've never hit anyone before.' Max grinned, as if wondering what he'd been doing with his life.

'And you never will again,' Bram said, trying to make his voice stern as he started the engine. 'Violence is never the answer. Is it? Max?'

'I guess not,' came the cheerful response.

The 'executive bungalow' that David and Linda called home was on a leafy street on the edge of Grantown, with views to the hills across the Millers' garden opposite. Grantown-on-Spey was an early example of a planned town, dating from the mid-1700s, as Bram had discovered when he'd first come here with Kirsty all those years ago, although in the south of England it would have been considered a village. It definitely had the feel of a town, though, with a spacious square and lots of shops and big churches, and some very grand houses. A town in miniature. Its setting was glorious, on the edge of the Cairngorm Mountains, and the stone houses with their walled gardens and orchards in the older parts of town were perfect.

David had lived all his life surrounded by this beauty, by wonderful, gracious Victorian architecture, and decided that his dream house was an ugly bungalow faced with orange and yellow stone cladding. There was no front garden, just a huge expanse of tarmac sweeping to the door.

Horrendous. But each to his own.

As they pulled in through gateposts topped by concrete horse's heads, David said, 'The women don't need to know about this.'

'Ah, now, David – I'm not comfortable keeping secrets from Kirsty.'

'Just think for a minute, Bram, about how she's going to react.'

Bram thought for all of five seconds. 'All right.'

'Okay, so we need to get our story straight. Max got tipsy and fell over. Whacked his face on the back of a chair.'

'Nice one,' from Max.

'We'll get grief for that in itself, but it's a whole lot better than the alternative.' David slapped Bram's shoulder. 'Great night, lads, great night. Thanks for the lift.'

Max moved into the passenger seat for the journey home, eager to give Bram an account of how the fight started. 'Finn was hell-bent on getting a rise out of me.'

'That doesn't mean you had to oblige him. Probably best to give him a wide berth in future. Just because we live next door to the Taylors doesn't mean we have to socialise with them.'

'Fine by me.'

As they pulled off the public road onto the track, Max took out his phone and used the camera function to check his face. 'Oh good grief, look at my eye! Is it possible to get a black eye from falling onto the back of a chair?'

'Well, I'm guessing your grandad should know.'

'I guess he should!'

Bram negotiated the bend in the track and then eased over the little bridge.

The track seemed to leap up under the front wheels, as if they'd hit a speed bump, and then there was an almighty crash and he felt himself jolted forward, the seat belt tightening across his chest, and then flung back, his head bouncing off the headrest.

What the…?

And then his whole body was tipping back.

He yelled something, and with his left hand grabbed for Max instinctively.

What the hell was happening?

The car crashed backwards and kept on going, as if the road under them had disappeared, as if they were falling back into nothing. He slammed his right foot on the brake pedal, repeatedly, uselessly, as if that could stop this happening. As if that could stop them falling.

'*Daaad!*' Max shouted.

15

'It was like some mad fairground ride!' Max enthused, sitting at the table grinning up at Bram as Amy dabbed antiseptic onto the cut on his face. 'One minute we're tootling along and the next – bam! We're up in the air!'

'You're certainly having a real run of bad luck,' said Amy, getting up from the table to wash her hands in the water Kirsty had boiled. She was glamorous as ever in a navy silk shirt and white Capris. 'Although I guess you could say it was *good* luck that neither of you was badly hurt. You're going to have quite a black eye, though, Max.'

Bram and Max had decided to pass off Max's injuries as having occurred during the accident. Their story was that he'd hit his face on the dashboard.

'We can check the scene of the accident tomorrow in daylight,' said Scott, handing his wife a towel. 'But I doubt there's foul play involved.'

'I suppose that bridge must be at least a hundred years old,' said Bram. 'And the Discovery is a big heavy vehicle.'

Part of the bridge had collapsed, taking the back of the Discovery with it, but as it was just a little bridge across a stream, the drop had only been four feet or so. Max hadn't been able to open his door as the Discovery had listed slightly onto that side, but he had scrambled across to the driver's door and they'd both got out that way.

They were slightly bruised from their seat belts, but otherwise unharmed.

Bram's first thought had been that whoever was terrorising them had done this, but he realised now that that was unlikely. Kirsty's panicked phone call to Scott and Amy had been unnecessary, and he felt bad about dragging them out this late at night. They'd had to park on the other side of the bridge and ford the stream, although Amy had made light of this, saying she'd felt like a kid again, getting a piggy-back ride on Scott's back.

Kirsty was banging about the kitchen putting away the contents of the dishwasher, not saying much, but Bram knew what she was thinking. Why hadn't he checked that bridge? In their division of labour as a couple, anything home-related was Bram's remit.

'Your seat belt must have worked,' Amy was saying to Max, examining the bruise across his chest. 'So how come you hit your face off the dashboard?'

Damn.

Max grinned. 'Well…' And he exchanged a look with Bram, who grimaced and nodded to signal he should come clean. 'That's not *exactly* what happened.'

Kirsty whipped round.

AT BREAKFAST THE NEXT MORNING, Phoebe, sitting wide-eyed across the table from her brother, was more inter-

ested in the fight than the collapsed bridge, and Max
was certainly not averse to telling and retelling the story.
Phoebe offered him first jam and then marmalade and
then lemon curd to go on his toast, as if setting out a
feast for the conquering hero, while Max drank coffee
and embroidered the tale.

'Finn was trying to provoke me from the moment he
arrived. I tried the strategy of treating him with lofty
disdain, but he kept on, laughing about Bertie being
shot and stuff.'

'He thought you wouldn't fight back!' Phoebe
crowed.

'Indeed.' Max gave her an indulgent half-smile.

There was an indefinable change in Max since last
night, Bram was concerned to note. He had – not a
swagger, exactly, but a consciousness, a new confidence.

Kirsty sat down next to Phoebe so she could look
Max in the eye. 'No matter the provocation, it's *always*
wrong to hit someone.' The last two words wobbled a
bit, and she took a breath. 'I don't know what else I can
say to make you see that.'

Max grimaced. 'It's okay, Mum, I'm fine. It looks
worse than it is.'

'That's not the point, Max, and you know it!' Kirsty's
chair legs scraped the floor as she got to her feet.

Bram put his hands on her shoulders and gave
Phoebe a reassuring smile. 'I think we *all* know that
what Max did was wrong. It's not something to be
proud of, punching someone and making their nose
bleed.'

'Hello?' said Max, indicating his own face. 'What
was I supposed to do, stand there and take it like a
human punchbag?'

'You needed to walk away, Max.'

'Pfff.'

'Finn's a bully,' Phoebe said firmly. 'He had it coming.'

Kirsty's phone buzzed, and she turned away to answer. After a brief conversation which consisted mostly of 'Oh no!' and 'Okay,' she ended the call and turned to Bram. 'Scott. He needs us down at the bridge. He thinks it *has* been tampered with after all.'

Max wanted to come too, but Bram and Kirsty insisted he stay inside with Phoebe. As he followed Kirsty outside, Bram realised that he wasn't actually too surprised that the bridge collapse hadn't been an accident. Maybe now the police would start taking the whole situation seriously.

'Why?' Kirsty said as they walked down the track. 'Why is someone doing this to us?' She grabbed Bram's arm. 'The bridge collapsing could have been really serious.'

Bram grimaced. 'It's just a small bridge over a stream. We were never going to be seriously hurt, even if it had collapsed completely.'

Kirsty stopped walking. 'How can you be so calm about it?'

'I'm not *calm*! I'm just–'

'The glass is always half full with you, isn't it?' She gave a shaky laugh. 'I never thought I'd be saying that as a criticism. But your determination to always look on the bright side – sometimes it flies in the face of reason.'

This echoed his own thoughts over the last few days. Bram took a breath, watching the morning light on the stretch of ground towards the wood, the shadows chasing across the grass as little white clouds moved over the sun and away. 'Maybe you're right. Maybe I do need to be less… less naïve, I guess.'

She turned to face him. 'Tell me the truth. Was it Dad's doing?'

'Uh – what?'

'Max getting into that fight!'

'No, no. It was as Max says – Finn was out to provoke him.' There was no point upsetting Kirsty further by telling her the whole truth.

At the bridge, the Discovery was still in situ in the ruins of the structure, its rear wheels in the stream, bonnet pointing skywards. Beyond it were several police cars, and a guy in forensic gear was taking photographs. There were dressed stones all tumbled about in the water, under and to either side of what remained of the bridge.

Scott splashed into the stream and pointed at a large wedge-shaped stone lying in the water. 'That's one of the keystones – the stones that sit at the top of each course of stones in the arch, across its width, and keep everything in place. See the white marks all over it? Those are chisel marks – recent ones. Someone's gone to a lot of trouble to chisel the keystones out.' He indicated another stone – this one looked as if it had been newly split, with a sharp, light-coloured edge to it. 'Looks like they must have removed maybe five or six of them last night. Hence the collapse when the Discovery came onto the bridge.'

'Oh my God,' breathed Kirsty.

'Quite an undertaking. They probably muffled the chisel with cloth, but the sound of it hitting the mortar and the stone would probably have carried to the house. You didn't hear anything?'

Kirsty shook her head. 'The double glazing would have cut out that kind of noise, presumably. At this distance, anyway.' She was staring at the Discovery, and Bram knew she was thinking of Max, already battered and bruised from the fight, sitting in that passenger seat as the bridge collapsed.

He touched her arm. 'At the risk of coming across as a glass-half-full idiot, I have to reiterate that it was never going to cause a serious accident. Was it?' he appealed to Scott.

Scott shook his head. 'Not unless something freakish happened – like the windscreen being broken and a stone hitting someone on the head or something. No. Whoever's doing this, I would say they probably don't want to actually hurt anyone, just put the fear of God into you.'

'But who would want to do that?' Kirsty was trembling.

'That's what we have to find out. At least this is the nail in the coffin of your Owen theory, Bram – there's no way they could determine who would be in the next vehicle over the bridge.'

Bram shook his head. 'If they were watching the house, they'd have seen me leave, and would know that Kirsty was at home without a vehicle. So they knew I was likely to be the next person over the bridge.'

'It could just as easily have been Max and David. If they were watching, they'd have seen them leave too. Anyway, I think it might be a good idea to take Linda and David up on their offer and go and stay with them for a few days. I don't think you're in any serious danger, but you can't be too careful.'

'Oh God,' said Kirsty. 'I really want to avoid that if at all possible. I want to keep Max out of Dad's orbit, at least until he's started school and has made some friends.' She was looking at Scott, not Bram, and Scott nodded as something wordless passed between them.

Were they thinking about Owen, who had also, perhaps, been in David's 'orbit' at the boxing club? Was that where the trouble had started?

And now she did turn to Bram. 'I know you're

covering for him. I know Max wouldn't have got into that fight if Dad hadn't been there.'

Bram opened and closed his mouth.

Kirsty, to his surprise, smiled. 'My glass-half-full idiot,' she whispered, and hugged him. 'You're probably spinning even that as a good thing, a bonding thing for Max and Dad. And you, in covering for them.'

This was so spookily accurate that Bram could only gape at her.

Scott was grinning at them like an indulgent uncle. 'You could come and stay with us for a few days.'

'And how would we explain that to Mum and Dad?' Kirsty grimaced. 'No – thanks, but we'll be fine here.'

'Will we?' said Bram. 'As the new glass-half-empty Bram, I feel obliged to point out that we've no water and now no access… And the borehole people won't be able to get their drilling equipment here until the bridge has been repaired.'

'We're managing, though, aren't we, without water? We can get Max's car from the hotel and use that until the Discovery has been repaired – park it on the other side of the bridge and ford the stream. It's not deep – we can set up stepping stones.'

'I guess.'

'Bram, I really *really* don't want to go back to Mum and Dad's. If we keep the kids inside until this person is caught…' She turned back to Scott. 'Hopefully that won't be too much longer? I know Max will go spare, but after last night, we should probably ground him anyway. He can't complain.'

'Okay,' said Bram. 'If you think it's best.' Let's all stay put.'

. . .

DAVID DUMPED a holdall on the floor of the Walton Room and grinned at Phoebe, who ran at him, jumping into his arms. David held her close for a moment, eyes shut. And then Fraser appeared behind him with Bertie, and Phoebe squealed in delight. David released her, grinning. 'Aye, I'm kidding myself if I'm thinking Grandad can compete with Bertie, eh, princess?'

'I love you both the same,' Phoebe assured him, her face pressed into a now cone-less Bertie's neck, and David smiled down at her fondly.

Bram was glad to see the two of them. He hadn't been relishing spending the night here alone with Kirsty and the kids, at the mercy of whoever might be out there. It was a good feeling, knowing they had David and Fraser on their team.

'Right, I've put you both in the twin guest room,' said Kirsty.

'We're not going to need a room,' said Fraser.

'We'll be on watch all night,' added David. 'Might do a bit of patrolling round the house too.'

'Oh no, Dad!' Kirsty turned and glared at him. 'No!'

David put an arm round her. 'Relax, princess, I'm not going to touch the wee bugger, although no one could argue that he's got it coming. We won't confront him – or them. We'll call the police if we see anything. Don't you worry.'

'Bertie! Come on, Bertie!' Phoebe danced up the stairs, Bertie's nails clicking on the stairs as he followed her.

Kirsty waited until Phoebe was out of earshot. 'You'd better not *confront* them, Dad, or that could be you going straight to prison.'

'Aye, I'm the problem here?' David exchanged a look with Fraser. 'Let's bend over backwards to blame everyone but the perpetrator. You blame yourselves for hurting the wee snowflake's feelings with those notices. You blame Max for defending himself. You blame me for wanting to catch the bugger. But don't you worry. If we see anything, we'll call the cops like responsible citizens, and the toe-rag will maybe get hauled into court and given a community service order. That make you happy, eh?'

'Yes, Dad, it would. When this person or persons are caught, they'll have a restraining order slapped on them so they won't be able to come anywhere near us. That's what we want. That's *all* we want. Okay?'

David held up his hands in surrender.

Bertie and Phoebe reappeared, and as David and Fraser pulled on gloves and hats in the Walton Room, Phoebe poured water into Bertie's dish in the kitchen. 'Just to make sure he's hydrated,' she told Bram, bending over him and fiddling with his collar. It was the petcam, Bram saw, which she was attaching. Unlike the representation in her drawing, it was so small it was barely noticeable.

'Come on then, boy,' said David, opening the door, and Bertie plodded obediently after him.

16

Kirsty and the kids had gone to bed, but, if he was to retain any shreds of self-respect, that wasn't an option for Bram. What sort of a man snuggled up in bed and went to sleep, relying on his sixty-seven-year-old father-in-law to protect his family? David and Fraser were out there in the dark somewhere, 'on patrol' with Bertie. The least Bram could do was sit up and keep watch.

He had the lights out in the Walton Room and the curtains pulled back so he could see the verandah, flooded in illumination from the security lighting David had insisted on installing despite Bram's objections on the grounds of light pollution. The lighting had an industrial feel, with a cold blue tinge to it.

It was a struggle to keep awake. The armchair was too comfortable.

Bram stood, and stretched, and walked to the windows.

And froze.

There was someone out there! Just beyond the verandah, moving stealthily around the pools of illumination.

Bram could only just see him, a shadowy moving
shape…

Police. He should call 999?

But by the time they got here, he'd be long gone.

Oh God! What should he do? Go out there? Try to get
a photo?

What if they tried to get into the house?

He needed something to defend himself with. A
knife from the kitchen?

And then the figure moved into one of the pools of
light, and Bram saw that it was David. *It was David!* He
was barking with weak, hysterical laughter as he flung
open the door and stumbled out onto the verandah.

'God, David–'

The laughter died as he saw who was with him.

Max. In dark jeans and jacket, his eyes shining with
excitement.

'What the *hell* are you doing out here?' Bram spluttered as Bertie plodded up the steps to greet him.

'On patrol!'

'I thought you were in bed!'

'Yeah, I snuck out while you were asleep!'

David smirked. 'Sentry asleep at his post. Firing
squad offence that, Bram.'

Had he actually been asleep? He must have been.
Damn.

'Have you seen anything?'

'Nope. All quiet on the Western Front!' Max grinned.
He seemed unusually hyper.

'Have you been drinking?'

'A nip of whisky to keep off the chill,' asserted
David. 'Nothing wrong with that.'

Bram grimaced. 'Where's Fraser?'

'In the wood,' said Max. 'Bertie seemed to pick up a
scent, but we think it was probably just a rabbit or

something. He's pretty hopeless as a patrol dog, to be honest!'

'Okay, well, I think you've done your bit, Max. You can come inside now and help me stay awake.'

'Uh, I think I'm more use out here, Dad.'

David slapped Max's back. 'Course he is. You go back to beddie-byes, Bram. We'll report back in a bit, make sure you're not sleeping too soundly!'

'Well…' Bram grimaced. 'As long as you stay with Grandad at all times, Max, and don't go off on your own.'

'Wilco!' Max sketched a salute. 'Come on, Bertie, let's go!'

Bram should insist that he come inside. But he was safe enough, surely, with David? Even so, Bram felt like the worst sort of coward as he watched the two of them melt back into the night.

Rather than resume his seat and maybe fall asleep again, he spent the next hour pacing around the ground floor of the house in the dark, senses straining, adrenaline coursing, jumping at every little sound – ice cracking in the freezer, a gust of wind in the chimney, a floorboard creaking under his feet. It was as if the house itself had turned against him, and was mocking his efforts to stand guard.

Max.

His son was out there.

This wasn't right. He needed to go and get Max.

Kirsty wasn't asleep. 'What?' she said at once when he came into the bedroom. 'Has something happened?'

'No, no. But Max – did you know Max is out there with your dad and Fraser?'

'What?' She swung her legs off the bed. 'God, Bram!'

'He's fine. I spoke to them an hour or so ago, and–'

'An *hour*! But anything could have happened since then!'

'Okay. I know. I'm not happy about it either. I'm going to get him and make him come back inside.'

'I'm coming with you.'

'No, you have to stay with Phoebe. Maybe you could sit up downstairs and keep watch? Apparently I'm not much of a sentry. Max got past me while I was asleep.'

She didn't smile. 'Okay. Go and get him, Bram.'

The night air was cool, and Bram was glad of his jacket. He'd taken a torch with him and he used it to light his way across the grass around the side of the house, but there was a moon high in the sky, almost a full one, and when he switched the torch off he found he could see well enough not to be stumbling about. And he felt horribly conspicuous carrying a light around for anyone to see.

He stood for a moment, letting his eyes become accustomed to the dark. And that was when he saw him, a tall, slim figure in dark clothing moving erratically towards the shed.

Max.

How much whisky had David let him have?

And where the hell *was* David?

Bram strode after his son, rehearsing what he was going to say. He needed to impress on Max that when someone pressured you to drink alcohol, you weren't being a man by giving in. Quite the opposite. He didn't want to scare him by shouting so he just hurried after him, closing the distance between them.

Max reached the shed and stopped, putting a hand against it to prop himself up.

'Okay,' said Bram as he came up behind him. 'It's okay. Let's get you inside.'

Max straightened, and wheeled round.

Bram staggered backwards.

The face turned towards him was hairy, with a snarling mouth, long fangs –

It was a mask.

'Christ!' Bram yelped.

It wasn't Max. Max wasn't this tall.

And then the mask was up close, right in his face, hands were on him and Bram was trying to wrench himself free, the shock of what was happening paralysing his brain, his muscles. All he could do was throw his bodyweight backwards, try to break the guy's hold, but he was too strong –

And then he suddenly let go.

Bram flew backwards to the ground, and the masked man laughed.

He *laughed*.

This was the bastard who had shot Bertie, shot the crows, shot at Bram, *threatened his kids, terrorised his kids*!

Are you a man or a mouse, Bram?

Next thing he knew, his muscles were exploding into action and he was jumping up, lunging forward and gripping the other man's arms. He was slamming him back against the shed, and his head was bouncing off the metal hose bracket with a dull *clonk* and then he was coming at Bram again, growling low in his throat like an animal.

And like an animal, Bram felt something primeval overwhelm him.

Rage.

It flooded his brain, it swept away all fear, it swept away everything, everything Bram had ever felt or thought or been.

There was only the rage.

He launched himself forward and saw, as if from a great distance, his own hands on the bastard's shoulders as his head bounced off the metal bracket, *crack, crack, crack,* until he was limp, until he slumped forward and Bram stepped back and let him fall to the ground.

He drew back his foot to kick him.

And then the rage was gone.

And there was only silence.

Silence, apart from the sound of his own ragged breathing, the cool night air ripping in and out of his lungs as he stood there staring down at the still shape. The torch he'd dropped was there on the grass. He stooped to grab it, but his hand was shaking so much he dropped it again.

'Oh Christ, oh Christ,' he whispered.

He fumbled for the torch and managed to switch it on. Made himself shine the beam on the guy. It shook all over the place, giving the illusion, at first, of movement.

But the man was still. Lying half on his side, face upwards. Mask upwards.

Choking on a sob, Bram dropped to his knees and pulled up the mask.

Finn.

It was Finn Taylor.

Bram put a trembling hand to the boy's chest.

'Finn? *Finn?*'

17

B ram shook Kirsty awake. In the gloom of the Walton Room she squinted up at him, shifting in the armchair. 'I wasn't asleep,' she said with a little smile.

'He's dead.' Bram's voice was strangely calm. 'I've killed him.'

'What?'

'I've killed Finn Taylor.'

She didn't believe him. Of course, she didn't believe him. He didn't believe it himself as he told her what had happened, that he'd thought it was Max, about the shock of seeing the mask, the out-of-body experience when he'd found himself bashing the guy's head against the hose bracket – the realisation that he wasn't moving, the realisation that he was dead –

And then they were running, out onto the verandah and down the steps and across the moon-washed grass to the shed.

Bram stood sobbing as Kirsty dropped to her knees beside the still figure. She used the flashlight app on her phone, shaking in her hand, to illuminate Finn's face, the dead, staring eyes, the sticky head wounds, the blood on the grass, brightly, improbably red in the harsh white light. She put the fingers of her left hand, shrinkingly, against his neck.

'We need to call an ambulance,' Bram got out. 'But he's dead. *He's dead, isn't he?*'

He fumbled his phone out of his pocket and powered it up. But then Kirsty was grabbing it from him.

'Yes. He's dead. There's no pulse. There's no point calling an ambulance.'

'But he – he might not be–'

'*Look at him, Bram!* Of course he's *dead*!'

'But we still – we still have to–' He put out a hand for his phone.

She pushed it into her pocket. 'Let's just think this through.' She took a shuddering breath, turning away from Finn's body. 'He's dead. There's nothing anyone can do for him. Is there? If we call an ambulance, you'll be arrested.'

The harsh light from her phone lit up her face from below, like she was a kid with a torch trying to freak people out, trying to make herself look weird and scary. For a long moment, Bram couldn't speak. Then:

'I killed him.'

He had killed someone. He had killed that boy.

'You'll be arrested and the charge will be murder because it wasn't self-defence, was it? He didn't hurt you? There won't be any defensive injuries on you?'

'He came at me, he grabbed me, but… No. He didn't hurt me.'

In the eery light from her phone, he could see that Kirsty's face was stiff with shock but that she must have been soundlessly crying. There were tears shining on her cheeks, on her chin. 'We could – make some? I could hit you? But forensics these days, they can tell all kinds of things, they can probably tell the size of the fist that made an injury... And even if we could mock something up, even if we could make it seem like self-defence... *Look at him, Bram!*

Bram made himself look.

'Look at all the blood! That's not a result of self-defence! How many times did you whack his head on that bracket?'

Bram was sobbing again. 'I don't know.'

'Way more than you needed to to defend yourself!'

'I – it was like – it was as if I was *possessed*! As if it wasn't *me*! I couldn't stop myself!'

It was David. It was David who'd possessed him.

Are you a man or a mouse, Bram?

This was all David's fault.

No it wasn't.

He couldn't shift the blame for this onto David. He'd done this.

He'd done this.

'You were *possessed*?' Kirsty's voice shook. 'How's that going to sound in court?'

For a long moment they stood there staring at each other. It was as if they'd stepped out of their normal life into a twilight zone world which couldn't possibly exist, which must surely be something they were imagining, something they watched on Netflix late at night and could switch off any time it got too disturbing, shivering and laughing at themselves and getting up to make some hot chocolate.

But this was *really happening*.

'Bram?' she said, finally.

'We need to call an ambulance and the police.'

'No one knows,' Kirsty said, her voice now urgent. 'No one knows it was Finn who was terrorising us, do

they? If he disappeared, there'd be no reason for the
police to think we were involved. If we dispose of the
body–'

'We can't do that!'

'– there'll be nothing tying you to his disappearance.
Who's going to suspect *you*, unless we hand it to them
on a plate? And why should we do that? Finn was
terrorising us. It was his own fault that you were so
freaked out by everything he'd done that you lost it.'

'No,' said Bram, trying to think, trying to get his
head round this nightmare that had descended on them.

'Bram, *no one knows it was Finn* doing any of it.'

'They might. He might have had – accomplices. His
friends–'

'Okay, even if that's the case, his friends aren't going
to go to the police and confess to that, are they? If Finn
disappears, the police will have nothing to connect him
to us. Finn is – *was* a binge drinker who got into trouble
a lot. No one will be too surprised if he vanishes. It
happens all the time, young men getting drunk and
disappearing, lying dead in a ditch somewhere or
falling into – into a river…' She stopped.

'We can't – try to cover this up! I have to tell the
police what happened.'

'And go to prison.'

Bram lifted his shoulders helplessly.

'God, Bram!' Kirsty was sobbing now. 'You wouldn't
last *five minutes* in prison!' She clutched him, clutched
his shoulders, and then she was hugging him close. 'It
would break you, and I'm *not going to let that happen*!'

'I would cope,' he managed to say.

'Of course you wouldn't! You can't go to prison. We
need you. The kids and I need you.' She pulled away
from him but kept a grip of his shoulders. 'We have to
get him out of sight. Into the shed. We can deal with him

– with it later, when Dad and Fraser have gone and Max is in bed... Bram. *Bram!*' She shook him. 'We have to do this. Okay? *Okay?*'

'Okay.'

Neither of them wanted to touch him. Neither of them wanted to go near his head. In the end, they took a boot each and dragged him to the door of the shed.

'It's locked,' said Kirsty, shining the flashlight from her phone on the padlock securing the door. 'Where's the key? Bram? Where's the key to the padlock?'

He'd got a padlock to secure the door, he remembered now, after the incident with the weedkiller. He'd put the little padlock key...

'Under that flat stone.'

He watched Kirsty stoop, the light from her phone illuminating her in fits and starts, turning her into a series of freeze-frame shots, into a strange, menacing figure that seemed to move in jerks, like something in a horror film.

She lifted the stone. 'Got it.'

They pulled him – *it* – inside the shed, into the incongruously everyday smells of creosote and oil and new, resiny wood. The floor of the shed was finished with smooth, pale-grey, heavy-duty ceramic tiles that David had recommended for ease of cleaning, and Bram could see that Finn's head had left a trail of blood, like a snail's trail, across them.

He stopped, one large, booted foot in his hand.

He could feel the indentations of the sole, the roughness of the leather, the criss-crossing laces, and imagined Finn sitting on a chair in the boot room at Benlervie to tie these laces for the last time. He cupped the boot in his hand, the words going round his head:

I'm sorry, I'm sorry, I'm sorry.

'Let's get him back against the workbench, so if

anyone looks in the windows they won't see him,' said Kirsty, her voice wavering on the last word.

They pulled Finn across the remaining few feet, turning as they approached the bench to bring him around so he was lying parallel to and slightly under it. Bram set the boot he was holding down carefully. Kirsty grabbed a blue tarpaulin and tucked it around Finn as if tucking one of the kids into bed, her hands gentle as she pressed it down over his head.

'I'm sorry,' Bram said. 'Kirsty. I'm sorry.'

She nodded. Stood.

He followed her out of the shed.

He shut the door. Hooked the padlock into position. 'Where's the key?'

'I thought you had it?'

They checked their pockets.

No key.

'We must have dropped it.' Bram took Kirsty's phone from her and shone it on the grass.

'It doesn't matter,' said Kirsty. 'We need to find Dad and Fraser and Max, and stop the patrol. Get Dad and Fraser to leave. Then when Max is asleep, we can bury... bury Finn in the wood.'

'*Our* wood?'

'Yes. We can control what happens there. We can make sure no one... I don't know, excavates there for drains or...' She was already walking away. 'Come on, Bram. We need to find them.'

As he walked after her, hardly able to take in what she had just said, he saw, briefly illuminated by the light from Kirsty's phone, Henrietta, the wooden goose, standing there amidst the wildflowers staring at him, or so it seemed to Bram for one mad moment. He choked back a sob and looked away.

•   •   •

BERTIE RAN TOWARDS THEM, tongue lolling, across the grass of the paddock. Kirsty shone her phone behind him and Bram made out three indistinct figures.

As Bertie nuzzled him, Bram swallowed another huge sob. This innocent animal. Little did he know…

'What the hell are you doing out here?' was David's greeting as he shone a powerful torch in their faces.

'I'm not happy about this – it's asking for trouble,' Kirsty said. 'Patrol's over. Please, Dad, go home. Max, I want you back in the house and in bed, okay?'

The torchlight lingered on Bram. 'God almighty, what's up with you?'

'Hay fever,' said Kirsty.

Max was plodding along after Fraser, arms hanging by his sides as if he'd forgotten how to walk properly.

'Boy's done in,' said David. 'Fraser and me, we'll just do a last circuit of the house and–'

'No!' said Bram and Kirsty together.

What if they decided to check the shed?

'No, Dad,' added Kirsty. 'I think you've done your bit. Thanks so much. But it'll be light soon.'

'Not for another couple of hours.'

'If anyone was going to mess with us tonight, they'd have done it by now. Even yobs need their shut-eye.' How was she able to smile? How was Kirsty even functioning, given her complete abhorrence of violence of all kinds?

She was so much stronger than Bram. But then, he'd always known that.

David chuckled. 'Okay, princess. We'll get out of your hair. We could probably do with some beauty sleep ourselves before we have to be back on site bright and early in the morning.'

'Aye, not so bright and not so early,' Fraser muttered, stooping to pat Bertie.

When David, Fraser and Bertie had left and Max had stumbled up the stairs to bed – he'd probably be asleep as soon as his head hit the pillow, thank God – Bram and Kirsty looked at each other.

'We have to do it now,' Kirsty said, as if reading his mind. 'We can't just leave him in there.'

Bram nodded.

'There's a spade and a fork in the shed. We might need a pick axe, for stones. Do we have a pick axe?'

'No.' His legs were shaking. He had to sit down. He stumbled to the armchair by the cold stove. 'Why was he doing it, Kirst? Finn? What had we ever done to him? It was obviously nothing to do with Owen, Finn wasn't even born when–'

'Of course it's nothing to do with Owen! He's – he was just a little yob, Bram, doing it for kicks. A *nasty little yob*.'

Yes. A fortifying flare of anger shot through Bram. He'd been terrorising them. Finn had been terrorising them for no reason.

But he couldn't stop his legs from shaking as they left the house and walked back over the grass to the shed. Bram averted his eyes from Henrietta this time. Neither he nor Kirsty spoke a word.

What more was there to say?

At the door of the shed, they both stopped, as if waiting for the other to open it. But when Bram tugged at the padlock to remove it from the loop, it wouldn't budge.

'Oh God,' he whimpered. 'It must have locked automatically, when I hooked it over the loop. But I'm sure I didn't click the arm thing into place, I just left it loose!'

'You can't have.'

He shook his head. It was like some outside force had taken him over, like he really was possessed, his actions not under his control any more, not even registering in his brain. 'I don't remember. And I didn't realise it did that! I didn't *realise*, Kirsty, that it would lock itself automatically! *And we don't have the key!*'

'Okay, Bram, calm down! Let me try.'

But the padlock wouldn't budge.

They spent a tense ten minutes sweeping the ground with the flashlights on both their phones, Kirsty snapping at Bram to stop whining about the key probably having been dropped inside the shed.

Bram bent to lift the stone the key had been under originally, although he knew it wouldn't be there –

And there it was.

'For God's sake!' Kirsty swooped on it.

'I don't remember…'

'Right. Let's do this. Bram, you're going to have to hold it together. You're going to have to help me because I can't do this on my own. *Bram?*'

He nodded.

Kirsty fitted the key into the padlock, pulled it free and opened the door. Bram choked as he stepped inside after her – this wasn't a garden shed any more, redolent of freshly cut timber and linseed oil and paint. It was a butcher's shop, the air cloying with the animal smells of death. There was blood – so much blood on the floor, the stench of urine and shit –

The tarpaulin loomed up at the back of the shed, over the workbench, as if animated, puffed up, as if Finn's life force had transferred to it and *oh God, how did it get there*? Someone had moved the tarpaulin! It always puffed up like that unless you stamped down on it as you folded it to get the air out.

Finn wasn't there.

Kirsty was wailing, a keening sound coming out of her mouth, and Bram slowly turned his head to watch her, to watch her step across the shed to the stack of boxes under the window across which Finn was slumped, face down, the back of his head a mess of blood and bone and hair and – was that *brain*?

'*Oh God oh God oh God!*' Kirsty screamed.

Bram, as if in a dream, a nightmare, went past her to Finn. He put a hand on the boy's back. Wet. He was wet.

He said, his voice seeming to come from far away, 'Finn?'

The boy didn't move.

'He must have been *trying to get out of the window*!' Kirsty screamed. 'He *isn't dead*!'

Bram pushed his hand between Finn's chest and the boxes he was lying on, and put his other arm across his back, and heaved him up and backwards off the boxes. 'Help me,' he said to Kirsty. 'Kirsty! Help me!'

They lowered him gently onto his back on the hard ceramic tiles.

Finn's chest was wet too. In the shuddering light from Kirsty's phone, he could see that it was blood. All over Finn's black top. All over Bram's hands. He made himself not flinch away. He pressed his hand on the boy's chest.

It wasn't moving.

'I think he is dead.'

'He can't be,' groaned Kirsty. 'How can he be? *He's moved!*'

Bram put a finger to Finn's neck. 'But he's dead now. I think.'

'I did that before and there wasn't a pulse!' Kirsty's own fingers were next to Bram's, moving through the blood on the boy's neck. 'But I mustn't have done it right!'

'Google it,' said Bram. 'On your phone. Google *How to tell if someone's dead.*'

But Kirsty's fingers were still moving on Finn, under his chin, down his neck, under his jawline.

Bram wiped his hands on his jeans and got out his own phone.

Google.

How did you get Google on a phone? It was as if all the ordinary everyday things he used to be able to do without thinking weren't available to him any more. He was outside it all now. He was outside normal life.

'Google,' he said aloud.

His finger, his bloody finger, swiped the screen as if of its own accord, and there was the little Google icon. He stabbed at it.

How to tell if the bloody finger typed.

someone likes you the autofill suggested.

someone dead the finger continued.

'Kick him,' said Bram, reading the results. 'Or poke him. But I think we've already checked the responsiveness thing by – by hauling him about. He's not responsive.'

'Of course he's not *responsive!*' Kirsty yelled.

'Try poking him, though,' Bram said dully.

Kirsty jabbed a finger at Finn's arm.

'And shouting his name,' he added.

Kirsty just sat there, squatting on the floor next to Finn, holding the flashlight from her phone so it shone on the boy's face – there was blood all over his face apart from his eyes, his staring eyes –

'*Finn!*' Bram shouted.

Nothing. Of course, nothing.

'We have to check whether he's breathing,' said Kirsty.

'Uh, yeah, that's the next thing.' Suddenly Bram was calm. He read quickly. 'Okay, we need a mirror. Or a piece of glass…' He took Kirsty's phone from her and shone it around the shed. That would do – a glass jar on the workbench in which Phoebe had been collecting rose petals. He tipped them out and brought it back to Finn. 'Okay. Shine the light on the jar…'

Bram held the side of the jar over Finn's mouth and nose. His mouth was slack, slightly open.

He held the jar closer. There was a solitary rose petal still inside, browning around the edges, stuck to the glass.

'See any condensation on it?'

Kirsty just shook her head.

'Okay.' Bram set down the jar and returned to the Google results. 'Next thing is eyes. Shining a light in his eyes and seeing if the pupils contract.'

He held the flashlight from the phone over Finn's left eye. The pupil wasn't black, it was red, like people in photographs got red-eye from the flash bouncing off their retinas.

'It hasn't changed, has it? The pupil? Kirsty?'

'No. He's dead, Bram. He's dead *now*, but he wasn't *then*! He can't have been. I thought he was dead! But *he was still alive and we left him in here to die!*'

'We should have called an ambulance,' Bram said dully, sitting back on his heels, angling the phone so the light fell not on the boy's face but on the floor by Kirsty's feet.

He had still been alive.

When they'd dragged him in here like a piece of meat.

He had still been alive.

When they'd dumped him down by the workbench and put a tarpaulin over him, when they'd left him there, when they'd shut and locked the door.

He had still been alive.

And he'd come back to consciousness, and managed to crawl to the window.

A dying boy. A desperate, dying boy, in who knew what pain, what agony?

Left here to die.

THERE WERE TOO many tree roots.

Even when, on their third attempt to find a suitable spot, they chose a dip in the ground with no trees in it, they found roots, pale, thick snakes hidden in the earth that frustrated their attempts to dig. Bram had to hack at them with the spade, but he couldn't get a good swing because the sharp part was along the end, not the sides. He had to stand over them and almost throw the spade downwards at the solid, woody structures that seemed almost to be there to protect the soil from what Bram was trying to do.

It was hopeless. The dark was already melting away, and soon they wouldn't need a torch or the phone's flashlight any more to see what they were doing. In summer, in Scotland, the dawn came very early. Not quite the land of the midnight sun, but close to it.

'We need a saw,' said Bram. 'But it would take too long.'

'We can't put him back in the shed!' Kirsty raked her earthy hands through her hair, looking down, shrinkingly, at the wheelbarrow into which they'd put Finn, well wrapped up in the tarpaulin, which they'd tied round him with string like a mummy. The mask was in there too. Bram had put it back over Finn's face before wrapping him in the tarp, as if he really were an Egyptian being prepared for the afterlife. It had been easier, though, as soon as the mask was in place; as soon as Finn's face had been covered and he didn't have to look at it any more.

'We need somewhere that's easier to dig,' he said. 'The paddock, maybe. But we'll have to work fast. It'll be light in half an hour.'

'The veg patch!' Kirsty said, turning back to the barrow. 'We can put him in the veg patch for now, while we think where we can put him permanently. Maybe we could dig a hole here over the next few nights, if we brought a saw... Fill it in with loose soil between times...' She hefted the wheelbarrow. His long legs were flopping over the front, as if he was a kid and Kirsty was giving him a ride in the barrow.

Even inside the tarp, he stank of shit.

The veg patch was much easier to dig in. They took it in turns with the spade to make a long trench down the length of it, deep enough to contain Finn's body with a couple of feet to spare.

'We should go deeper, maybe,' said Bram.

But it was already so light that he could see the pale lines across his knuckles against the earthy grime on the backs of his hands.

'No time,' said Kirsty shortly. 'Let's get him in there.'

Bram brought the barrow to the trench and tipped it sideways, and Finn flopped into the hole. They shovelled soil in over him. It took surprisingly little time to fill the hole, and then there was the problem of the mound of earth displaced by the body. Bram used the spade to distribute it over the veg patch as best he could, Kirsty helping by kicking it with her trainers.

When they'd finished, they took the wheelbarrow back to the shed.

There was blood all over the floor. A huge pool of it where they'd left Finn by the workbench at the far end, and streaks leading to and from it, where they'd dragged him there and he'd dragged himself to the window –

The boxes under the window were covered in it too.

Was that where he'd – bled out, was that the term?

Or had it been the concussion that had killed him? Surely it had to be. A head wound so severe that bits of brain were –

No.

No.

He couldn't think about that now.

'We need to just lock the shed for now and deal with this later. Tomorrow night. We'll need to get water up from the stream to clean the floor with. And we can burn the boxes.' Kirsty slumped against him. 'Oh, Bram. *How can this be happening?*'

He held her. He just held her. He couldn't do anything to shield her from this, and that was one of the worst things of all.

For a long moment, they just stood there, looking at the blood all over their garden shed, where they'd left a nineteen-year-old boy to die. It was so horrific it was almost impossible to comprehend.

Kirsty pulled away from him. 'We need to check and see if there's blood on the ground outside.'

There was some on the grass. Bram took a bucket to the stream and poured water over the area, mashing the grass with his feet to make sure any trace was obliterated, and then pouring more water over his shoes.

'The cameras!' said Kirsty. 'The cameras you moved from the wood to the house! We'll have been caught on those cameras!'

'Okay.' He took a long breath. 'That's okay.' The ladder was kept on hooks on the wall of the shed. He went in there and reached up to it. 'I'll get them down.'

'We need to destroy them. Smash them up.' Kirsty

took the other end of the ladder. 'Put them in bin bags. Then into the car. We can take them to the dump, or put them in a random bin – Bram? Bram, we have to just do this one last thing and then–'

'And then what, Kirsty? *And then what?'*

18

The whole of the gable wall of the bedroom was glass, and in the middle was a door that opened onto a tiny balcony. As Kirsty, exhausted from crying, slept in their disordered bed, Bram slid the door open quietly and stepped outside into the early morning air. From here he had a bird's-eye view of the vegetable patch and the newly turned soil.

And it was possible to see over the treetops to Benlervie, to a triangular section of the lawn in front of the house and part of the driveway. The cooing of a collar dove was the only sound. So peaceful. So idyllic.

Had Finn been missed yet?

It was so hard to think of him as *it*, a dead body, a thing that was lying under the soil of the vegetable patch because Bram had battered the life force out of it and it was just a collection of chemicals now, carbon and nitrogen and... whatever. It wasn't Finn any more. A nineteen-year-old boy with his whole life ahead of him. All he would ever be now was a nineteen-year-old corpse. Slowly decomposing into its elements.

'Muum? Daaaad?' came Phoebe's call.

Bram crossed the room to the door; slipped outside into the corridor. Phoebe was standing there in her jim-jams, hair straggling to her shoulders.

'I'm hungry.'

'Okay, *kleintje*, let's go and get some breakfast.' The thought of food made his gorge rise. He couldn't get the image out of his head of Finn's face, Finn's bloody face with those staring eyes; the terrible head wound with the pieces of bone and brain in it –

'Are you okay, Dad?'

'Ah, yes, I'm fine. Just didn't get much sleep last night, what with the patrols and everything.'

As he was standing at the worktop staring at the pan in which two eggs bobbed about – Phoebe loved boiled eggs and soldiers – his phone buzzed in his pocket. He pulled it out. The screen felt strange, rough, and as he stared at it he realised that it was smeared with dried blood.

Finn's blood.

And the name illuminated under it was Sylvia Taylor.

Time seemed to slow down. Here he was, standing in their new kitchen, Phoebe sitting at the table in her pink pyjamas with Dalmatians all over them. Here he was, holding a phone smeared with the blood of the dead son of the woman who was calling him –

'Are you going to answer that, Dad?'

No! He couldn't talk to Sylvia Taylor! He couldn't talk to her and sound normal.

But he had to.

He put the heat off under the eggs. 'Back in a sec,' he told Phoebe, and took the phone through to the Room with a View.

'Bram!' exclaimed Sylvia in his ear. 'Have you seen Finn?'

He swallowed. Plastered a smile to his face. He'd read somewhere that if you smiled as you spoke on the phone, you sounded more friendly. 'Hi, Sylvia. No, not this morning.' Which was true enough.

'Are you sure?'

'Uh, yes. He's gone AWOL, has he?'

'His bed hasn't been slept in. Are you sure you haven't seen him?' Why was she being so insistent? Why would she think Bram *would* have seen him? 'Max hasn't seen him?' she added.

'Uh… I'll check with him and call you back.' He ended the call and stood staring out at the distant hills. He should have expressed more concern. Asked more questions. But maybe she would think he didn't want to waste any time.

He walked back through the kitchen, heading for the stairs.

'My eggs, Dad.'

'For God's sake, Phoebe! I'll be two minutes, okay? I have to speak to your brother, *then* I'll get your eggs!'

Phoebe's lip trembled.

He didn't have time for Phoebe's histrionics. He ran up the stairs and pushed open Max's bedroom door. He could have just pretended to Sylvia that he'd asked him, but then Max might give the game away later.

'Max? Max?' He went to the bed, clicked on the bedside light.

'Hmmph?' Max was just a shapeless mound under the covers.

'You haven't heard from Finn, have you?'

'Nuh.'

'Okay. Go back to sleep. It's okay.'

He called Sylvia straight back before he lost his nerve. 'Hi, Sylvia. No, Max hasn't been in contact with him. Sorry.'

'Right. We're calling the police.' Why did she sound so aggressive?

'The police?'

'We need to do a proper search. We've been out looking, in the woods, the nearest fields. But we have to organise a proper search.'

'But Sylvia – don't you think he's probably just been out drinking with his friends and has crashed somewhere?'

'No. He wasn't with his friends. He went out for a walk *on his own* last night and, as I said, his bed hasn't been slept in. He didn't come back. We need to search your property.'

Oh God oh God!

'He's not here, Sylvia.'

'The police need to do a proper search.'

'Uh, right, yes, of course. No problem.' Shit. Why had he said that? Why *would* it be a problem? 'But we can do that. We'll have a good look and let you know–'

'We'll send the police over when they get here.'

'Right. Okay. I'm sure he's probably–'

But she'd cut the call.

He stared at the screen of the phone for a moment. At the dried smears of blood on it.

Okay. Okay.

The shed.

The first thing was to deal with all the blood in the shed. They'd be bound to look in there. And in the wood, there were the holes they'd started to dig – those needed to be filled in. But if the Taylors had been out searching already, maybe they'd already found them, and it would look really suspicious if they were subsequently filled in?

Should he wake Kirsty? Get her to help?

No.

She'd fallen apart last night, when they finally had all the cameras down, when they'd smashed them with a mallet from the shed and bagged them up in bin bags. She'd collapsed, hands over her head, sobbing. He had had to half-carry her to bed, where she'd lain in his arms, crying away most of what remained of the night.

He would leave her be.

'Daad,' said Phoebe.

He marched into the kitchen, fished the eggs out of the hot water with his fingers, dumped them in egg cups. 'Can you get your own toast? There's a bit of a crisis – Finn Taylor's gone missing.'

Phoebe was at the fridge. 'Okay. Where's the margarine?'

'Bottom shelf. Did you hear what I said, Phoebs?'

Phoebe nodded. 'Finn Taylor's a bad person, Dad. Who cares if he's missing?'

'Now, Phoebe,' he managed. 'That's not very nice.'

She shrugged.

Bram ran to the shed. It took him three attempts to unlock the padlock. How long would he have before the police got here? Or the Taylors? Or both? When he pushed open the door, the smell hit him: that stomach-churning butcher smell. And the blood – it was everywhere! On the cardboard boxes, on the floor… Spattered on the walls, on the window, on the floor next to the boxes…

Everywhere.

There were even some splashes on the ceiling.

How had it got right up there?

When Finn… He must have been stumbling about, and falling, and the blood – from his head wound –

He must have been so desperate. Bleeding everywhere, falling so hard onto the floor or onto the boxes that the blood was sent arcing – It hadn't just been a case of him crawling, half-conscious... He must have been on his feet and then fallen, repeatedly, for this to have happened.

And then, like the terrible, evil person it seemed he was, the thought popped into his head: *Thank God David insisted on varnishing the wood.* Three coats of varnish, David and Fraser had applied. Bram had objected, at the time, to this profligate waste of the planet's resources. But if the wood had been bare, there was no way he could have got the blood off it. It would have soaked in.

Okay. He needed to get pails from inside – some of them would already be full of water, hopefully, the ones in the downstairs loo, unless someone had used them to fill up the cistern. He ran back to the house.

Thank God, two of the pails were full. He detoured to the kitchen for cloths and hurried back to the shed, the pails slopping water as he went. In the shed, he started with the big pool of dried blood by the work-bench. The water in both pails was soon scarlet, the cloths scarlet... His hands shook as he wrung them out in the already bloody water, the water that had Finn's lifeblood in it –

Gagging, he only just made it outside before he was throwing up, as if his insides were rebelling against what his brain was asking his body to do.

But falling apart was a luxury he couldn't afford.

He needed to get that shed cleaned up.

He tipped the pails of bloody water out on the grass and ran to the stream for more. It took four trips before the tiles and the walls and ceiling were clean. Clean enough, anyway. He'd need to use proper cleaning fluids on them to remove any invisible traces. Bleach, although he didn't believe in the stuff and they didn't have any in the house. Would eco surface cleaner do the job?

Now the boxes under the window, which also had blood all over them. He unstacked them and then restacked them with the bloody ones at the bottom and against the wall. But there was still blood visible on a couple of them.

Paint.

He could pretend he'd been in here painting something, and spilt paint over the boxes. There was plenty of paint in the cupboard, left over from decorating the house. He got a screwdriver and eased open the lid of a tin of the dark green eggshell they'd used for the woodwork in Kirsty's study.

He splashed it over the boxes, over the bloodstains. The stains from where Finn – where Finn had tried to get to the window –

He needed to go to the police and tell them what happened. He needed to tell the Taylors. He needed to confess and take whatever punishment was coming to him.

We need you. The kids need you.

How long would he go to prison for?

A long time. Ten years? More? Because Kirsty was right: he couldn't argue self-defence. He'd bashed Finn's head on that hose bracket how many times? And then they'd locked him in here *while he was still alive.* That was unforgivable. He'd get more than ten years for that, surely?

And Kirsty would go to prison too.

And then what would happen to the kids? Ma and Pap were too elderly to cope with Phoebe. David and Linda would have to take them in. Kirsty was adamant that that mustn't happen – she'd gone on and on about it all night, sobbing that *'the kids can't go to Mum and Dad'* – presumably she didn't trust David to look after them, after what had happened with Max and the fight in the Inverluie Hotel bar. And Phoebe – their vulnerable, fragile little Phoebe... How would she cope? How would she begin to get her head round Bram and Kirsty going to prison for...

Oh God oh God oh *God*!

Kirsty was right, as she always was. That couldn't happen.

The hose bracket. He needed to clean it.

He used one of the now pale-pink clothes to wipe it down, shrinkingly, his gaze averted, and then he shoved all the cloths into one of the pails and put it under the workbench.

That would have to do until he had time to clean up properly.

Now for the holes in the ground in the wood. He shut the shed door and padlocked it and pocketed the key. First line of defence would be that he couldn't find the key – *but take a look in at the window – you can see there's no one in there.*

He ran to the wood. It looked different by daylight, but he knew that the biggest hole, their third attempt, was in the beechwood. That was the one it was vital to fill in. The others might be dismissed as the work of animals, but he'd used the spade in the third one to try to get through those roots.

'Finn!' he began to shout as he ran along the path. 'Finn?'

He could hear voices, away off through the wood.

He needed to find that hole. They'd come along here with the barrow, after attempting to dig amongst the undergrowth under the birches. They'd passed this big tree with the twisted trunk...

There it was – the dip in the ground. With a mound of soil next to it!

Bram ran to it, trying to look around him to see if

there was anyone about, but with all the trees it was hard to see. He had to just do it. He kicked at the pile of earth, swiping it into the hole with the side of his shoe. He hadn't realised how much soil they'd managed to dig out.

When most of the soil was back in the hole, he stamped it down and kicked beech leaves over it.

Thank God.

It was done.

Now what? Should he go over to Benlervie and offer his assistance? But wasn't that what murderers did? They 'inserted themselves into the investigation'? Got a sick kick out of it?

Instead, after finding and filling in the other two holes, he sent Sylvia a text:

Any sign of him? Searching our wood now.

He wasn't sure how long he'd been standing there, staring at his phone, when Andrew and another portly man appeared, coming along the path towards him. His phone still had blood on it! He shoved it into his pocket and walked down the path to meet them, assuming an expression that he hoped conveyed worry rather than guilt.

'No sign of him?' he called when he was near enough.

Andrew shook his head. 'You're sure you haven't seen him?' He was looking narrowly at Bram. *Damn.* Bram had never been a good liar. Ma always said his conscience gave him away in his body language before he'd even opened his mouth.

'No, and Max hasn't either. I've had a look around the house, in the shed… Well, I was working in the shed earlier this morning, so unless he was hiding in the cupboard in there or under the workbench –' A high, awful sound halfway between a giggle and a yelp came out of his mouth. '– I already knew he wasn't there.'

'Okay,' said Andrew, frowning at him.

'Could he be with some of his mates? Was he out drinking?'

'No,' said Andrew shortly. 'We think he went out for one of his night-time walks. He comes here sometimes. Through the woods. The police are going to do a proper search when they get here.'

'Good, good!'

What had he just said?

Of course it wasn't *good*!

He frowned. 'I'm sure he'll turn up safe and sound. Uh, I might just go back and speak to Max again. See if he has any ideas as to what might have happened – I mean, where he might be.'

What might have happened?

Shut up, Bram, just *shut up*!

He practically fled away from them down the path.

19

K irsty had done her best with foundation and blusher and eye make-up, but she still looked terrible: her skin pasty and slack and dry, her eyes sunken into dark pits in her face so you could imagine what the skull underneath would look like.

God, where had that thought come from?

The four of them, Bram, Kirsty and the kids, were sitting at the kitchen table. Through the side window, Bram saw the two uniformed police officers walking off towards the paddock. They had come to the door ten minutes ago to say they were going to conduct a search of their grounds, and Bram had nodded and smiled and said to let them know if they needed anything. 'Sylvia's overreacting a bit, isn't she?' he'd added. 'Finn's a very, uh, sociable boy. He's probably crashed at a friend's place.'

The female officer had smiled back and made a non-committal 'Mm' sound.

'Unless they're thinking... We've had some trouble with, uh, youths recently. They shot my mother-in-law's guide dog. Broke into the house... I hope Finn didn't encounter them and...' He swallowed.

'Yes, I've seen the crime reports. We'll be looking into that possibility, of course, but as you say, hopefully this is just a case of a young man who's maybe had a bit too much to drink and not made it home.'

Bram had nodded. 'Yes, well, I hope you find him soon.'

'Mum, are you okay?' Phoebe said now in a small voice.

'I'm fine, darling.' Kirsty smiled at her. 'Just didn't get much sleep last night.'

'Are *you* okay, Max?' Phoebe persisted. 'Are you worried about Finn?'

'Yeah,' was all Max said in response. He was still in the boxers and T-shirt he wore in bed. He was staring off, a punch-drunk expression on his face.

When they'd all eaten and Bram was clearing up the breakfast things, there was another ring at the door.

It was the male PC. 'Wondering about your shed. You looked in there?'

'Yes, he's definitely not in the shed,' said Bram. 'I was working in there this morning, before I heard from Sylvia that he was missing. But come and take a look if you want.'

As Bram strode across the grass towards the shed, the two cops at his side, he felt weirdly unconcerned, weirdly calm. It was almost as if he wanted them to find the blood. To discover what had happened. To take it all out of his hands.

He didn't even pretend to have mislaid the key. He took it from his pocket and inserted it into the padlock. Pushed open the door.

Paint fumes assaulted them.

'Phew.' The female cop smiled at him. 'Looks like there's been a riot in a paint factory in here!'

Bram smiled. 'Yeah, I'm not the handiest of DIYers, it has to be said. Knocked over the tin of paint while I was–' While he was what? What had he been painting?

'Aye, paint's a bugger,' said her colleague. 'At least it was in the shed and not all over the new carpets, eh? Been there, done that.'

'Feel free to look around.'

'Nah, you're all right.' And as Bram closed and locked the door: 'Thanks very much, Mr Hendriksen. We'd better get off to the next place on the list.'

BRAM COULD HARDLY LOOK at David. He'd thought he didn't have any energy left for any more emotion, but the hatred that surged to the surface whenever he looked at the man threatened to overwhelm him afresh. If David hadn't put such pressure on Bram to *step up*, would this ever have happened?

And David, he was sure, suspected something. He'd seemed on edge ever since he'd got here, alerted by Max to Finn's disappearance. They'd all been out there helping to search the woods, apart from Kirsty who'd stayed in the house with Phoebe. After they'd had something to eat they would have to go back out again, Bram supposed. But at least he hadn't had to speak to Andrew again. A police constable had issued them with hi-vis tabards and told them which part of the wood to search. And then everyone had spread out, so Bram didn't have to interact with anyone.

Nothing had been found, of course. Apart from a couple of dead badgers.

Now David was prowling around the kitchen, then sitting down with the rest of them, then getting up to resume his prowling. Fraser was slumped at the table nursing a cup of coffee. Could Kirsty and Bram's drawn faces, their traumatised expressions be explained by the late night, from David's point of view? And the worry, maybe, about the intruder? And now Finn's disappearance? Or had David worked out that there was something else going on?

'There was talk amongst some of the searchers,' said David finally. 'Speculation that the lad might have encountered the joker who's been messing with you. PC said they were following that up as a line of enquiry.'

Phoebe, thank goodness, was up in her room, but Max was sitting next to Fraser, poking at the salad on his plate. His head snapped up.

'It's possible, I suppose,' said Kirsty numbly.

Max looked like he was going to cry.

'I'm sure he'll be found safe and sound,' Bram said briskly.

'We should get back out there,' said Fraser, but with no enthusiasm.

Kirsty got up abruptly from the table, widening her eyes at Bram to telegraph that she needed to talk to him. Up in their bedroom, she went to the wall of glass in the gable and stood looking out at the wood, where someone in a yellow tabard was walking slowly along the edge of the trees. 'I'm going to get some bits of shopping. I'll dispose of the cameras in a bin at the supermarket.' She turned away from the view. 'Does Scott know about the cameras? Does anyone else, apart from us, and Mum and Dad and Fraser?'

'Well, we had notices up saying we had CCTV, but that could have been a bluff. No. I don't think anyone else knows we actually put cameras up – not unless David or Fraser or Linda mentioned them to Scott or something.'

'What if Mum or Dad or Fraser asks about them?' She rubbed her face. Picked at the dry skin at the side of her mouth.

'We can say they were stolen,' Bram suggested. 'We didn't let on because we didn't want Phoebe to worry that we didn't have cameras covering the house.'

A door banged downstairs, and a woman shouted: '*Where are they?*'

And then a man: '*Sylvia!*' That was Andrew Taylor.

Footsteps pounded on the stairs and then the bedroom door was flung open and a mad woman was launching herself at them, grabbing Bram, shaking him, her eyes wild. He barely recognised Sylvia Taylor.

'Where is he? What have you done to him?'

She knew? But how?

'Sylvia!' Andrew came into the room and took hold of his wife from behind, trying to pull her off Bram, who stood, passive in her grip, gaping at her. She had tied her hair back in a scrunchie but half of it had straggled free, and her face was bloated and puffy from crying. 'Sorry, she's – not exactly thinking – rationally.' The last word was gasped out as Sylvia rounded on him. And now she was hitting Andrew, pounding at his chest as he held on to her shoulders. 'This isn't helping!' he half-shouted over the noise she was making, a wailing sound that went straight through Bram, jangling all his nerve endings. Andrew pulled her against his chest and she collapsed against him, the wail now a thin, hopeless sound that Bram just couldn't listen to any longer.

He pushed past them and fled the room, fled to the bathroom, rushed inside and locked the door behind him.

He couldn't do this.

He couldn't do this any more.

· · ·

WHACK WHACK WHACK! on the door.

'Bram!' Kirsty. 'Bram, please, come out of there! They've gone. The Taylors have gone.'

Bram opened the door. 'I need to tell the police what I did. We can't put them through this. Sylvia and Andrew. Sylvia knows, somehow. Or suspects. I don't know how, but–'

Kirsty put her fingers to his lips. 'No,' she said softly. 'You're not going to the police. You're not going to ruin your life, *all of our lives, the kids' lives*, just because you can't take the guilt. Sylvia–' She dropped her voice again. 'Sylvia can't possibly know anything.'

'But you heard her! "What have you done to him?"'

Kirsty shook her head. 'Maybe she suspects that it was Finn who was responsible for terrorising us. If it was Max, if he'd been doing something like that, he'd have a hard time pulling the wool over our eyes, wouldn't he? But she can't possibly know that we – that we have anything to do with his disappearance.' She kissed Bram on the mouth, tenderly, gently. 'We have to hold it together. No one knows a thing. And that's how it's going to stay. Okay? Bram?'

In the end, Bram nodded.

'Right. I'm going to the shops, and I'll get rid of the cameras. Then I'll be straight back. Get back out there with Dad and Fraser and make out you're as keen as mustard to participate in the search. Okay?'

'Okay.'

'Bram, if we don't do this, if the police find out what we did, we're both going to prison – and *that can't happen*. It *can't*. Right?'

He nodded. 'Right.'

· · ·

BRAM TOLD David and Fraser that he was going to do a blog post about Finn to 'spread the word' and retreated to his and Kirsty's bedroom. He couldn't face going back out there. He couldn't face Andrew and Sylvia and Cara.

He watched David striding across the paddock to the woods, Fraser following, both in their hi-vis tabards. He didn't go out onto the balcony. He opened the sliding door an inch so he could hear what was going on but stayed inside, hopeful that the sun glancing off the glass would stop anyone down there spotting him. The police were always on the alert, weren't they, for anyone acting strangely in these circumstances? The missing teen's neighbour skulking in his house watching the search would presumably ring all kinds of alarm bells.

He could see occasional glimpses of fluorescent yellow tabards moving amongst the trees. Maybe it was the presence of the searchers, but what he was looking at now, the paddock, the woods, the hills beyond – it all seemed different. Like it was an entirely different place. It was as if everything had shifted onto a new plane and was no longer quite as it had been, but the changes were so subtle that he couldn't have named them. Would everywhere be like this, now? When he went back to Islington, or to visit his parents in Primrose Hill, would he find that everywhere had slid sideways, become a different version of itself?

Of course it would.

The whole world had changed. He'd be seeing everything, now, from the perspective of the man who had killed a nineteen-year-old boy. All his life, whatever else he did, if he found a cure for cancer or stopped global warming or reversed habitat destruction, he would still be first and foremost Finn Taylor's killer. Finn Taylor would still have ended his life in unimaginable pain and terror, stumbling around that shed, falling and falling again –

How could he ever come to terms with that?

He couldn't.

There was no way to make Bram Hendriksen back into a worthwhile human being.

All he could be now, he supposed, was someone who helped Kirsty and Max and Phoebe make good lives for themselves.

Yes.

They were all that mattered.

Kirsty and Max and Phoebe.

But *he was a murderer*! How could it be a good thing that he was in their lives?

Was he really a *murderer*, though? Finn Taylor had been terrorising them. He'd been *wearing a mask*! For all Bram knew, he'd been heading for the house to break in and – what?

What had Finn been intending to do?

Was it possible that Phoebe had been right all along and Finn Taylor was a psychopath? It wasn't as if he had the excuse of a horrendous childhood that had turned him feral. He was a privileged young man with perfectly nice and very wealthy parents. He had to have been a pretty disturbed individual to have taken all that trouble to victimise the Hendriksens, for no good reason that Bram could think of.

Was it possible that Bram's actions had actually averted an even worse tragedy?

He wasn't sure how long he'd been standing there when his phone buzzed. Mechanically, he took it from his pocket. The dried blood was still on there, streaked over the screen. A forensic specialist's dream.

He supposed he needed to clean that off.

It was Kirsty.

'Mission accomplished,' was all she said. 'See you soon.'

'Okay.'

After he'd ended the call, he stood staring down at the vegetable patch. Little did they all know, little did Finn Taylor's father and mother and sister know that their beloved boy was dead, battered to death by Bram, his body shoved unceremoniously into a hole in the ground like a dead cat or dog.

People were coming towards the house from the wood.

Scott. And David and Fraser.

Was Scott coming to arrest Bram? But how could he be? He was probably just coming to update him on what was happening.

He looked down at the phone still in his hand. He should clean the blood off it, but he was strangely reluctant to do so, as if it were some sort of penance, to carry around something with Finn's blood on it. He shoved it back in his pocket and was descending the stairs when David called: 'Bram? *Bram?* Get your arse down here.'

David and Fraser were sitting in the Walton Room, and Scott was in his usual pontificating position by the hearth. 'Finn Taylor's beanie hat has been found in your wood,' he said.

'Beanie hat?' Bram repeated.

'His parents have identified it.'

Bram walked across the room towards them. Should he sit down? Offer them something to eat and drink? He stared at David, welcoming the spurt of anger he felt, now, in his father-in-law's presence. It was as if Bram was carrying too much guilt for one person and he had to shift some of it onto this man, this abominable man who'd got inside Bram's head with his macho bluster and destroyed them all.

It felt good to hate him.

'They last remember seeing him wearing it a couple of days ago,' Scott went on. 'He generally wore it when he was out on these late-night walks of his, apparently. So – well, I'd say it's concerning.'

Bram supposed he was expected to make some sort of comment about the hat.

'So do you think he might have had some kind of run-in with whoever's been terrorising us? And lost his hat in the scuffle?' But how *had* Finn lost his hat in the wood?

Scott grimaced. 'It's possible. Anyway, we'll be bringing in sniffer dogs. Hopefully we'll be able to get them here early tomorrow afternoon. See if they can pick up a scent trail from where the hat was found.'

Sniffer dogs?

'Right. Won't that be too late? Won't any scent trail have disappeared by then?'

Scott shook his head. 'The Taylors are agitating for an immediate deployment – regardless of logistical practicalities – but in a wood, a scent trail will last for days. Relatively high humidity and low air movement.' Scott, of course, would be an expert on scent trails as well as everything else.

'Right. Uh, good.' They would have to move the body. And blitz the shed. They'd have to do that tonight. But where the hell were they going to put the body?

Scott was looking at him a bit too closely for Bram's liking. 'Did you see or hear anything out of the ordinary last night? Anything strange?'

Bram pretended to think. 'No. No, I don't think so. Well, David and Fraser–'

'*Anything strange?*' David interrupted him. 'No offence, eh, Bram? Yeah, we called in. We didn't see or hear anything either.'

And the penny, belatedly, dropped. Of course David, with his record, wouldn't want the police knowing that he and Fraser had been out in the woods 'on patrol' last night. That was why he was so on edge.

'How's Sylvia doing?' David went on.

Scott grimaced. 'Not good, as you can imagine.'

That poor woman. And things were only going to get a whole lot worse for her.

'She's pretty frantic.' Scott looked at his watch. 'Okay, I'd better get back to it.'

WHEN KIRSTY GOT BACK with the shopping, Max took a couple of the bags from her, but Kirsty clung on to the third one. 'Stuff for the utility room,' she said, diving off down the corridor past her study. Bram hurried after her and closed the utility room door behind them.

'Did you get it?'

'Three big bottles.' Kirsty opened the bag to show him the bottles of bleach and several packs of cloths. 'That should be enough.'

One of the Netflix serial killer episodes, Bram had remembered, had featured the perp using bleach to destroy DNA evidence. They would slosh some over Finn's body to destroy any of their DNA that might have transferred onto him, and they also needed to clean the shed.

'Should be,' he agreed.

He'd called her after Scott had left, and told her about the sniffer dogs. 'They're going to follow Finn's trail to the shed, and then back into the woods, and then to the veg patch. Or actually, no, they'll probably go straight to the veg patch because he's only a couple of feet down. Dogs have an incredible sense of smell. They'll be able to tell there's a rotting corpse in there–'

Kirsty had made a wordless sound.

'So we've got to do it tonight. We have to move Finn and blitz the shed. We need proper bleach, not the eco stuff.'

Now, as he took the bag from Kirsty and shoved it into the cupboard under the sink, Finn Taylor flashed into his mind again, Finn Taylor coming back to consciousness in the shed…

Why hadn't they called an ambulance? How could they have just left him there to die?

He slumped against the cupboard. 'We have to be sure that this is what we want to do. This is our last chance to confess. If we dig him up and re-bury him somewhere else, we're compounding what we've already done, big time. We can't say it was spur of the moment. How'll they spin it in court? The Hendriksens brazenly assisted with the search for Finn and then that same night they dug up his body and–'

'We can't confess to it. *We can't go to prison.*'

For a long moment, they stared at each other. How on earth had they come to this?

'We have to do it, then. Tonight. We have to dig him up and dispose of him properly.'

20

M ax went to bed at 11:30, and they left it another half hour to make sure he was asleep before donning waterproof overtrousers and coats and gloves in the utility room. Then Bram retrieved the bag of bleach from the cupboard under the sink.

Kirsty put a hand on his arm. 'What if the Taylors hear the car on the track?'

Those poor, poor people!

He took a deep breath. 'If they hear the car and ask about it later, we can say one of us couldn't sleep and went for a drive.'

'Okay.' Kirsty nodded. 'But if they're still out there searching… once we start digging, if someone finds us, there's no way we could explain it. And once we get it – him – out of there…'

'Well, what's the alternative?' Bram snapped.

Kirsty lifted her shoulders helplessly. 'Maybe we should wait another hour or so? So it's less likely anyone will be out there?'

'Okay.' Bram put down the bag and took her in his

arms. 'Thank you for doing this. Thank you for – for helping me to – Oh Christ, Kirsty! I'm a *murderer!*'

'No, you're not! You were *terrified!*'

'But I wasn't – not at that point. I was *angry*. I *wanted* to hurt him.'

She hugged him close. 'You were protecting us.'

They took off the waterproofs and crept through the house to the Room with a View, where they lay without speaking on the sofas. Bram must have drifted off to sleep, because soon Kirsty was shaking his arm. 'It's half past one. Let's do it.'

They put the waterproofs back on and walked in silence to the shed, where they numbly set to work by torchlight. Kirsty sloshed diluted bleach over the floor and walls while Bram took everything out of the boxes – tins of paint, old plant pots, wood stain, ice cream tubs containing recycled bits of string and screws and nails – and stacked it on the floor and on the workbench. Then he ripped up the boxes and bagged them. They'd stop at a wheelie bin on the way back and dispose of them. Some of the cardboard was stiff with dried blood.

All the time he was working, he kept expecting a policeman to loom up in one of the darkened windows, or Andrew Taylor to suddenly appear in the doorway.

When he'd finished, he took the bin bags down to the stream and left them in Max's car, which was parked on the other side of the collapsed bridge.

Then he returned to the shed.

'Okay. I think we're done here,' he whispered to Kirsty. 'How much bleach is left?'

'Enough.'

Bram got the spade and the bleach and they walked together, again in silence, to the vegetable patch. He glanced at his phone. It was 2:40 and already the sky was lightening. Sunrise would be at about five o'clock, but it would be almost fully light long before then.

'We'd better hurry,' he hissed.

Kirsty nodded.

But for a long moment, they just stood there, looking at the veg patch.

Okay. Don't think about it. Just dig.

He sank the spade into the soil and immediately hit something soft that gave under it. God. He wasn't even two feet down. The sniffer dogs would have found him immediately.

It took a surprising amount of time, though, with just one spade between them, to remove all the soil from the tarpaulined body. Whenever he was digging, Bram kept having to stop, sure he'd heard a sound, a stealthy footstep. He kept pausing, freezing, ears straining. But it was just the many normal, small sounds of the night – a branch scraping against another branch, the wind in the trees, a bird flapping.

'We need the barrow,' Kirsty whispered. 'And scissors to cut the string round the tarp. And more string to tie it back round him again once we've… once we've…'

Bram didn't want to finish the thought, but, 'Bleached him,' he managed to get out.

Kirsty swallowed.

Bram nodded. 'I'll get all that.'

He made his way back to the shed. He could see the fuzzy outline of Henrietta the goose in the long grass. He imagined her staring at him, and into his head came an image of himself as a child, innocently playing next to Henrietta in the garden at Primrose Hill, chatting to her as he constructed one of his elaborate villages from twigs and leaves, little thinking that one day –

But he couldn't go down that road or he'd lose it.

Another dreadful thought came to him: what if the

police had decided to start the search with the sniffer dogs at dawn, when humidity would be high? The optimum time to pick up a scent trail? What if they rolled up when Bram and Kirsty were manhandling Finn Taylor's body into the boot of the Polo?

Well, there was nothing he could do about that possibility. He concentrated on locating a pair of scissors and some string, and dropped them into the barrow, which he wheeled back to the veg patch. Between them, they hauled Finn out of the earth, another surprisingly difficult task. It seemed all wrong, that the boy had been under the ground, in the suffocating earth.

He's dead. He's dead.

There was no need now for the torch. The night was fast retreating. They needed to get this done! They unwrapped the tarpaulin and removed the mask and sloshed bleach over it and the body, turning Finn so they could do both sides of him, almost like – Bram gagged as the thought occurred to him, and he had to turn away, take a step away.

Like he was a piece of meat.

He swallowed bile. 'We have to do this,' he muttered, his hands shaking as they spread out the tarp and pulled him onto it, threw in the mask and tied the tarp back around him with the string. Finally, they hefted him into the barrow and returned the soil to the hole.

'If the dogs show an interest, and the cops ask why the soil's been all dug up,' Bram whispered, 'we can say the veg patch was poisoned with weedkiller and we were digging it over to disperse the poison.'

'But that doesn't make sense!'

'So? We're ignorant townies.'

Bram hefted the barrow and they made their way to the stream, waterproofs creaking as they walked, the sound horribly loud in the still, cool, pre-dawn air. The night was melting away, the sky no longer black but an ever-lightening blue. He could see the water in the stream, the stepping stones, the trees on the other side, no longer shades of grey but green and brown.

The barrow got away from Bram on the bank that sloped down to the water and it tipped over, catapulting the body out into the stream.

'Fuck!' Kirsty hissed.

'It's okay!' Bram righted the barrow and manoeuvred it next to the tarpaulin-wrapped body. 'Help me lift him!'

Eventually they had him back in the barrow and, with Kirsty pulling and Bram pushing, got it up the other bank. They shoved the barrow right up to the boot of the car and hauled the body inside. It took a lot of pushing and pulling to fit him in there, with those long legs of his. They were lucky, he supposed, that there was no rigor mortis. It must have come and gone while he was in the ground. Eventually they managed to fold him into the space and slam the boot shut.

'Now the barrow,' Kirsty hissed. 'We'll have to bleach it too. Where's the bleach?'

'In the shed.'

'Did we lock the shed? Maybe we should slosh some water over the floor to rinse it off a bit – the smell of bleach is overpowering. They might wonder–'

'And we need to get these waterproofs off and dispose of them.'

'Not until we've got rid of – it,' said Kirsty. 'We don't want our DNA getting on it. Then we can put the waterproofs in a wheelie bin too.'

'We can't put the bags of cardboard and the waterproofs all in the same wheelie bin! The people would notice their bin suddenly being full.'

'Okay, so we put it in a few different bins.' Kirsty groaned. 'But look how light it is already! We're not going to have time to clean up here, find somewhere suitable, dig a hole, bury him–'

She was right. 'Okay. We can leave him in the car for now. Dispose of him tomorrow night. We've got time to clean up in the shed and bleach the barrow and stuff.'

They rinsed out the pails in the stream and carried fresh water up to the shed, and sloshed it over the floor, and used the cloths to mop up as best they could. By the time Bram had cleaned the barrow and, while he was at it, his phone with some diluted bleach, it was properly light, although it wasn't yet five o'clock.

'We can leave the waterproofs in here,' Kirsty said, wriggling out of hers. 'They've already searched the shed, haven't they?'

'We were mad to think we could get everything done tonight. We haven't even thought through what we're going to do with... Where we're going to re-bury...' He broke off, staring out at the lovely dawn light on the tops of the trees, the mist hanging in skeins across the forest. 'Oh Christ, Kirsty! How could we have thought we'd ever get away with this?'

'We *are* going to get away with it.' She caught hold of his arm, as if without its support she would keel over. 'But the sniffer dogs! The police are probably going to park right next to the Polo! The dogs will be all over it!'

'Okay. Okay...' God! 'We'll have to park somewhere else.'

'And how do we explain the car being gone?'

Bram tried to think. 'Scott said the sniffer dogs will be here early afternoon. What if we say that watching the search for Finn is too upsetting for Phoebe, and we've decided to take the kids to your parents' place? We can do that first thing this morning. Stay the day in

Grantown, then dispose of him tomorrow night. Does that make sense?'

'Yes… I don't know. God, Bram – I can't tell any more what makes sense and what doesn't!'

'I know.' He took in a deep, shuddering breath. 'I can't either.'

21

I t seemed to be taking forever to get the kids organised. First Max couldn't find his phone, then Phoebe had a meltdown and refused to leave the house, obviously picking up on her parents' tension.

'It's too *early*!' she sobbed. 'I feel *sick*! Why do we have to go?'

'The police are going to be doing a proper search and they want us out of the way,' Bram improvised. 'Come on, *kleintje*. Don't you want to see Bertie?'

'Bertie could come here.'

'Not with all the sniffer dogs around. Bertie would be a bad influence. He'd probably lead them all on a wild goose chase for biscuits.'

A tiny smile.

'Now, what are you going to take to Grannie and Grandad's? Your paper and pens? You could do portraits of everyone.'

'Okay!' And she ran up the stairs.

'Dad, the Taylors are coming,' said Max from the door.

Oh *Christ.*

'Go up to Phoebe's room and keep her there till they've gone,' Bram told him.

'What are they–'

'Just do it, Max!'

Bram stood out on the verandah and watched Sylvia Taylor marching up the track towards the house, Andrew hurrying along in her wake.

'What have you done to him?' Sylvia yelled as soon as she was within shouting distance.

Bram just shook his head.

She stormed up the steps and pushed him with both hands so he staggered back against the wall of the house. Her hair was even wilder than last time he'd seen her, and there were streaks of mascara dried on her cheeks. 'If you won't tell me, you'll tell the police!' she yelled into his face, flecks of spittle landing on him.

Bram looked behind her to Andrew, who was standing staring at Bram.

'Did you kill him?' Somehow it was much more shocking, the calm way Andrew spoke, almost conversationally, as if they were chatting about the weather.

'Of course not,' Bram got out.

'The police will be here any minute,' Andrew added. 'We've called them. I imagine they're going to arrest you.'

So this was it. He was going to be arrested, and he would confess everything. It was over. He felt almost glad.

'Why on earth would Bram *kill Finn*?' It was Kirsty, striding towards them across the verandah. 'I know you're going through a terrible time, but really – If you think harm has come to him, isn't it more likely to have been the youths who've been harassing us?'

Of course. Of course that was what he and Kirsty would be thinking. Bram should have suggested that right off the bat.

'No,' said Andrew. 'And you know it.' He looked from Kirsty to Bram. 'There weren't any *youths*. There never have been. It was us.'

Us?

'What?' Bram could only gasp as Sylvia collapsed to the verandah floor, her legs folding under her.

Andrew stooped over his wife, putting a hand on her shoulder, but she shrugged him off. Behind him, Bram could see two policemen, running up the track towards them.

'I don't understand,' was all he could find to say.

And by that time the two PCs were on the verandah.

'Okay, folks,' said the older one firmly. 'What's going on here, then?'

'He killed him,' Sylvia mouthed, all the fight seeming to have gone out of her.

'You need to arrest him,' Andrew said. 'This man has killed our son.'

'But you can't think...' Kirsty blustered. 'You can't think *Bram* has anything to do with whatever's happened to Finn?'

'Let's just calm this down,' said the cop. 'Mr and Mrs Taylor, can you come with us back to your property and we'll–'

'I'm not going anywhere,' said Sylvia. 'Andrew? Tell them what you did. *Tell them!*'

Andrew closed his eyes for a second, then nodded. 'You might want to write this down.'

The cops looked at each other, and then the older one took out a notebook.

'We – *I* hatched a plan to...' Andrew flicked a look at Bram. 'To drive these people out of Woodside and buy the place back at a bargain price. Hence all the sinister happenings – it was Finn who shot the guide dog, shot at us with the BB gun, dumped the heart in the pan, all that. And I'm responsible for the water supply "failing", and the bridge collapsing. The idea was that, given all this, they'd feel it would be an uphill struggle to sell the place on the open market, so when I approached them with a low – very low – offer, they'd bite my hand off.'

'The bridge…' Kirsty had gone pale.

'Okay, let's get this straight,' said the older cop. 'You're saying you were responsible for everything that went on here? The shooting at animals, the home invasion, the tampering with the bridge…?'

Andrew nodded. 'We're in pretty dire financial straits. Overextended ourselves to buy Benlervie, and the restaurant is going down the tubes. We're having trouble making the mortgage and business loan repayments.'

'So *he* had this *ridiculous* idea!' Sylvia wailed.

'To drive the Hendriksens out?' The cop made a note.

'Yes,' said Andrew. 'And buy back Woodside at well below market value. Resell quickly at a healthy profit.'

Bram shook his head. 'But who would want to buy the place, given all the trouble there's been here?'

'We were intending to make out to potential buyers that you were a couple of nutters seeing threats that weren't there. We'd point them in the direction of your blog, which, given the trolls' input, does seem pretty paranoid.'

'*You're* the trolls,' said Bram.

'We started it off, yes, but it soon snowballed – randoms piling in with the mob mentality you get online.'

'Oh my God,' said Kirsty.

The younger cop was looking shell-shocked, but the older guy just shook his head in a *seen it all before* way as he continued to make notes.

'So Finn...' Bram was shaking. Could the cops see that he was shaking?

'Finn was the foot soldier, so to speak,' said Andrew dully. 'But it was down to me. I was directing the campaign. I palmed a front door key when I called over, weeks ago, while the place was still a building site... Got a copy made and returned it a couple of hours later, so no one was any the wiser.'

'So you planned this... Right from the start?' Kirsty shook her head. 'From before you even sold us the plot?'

Bram wanted to throw back his head and howl. While he'd been able to tell himself that Finn was just a little yob who had, to an extent, brought what happened on himself, it had been possible to attempt to rationalise what he'd done. But now it turned out that Finn was only doing what Andrew had told him to?

'Oh, yes,' said Andrew with a sort of grim satisfaction. 'Had it planned down to the last detail. And then when I found out that Kirsty's boyfriend had been Owen Napier, I used that to subtly suggest that maybe whoever had killed him was after Bram. Got Finn to write "Your next" in blood on the worktop. Hoping that would really freak you out.'

'Christ,' was all Bram could say.

'But you know it was us. Don't make out like this is all a big shock. You caught Finn, didn't you, prowling round the house? He'd got a couple of roadkill badgers and was intending to pose them in the wood, hang them from the trees, and then run round the house shouting, taking potshots at your security lights. Wearing the monster mask, so you wouldn't be able to identify him.

But you caught him? What happened? There was an altercation?'

'No,' said Bram.

'We had no idea,' added Kirsty.

'I – Obviously we didn't want to have to admit any of this, but weighed against Finn's life... *Please.*' Andrew's voice suddenly broke. 'Please just tell us what happened. Where is he? Is he dead or... Are you keeping him somewhere?' The hope in his eyes was a dagger in Bram's heart. 'Locked up somewhere – to teach him a lesson, maybe?'

'No,' Bram repeated weakly.

'This is ludicrous!' Kirsty protested. 'Where the hell would we be keeping him?' And as she met Bram's gaze, it struck them both at the same time: the car. What if they looked in the car?

'Feel free to search the house,' Bram said hurriedly. 'If you think we're keeping him prisoner here, for some bizarre reason, please – search the place.' And as the younger cop started to speak: 'No, it's fine. The sooner you can establish he's not here the better, presumably. Please. Go ahead.'

'We'll do that, if you don't mind, Mr Hendriksen,' said the older cop.

'Just let us get the kids out of here,' Kirsty put in. 'Actually...' She went inside and returned with a front door key. 'We'll take them to my parents and leave you to poke about as much as you like.' She took a breath and looked down at Sylvia, who was still slumped on the floor. 'I'm so sorry, Sylvia, Andrew... I know you must be going through hell. But really, we have no idea what's happened to Finn.'

The older cop took the door key from her. 'Thank you. And we'll need you to give us written permission to search your property.'

When they'd done that, Kirsty fetched a wide-eyed Phoebe and Max from upstairs and they left the house. It was all Bram could do not to sweep Phoebe up in his arms and run down the track to the bridge, to the car on the other side.

'Mr and Mrs Hendriksen!' came a shout from behind them.

Bram stopped, his heart thumping.

He turned.

The younger cop was running after them, flat out, arms pumping. Bram's body wanted to break into a run itself, to take off, to flee. It took a conscious effort of will to stay where he was, feet planted on the dusty surface of the track.

He flashed a panicked look at Kirsty.

Did they want to search the car? Of course they did!

The policeman skidded to a halt in front of Bram. 'Can you leave us a phone number? So we can contact you when we've finished?'

IN THE KITCHEN at David and Linda's, Linda pulled Kirsty into a hug. 'Are you okay? How are you holding up?'

They had called before they left Woodside to let them know what was happening.

Kirsty clung to her, tears starting. Phoebe looked on, frowning in concern. And Kirsty straightened, smiled, nodded. 'I'm fine.'

'Come here, princess,' said David, hugging Kirsty tight in his turn. 'Those bastard Taylors!'

'David,' remonstrated Linda.

'Sorry, love, but my God! First they scare the – bejesus out of us all with their antics, and then they try to set the cops on Bram because their wee yob of a son has done a disappearing act! The bugger could be anywhere. Who knows what else that lad's been up to? Probably on drugs. Probably lying somewhere in his own piss, a needle sticking out his arm.'

Bram stared at his father-in-law. He really was a deeply unpleasant person.

'David!' Linda put a hand on his back. 'Phoebe doesn't need to hear this.'

'I don't mind, Grannie,' said Phoebe. 'Finn is a bad person.'

'He's still a human being,' said Linda.

'He's a bad human being,' Phoebe amended, and that made everyone smile.

'Are you staying the night?' Linda asked.

'No – thanks, Mum, but we want to get back to Woodside once the police have finished there.'

'Why should they be hounded out of their own home?' David put in.

It wouldn't, of course, have been possible to bring overnight bags even if they had intended staying with David and Linda – how could they have explained to the kids why they had to hold their bags on their knees instead of putting them in the boot? It had been hard enough trying to account for the smell in the car on the way over. 'They must be spraying pig manure on the fields' was all Kirsty could come up with.

David was running water into the kettle. 'Scott just called,' he said over his shoulder. 'Apparently the police want to search here too. Can you credit it? I suppose they've got to tick all the boxes, cover their backs in case the Taylors decide to sue or something...'

What?

'That's ridiculous,' Bram managed, exchanging a frantic look with Kirsty.

If the cops came here, would they search the vehicles?

Possibly.

'I'm going to phone Scott,' said Kirsty, taking out her phone. 'Bram, can you come with me?' And the two of them practically ran outside.

Kirsty quickly called Scott to ask what was happening. From her side of the conversation, Bram gathered that the police were intending coming here after they'd searched Woodside, maybe in a couple of hours' time. When she'd finished the call, they stared at each other.

'We have to get rid of him *now*,' Bram said at last. 'But where can we…' He dropped his voice. 'How are we going to get rid of a dead body in *broad daylight*?'

Kirsty squeezed his hand. 'It's okay. I know a place. An old flooded quarry in a forest. We used to swim there as kids in the summer, but I don't think kids these days use it. There's a track right up to it. We could get rocks, put them in the tarp with the body, back the car up to the quarry and throw him in.'

'But what if someone saw us?'

'It's surrounded by forest. We have to risk it, Bram. What choice do we have?'

'Sorry, boy,' said Bram, hooking a hand under Bertie's collar to pull him away from the car. 'Not this time.'

Bertie strained to get back to the car.

'He really wants to go with you!' smiled Phoebe. 'No, Bertie, the sniffer dogs aren't trying to find biscuits!'

They had told Linda, David and the kids that they were heading back to Woodside to help with the search. David thought this was madness.

'The Taylors are only going to have a go at you

again,' he objected now. 'Why should you help the buggers?'

Bertie pulled free of Bram's restraining hand and launched himself at the boot of the car, jumping up at it and scratching with his paws, scrabbling sideways until his nose was level with the edge of the boot door. He snorted into it, sniffed, snorted. Scrabbled again.

Bram went after him and hauled him away, a smile plastered to his face. 'Sorry, Bertie. Not this time.'

'There's an odd smell,' said Linda, lifting her face into the breeze.

'I think he's rolled in something,' Bram improvised.

'Oh, bloody Nora,' said Linda.

'Over to you, Mum!' Kirsty smiled, and beeped the car open. 'Come on, Bram, we'd better get going.'

As they made off down the street, Bram let out a long breath. 'Okay, if it comes out that we told your parents we were joining the search but never actually turned up... What do we say?'

'We chickened out. Too scared of the Taylors.'

'That would make sense. We went for a drive and fell asleep in the car...'

'But were too embarrassed to admit it.'

Bram nodded. Was that reasonable? He couldn't think straight. He was so tired he felt nauseous. Light-headed and dizzy. As Kirsty turned out of the street he had to close his eyes to stop his head spinning.

'No,' said Kirsty. 'Oh, no.'

There was a high mesh fence all the way round the quarry, no doubt for safety reasons. They got out of the car and stood looking through it to the deep, turquoise water beyond.

'We could cut the fence?' Bram suggested half-heartedly.

'With what? And if they found the fence cut, they'd wonder why. With the search for Finn getting more publicity, some bright spark would be bound to put two and two together and get divers into the quarry.'

'So what do we do?'

'We'll just have to dump him. Deeper into the forest.'

'But someone's bound to find him!'

'Eventually, yes. But what else can we do? We can't bury him. We've no spade, and it would take too long anyway, with all the roots. We'll just have to dump him in the forest and hope it looks like – I don't know, a drunken fight gone wrong. Finn was a nasty piece of work – he probably got into lots of fights. One of the other yobs killed him by accident, drove him up here, dumped his body...'

'But they know he went out that night to terrorise us!'

'Obviously it's suspicious, and we'll probably be prime suspects, but they can't know what happened. They can't know some of his yobbish pals weren't helping him – they could have fallen out, gone for each other... They can't *know* who killed him.' She turned away from him to walk back to the car. 'We have to just dump him and hope for the best. What other choice do we have, Bram?'

They drove on up the track into the forest, and at a fork selected the weedier of the two alternatives, which looked as if it didn't get much traffic. They carried on for about quarter of a mile and then stopped the car.

'Here's probably as good a place as any,' Kirsty said dully.

But neither of them made a move. Bram closed his eyes.

And he must have slept – how could he have slept? – because the next thing he knew, Kirsty was shaking him awake.

'We have to,' she said, her eyes puffy and red from the silent tears she must have been crying.

They opened the boot and removed the bin bags. The body in the tarpaulin, which they'd managed to squeeze into the small space last night, was more problematic to get out again. Bram grabbed it by the shoulders and pulled it round, but the tarpaulin snagged on the catch for the boot lock. He heaved, and the tarp ripped a little.

Kirsty grabbed the legs and helped Bram lift the body out and lower it onto the track. 'We should take the tarp off him. All the soil on it – they might be able to match it to Woodside's soil.'

'Something else for the wheelie bins?'

'We should maybe just burn it all. We can go to a shop and buy matches and firelighters.' Kirsty glanced off back down the track. 'Let's get him out of sight before we start messing with the tarpaulin. Into the trees.'

The conifers in the plantation were planted close together and had spiky, brown, twiggy branches sticking out at head height and below which jabbed and snagged them as they heaved Finn's body through the trees. They had to bend double in places to avoid the branches, and one or other of them kept dropping their end of their burden. At least no one was likely to come walking through here. A few metres in it was a twilit, claustrophobic world, the light so dim that nothing was growing on the forest floor. It was just a carpet of dead, brown needles.

'We can't just... leave him here,' said Kirsty, when they finally laid him down.

He knew exactly what she meant. Abandoning him

here, in this dark, dead place where nothing grew...
Somehow it seemed so much worse than putting him
into the soil, where bodies were supposed to go. This
just seemed wrong.

'We have to,' choked Bram. 'We have to. We need to
get the tarp off him. Do we have scissors? The string...
We need something to cut it with.'

They stared at each other in the gloom. 'We don't
have scissors.'

'Or a knife?'

Kirsty shook her head. 'There might be something in
the car we could use.'

In the end they had to unpick the knots, and it
seemed to take forever, crouched there breathing in the
odours from the body. Finally they got the tarp off him,
and bundled the string and the mask inside it. Bram
averted his eyes from the body as they stumbled their
way back through the trees to the car.

Bram drove this time, back onto the main track, but
as they turned onto the straight section that led past the
quarry he saw people up ahead. An elderly couple in
light-coloured jackets, maybe a hundred yards away, out
for a nice morning walk. They were heading away
down the track, but turned to stare at the car.

'Go back!' Kirsty hissed. 'If we carry on up the main
track, I think it comes out eventually on the back road.'

Bram reversed back round the bend to the junction,
where he turned and headed off up the track through
the forest. In places the surface was rutted and difficult
to negotiate, especially where the track headed uphill,
where rainwater flowing down it had gouged out chan-
nels and trenches. What if they got stuck and had to call
a garage? How would they explain... And then when
Finn's body was found, which was bound to happen

eventually, the garage would have a record of recovering their car from the same forest –

But they got over the brow of the hill and down the other side, and then they were onto a much better track, and out of the trees into a clear-felled area, and then, *oh thank God*, onto a tarmacked public road.

They had done it.

22

One, two, three days and nothing. It was like waiting for a storm to break, and the kids were picking up on the tension. Max was spending almost all day in his room, and when Bram or Kirsty went in to check on him, he was usually in bed, either asleep or staring at the ceiling. Phoebe, in contrast, was hyper, bouncing around the house giggling manically one minute and in floods of tears the next over something as minor as creases in her skirt. She seemed to have got it into her head that the Taylors were going to come over and start shouting again about Bram killing Finn, and maybe try to hurt the Hendriksens.

'They're both very sensitive,' Kirsty said in bed on the third night, after they'd finally persuaded Phoebe back to her own room. 'Yes, they're upset about the Taylors, but I think, subconsciously, they know it's more than that. They know that something's far wrong.'

And Phoebe seemed to be getting worse. The next day, she was so clingy with Kirsty and Bram that one of them had to be in the same room as her at all times, although they drew the line at the bathroom. In desperation, Kirsty went into Grantown to pick up Linda and Bertie as distractions. As soon as Bertie appeared, Phoebe insisted on fixing the petcam to him 'in case the Taylors come for revenge'.

Oh God. Phoebe's imagination was often more of a curse than a blessing. 'That's not going to happen, *kleintje*. They've no reason to come for "revenge" against us.'

'But they think you killed Finn!'

'They'll soon realise they're wrong about that,' said Kirsty firmly.

Linda suggested that Phoebe help her make lunch.

'With Dad too?' Phoebe said at once.

As they cut up potatoes and carrots and onions for soup, Phoebe seemed to recover some of her bounce. 'Tell the story about how you and Grandad met,' she begged Linda.

Linda smiled. 'How many times have you heard that story, Phoebe?'

Phoebe grinned. 'Not *enough* times!'

Linda paused in her chopping of a carrot. Bram always marvelled at how proficient she was in the kitchen, without being able to see what she was doing. He had asked her once how she pictured things, and she'd explained that she formed a sort of three-dimensional map in her mind, only it was a map with no colour, not even black and white or light and dark, as she had no way of picturing those. He couldn't get his head round that.

'I was sixteen at the time,' she was saying now. 'Grandad and his family had just moved in next door to us.'

'On Capercaillie Drive!' Phoebe interjected. Phoebe loved the name of that street, and they often took a walk

along it past Grannie and Grandad's old houses, ugly
council semis covered in greyish-brown rough-cast
cement.

'Yes. Grandad was always friendly, saying hello and
chatting–'

'And he helped you clear up leaves on your
driveway!'

'He did. Several times. I worshipped him from afar,
but he was an alpha male. I never thought he'd be interested in me romantically. He was captain of the school
rugby team and heavily into sports of all kinds. I wasn't
at his school, of course – I was away at the Royal Blind
School in Edinburgh during term time, so I didn't know
him very well at first.'

'Then one day…'

'I think you could tell this story better than me,
Phoebe,' smiled Linda, finding another carrot with her
fingertips. 'One day, I had gone to the shops, using my
white stick – I didn't have a dog then, but I knew the
route, although I had to concentrate hard. On the way
back, some teenagers thought it would be funny to spin
me round and let me go, so I had no idea which way to
go to get home. They were all grabbing me and spinning
me, and I'd dropped my stick and the bag with the
shopping in it, and I was crying, of course, but then
there was shouting and suddenly the spinning stopped
and the other kids were yelling and I could hear some of
them running, and sounds of fighting. I was staggering
around, trying to feel for the edge of the pavement with
my feet in case I walked out into the road – or was I *on*
the road? I couldn't tell. And then I felt someone pull
me against their chest, and heard Grandad's voice
saying, "It's okay, Linda. It's okay." He had his arms
around me. He was so solid. So reassuringly solid.'
Linda's face glowed with the memory. Usually at this

point in the story Bram teared up, but all he could feel now was disgust. What had David done to those kids? Linda, being blind, couldn't know exactly how badly he'd hurt them. 'And he didn't let go my hand all the way home,' she finished with a smile.

Phoebe was jumping up and down in delight. 'Grandad kicked their arses!'

And here was where Bram would usually step in and say there was always a better way to solve a problem than violence, and Grandad should just have told the teenagers to stop and explained how wrong their actions were, but the words stuck in his throat, and it was left to Linda to say, 'Well, yes, and he really shouldn't have,' but without any conviction.

'He should! He *should*!' Phoebe objected, and burst into tears.

IT WAS four days after they'd left Finn's body in the forest that Scott appeared at the door, his face telling Bram all he needed to know. But he went through the pantomime of 'Hi, Scott – any news?' and showing him through to the Room with a View where Scott said yes, there was news, and it wasn't good, and could he speak to him and Kirsty together? Bram fetched her from the TV room where she was trying to relax with the kids, and the two of them sat side by side on the sofa facing Scott, Bram wearing what he hoped was a concerned but blameless expression of apprehension.

'Finn's body has been found,' said Scott.

'Oh, no,' said Kirsty.

Bram left a shocked silence before asking: 'What happened?'

'They're doing a post mortem, obviously. But it looks like he suffered a nasty head wound.'

'Where was he found?' Bram asked next. They would ask that, wouldn't they?

'In the forestry plantation at King's Seat Quarry.'

'Oh!' breathed Kirsty. 'You think he was swimming there, and – what? He had some kind of accident?'

'He wasn't near the actual quarry. It isn't looking like an accident. The death is being treated as unexplained, obviously. I just thought I should let you know. It'll be reported on the late news. Might already be on the internet, for all I know.' He got up from the sofa. 'I'd better get off. It's crazy busy, as you can imagine.'

'Thanks – for coming over and telling us,' said Kirsty, jumping to her feet a little too eagerly. A little too eager for him to leave. 'The poor Taylors.'

Scott nodded. 'It's hit them hard, of course.'

When he'd gone, Kirsty grabbed Bram, pressing her face against his shirt. He held her, and murmured what he hoped were reassuring words. 'There's nothing to tie us to the body. Thank God we burned the tarp and the other stuff.' They had bought matches and firelighters and kindling at a garage and chosen a remote spot in another forest, and piled the kindling and then the waterproofs and the tarp and the mask on top of the bloodstained cardboard. It had gone up in a good blaze, and within ten minutes everything had been consumed in a throat-choking conflagration.

'We need to check the internet.'

And so began two days of obsessive checking of the internet and the local TV news. The police were, of course, giving out very little information, only saying that 'enquiries to establish the full circumstances of the death are ongoing,' but there was plenty of speculation on Finn's Facebook page: 'So sorry, man. No way was this an accident. Hope whoever did this rots in jail' and 'There's a crazy new star up there shining down. Miss ya forever. Police know who did it, they're gonna arrest the bastard in next few days.'

Did Finn's friends suspect him and Kirsty? Had Finn told them what he was up to, or had it come out, had Andrew and Sylvia and Cara been telling people? If so, Bram and Kirsty were the obvious suspects.

The ring at the door came before seven the next morning. Both Bram and Kirsty were already up and dressed and surfing the internet at the kitchen table. They looked at each other, neither making a move to get up and go to the door.

But they had to answer it. Bram got up and crossed the Walton Room and opened the door.

'Mr Hendriksen, I'm PC Macintosh and my colleague here is PC White. We understand that your son Maxwell Hendriksen is staying at this address?'

'Max? Yes. But what–'

'We need to speak to him, please, Mr McKechnie. Can we come in?'

'Why do you want to speak to Max? If it's about Finn Taylor, he doesn't know anything about what happened to him.'

'Sir, if we could come in, and you could let Max know that we need to speak to him?'

'Right now? He's asleep.' Bram moved back instinctively until he was standing at the foot of the stairs, as if guarding them.

'Nevertheless.'

'I'll go and get him,' said Kirsty, gently pushing past Bram.

Bram didn't invite the policemen to sit down. They stood in an awkward triangle. From the floor above he could hear Kirsty's voice, and then Max, answering her groggily.

'I don't know anything,' Max said at once as he came padding down the stairs in his boxers and T-shirt.

'We understand that you and Finn Taylor had an altercation in the Inverluie Hotel bar,' said the larger of the two big men. 'A physical altercation?'

'Uh, yeah.'

'But that was days before Finn went missing!' Bram interjected. 'A couple of days, at least.'

'Did you know that it was Finn Taylor who'd been terrorising your family?'

'What?' Max shook his head as if to clear it. 'No.'

'Is that your VW Polo on the track beyond the bridge?'

Max turned to Bram, as if expecting him to sort this out for him. Bram said, 'What on earth has that got to do with anything?'

'A red VW Polo was seen on the forest track at King's Seat Forest four days before Finn Taylor's body was found there. The witnesses stated that the vehicle reversed away from them, which at the time they felt was strange.'

'Well it wasn't *my* car!' Max was looking from the policemen to Bram and Kirsty. 'How could it have been?'

'Of course it wasn't!' said Kirsty.

'We need to impound the car for forensic investigation,' said the other cop. 'Max, now's your chance to tell us anything you need to tell us. Things will go so much better for you if you tell us the truth at the outset.'

Max was shaking his head, stunned. 'I didn't do anything.'

'Okay.' The bigger cop grimaced. 'Maxwell Hendriksen. I'm PC Darren Macintosh and this is PC Ian White. We're arresting you for the murder of Finn Taylor. You don't need to say anything at this time other than giving your name, address, place of birth and nationality. We're taking you for questioning to Aviemore Police Station–'

'Oh my God!' said Bram. 'No! No, it wasn't Max! *No!*'

But Kirsty was suddenly at his side, gripping his hand, whispering one word – '*Don't*' – before going to Max and taking him in her arms, and saying to the policemen, 'I suppose he's allowed to get dressed?'

When they nodded, she hustled him back up the stairs to his room.

23

After Kirsty had called David to break the news that Max had been arrested, Bram said, 'We have to tell the police what really happened. We have to tell them what I did. We can't let Max take the blame for it.'

'That's not what we're doing.' Kirsty leant back against the front door wearily. 'There can't be any evidence against Max, because he didn't do it. That's what I told him. I told him to tell the truth, but not to say anything about the "patrol" he was on that night with Dad and Fraser – that would just confuse the issue.'

'But Max–' *Oh Jesus.* 'They're going to question him. Browbeat him!' *He must be so scared.*

'It'll be fine. Scott will look after him. They'll have to release him within twenty-four hours or charge him, and they don't have enough – they *can't* have enough – to do that. How much worse is it going to be for Max if we're convicted of this? We have to hold our nerve.'

'You mean *we're* the real suspects, and Max has been arrested to push us to confess?'

'It's possible, isn't it? But there's no need to panic. Hopefully the tarp will have prevented any forensic evidence from Finn being transferred to the car, but even if they do find something, Max was in that fight with Finn. Any of Finn's blood inside the car could be explained by that. His blood getting on Max's top, and Max chucking the top into the boot. Or even just onto his hands. Max opens the boot, grabs something, transfers the blood…'

'But there might be other evidence. Something from the car, fibres or whatever, transferred to Finn's body.'

'He was completely wrapped in the tarp.' Kirsty frowned. 'And we've destroyed all the cameras–' She broke off as her phone buzzed. 'Oh, hi, Dad. Yes… No, not yet, but I suppose we… Okay. Okay. Thanks.' She ended the call. 'Dad's going to organise a lawyer for Max. I couldn't really refuse, but I don't think it's in Max's interests to go *No comment* as a lawyer would probably advise him. He just needs to tell the truth.'

Bram nodded. 'But hopefully Max will heed your advice and do that, lawyer or no lawyer. If he–'

'Bertie-cam!' Kirsty interrupted. 'Phoebe's so obsessive about it, I bet she made Bertie wear it that night, when he was out on patrol.'

'She did – I saw her attach it. But that's okay. Bertie was nowhere near us. If he had been, he'd have come up to greet us. Chances are he was with David and Max all night.'

'Exactly,' said Kirsty, a smile curving her mouth. 'And if that's the case, the footage might prove that Max couldn't have killed Finn. It'll show Max on patrol, and then us coming to get him… And you can say you sat up on watch all night and Max didn't leave the house again. Max just has to tell them about the patrol, and we'll produce the Bertie-cam footage…'

'Okay.' This could work! 'Okay, yes, but what about Fraser? The footage might exonerate David and Max, but Fraser was off on his own.'

'Let's just concentrate on Max for now, Bram.'

Phoebe's room was in darkness. Bram opened the curtains and Kirsty sat on the bed and gently touched Phoebe's sleeping face. 'Phoebe? Darling?'

'Mm?' she opened one eye.

'Where do you keep Bertie-cam? Is it somewhere in here?'

'In my treasure box,' she said, suddenly awake, sitting up in bed and looking past Kirsty to the door. 'Is Bertie here?'

'No. We just need to take a look at what's on the camera.'

'Can I look?'

'You can get dressed and then have your breakfast. Then we'll see.'

Phoebe kept her 'treasure box', a little oak box they'd picked up at an antiques fair, on top of her chest of drawers. It contained her favourite hair slides and some pottery animals and a misshapen, mutant sweet she had become too fond of to eat. And Bertie-cam.

'What on earth are we going to tell her about Max?' Kirsty hissed as they headed back downstairs.

'We can just say Max has gone with the police to answer some questions.'

Bram sat down at the kitchen table and removed the SD card from the camera. He plugged it into his laptop and they began going through the footage. The early stuff was just Bertie plodding about the house hoovering up crumbs. Then he was running about outside. The camera was a fish-eye one that gave a wide-angled view of Bertie's world, and there was

audio, and they couldn't help smiling at the sweet snuffling sounds he made as he went about his business.

Then Bertie was back in the kitchen, presumably just
after Phoebe had attached the camera on that fateful
night.

'Come on, then, boy,' said David's voice.

Now David and Fraser were in shot in the Walton
Room, and Kirsty, telling them to be careful and not
confront anyone. Each person's knees came into close-
up one after the other as Bertie went around the room
getting petted: David, Fraser, Phoebe and Kirsty. Then
he was following David and Fraser out onto the verandah, and off out into the dark, at which point the view
changed to infrared, David and Fraser's outlines
glowing white and yellow and orange.

They fast-forwarded through the patrol of the
paddock and then the wood. And then a third figure
appeared – Max – and they switched to real speed. The
image juddered as Bertie bounded over to greet him.

'Hi, Bertie!' said Max. 'I've come to help with the
patrol,' he added to the men.

'Good lad!' said David. 'More the merrier.'

Kirsty clicked fast-forward again. Bertie, as they'd
hoped, stayed close to Max and David throughout –
they didn't let him run off on his own. Fraser peeled off
at one point and David and Max left the wood to walk
round the paddock and the house. That was when Bram
saw them and came out onto the verandah to talk to
them. Then they continued back into the wood.

'This is brilliant,' said Kirsty. 'It surely shows that
Max is innocent.'

And then it all happened at once, the action speeded
up almost comically. A third figure came into shot from
the left of the screen, there was a blurry tussle, and

David grabbed a long object from him and hit out with it, causing the third figure to stumble back.

As Kirsty hit 'pause', the figure froze, off balance, David's compact form leaning towards him, chin jutting aggressively.

'Oh my God,' breathed Bram.

Kirsty replayed the sequence at normal speed.

They sat there in silence as the figure appeared – a tall, lean figure whose head, in the infrared glow, was less bright than David and Max's because, of course, it was insulated by the mask and, presumably, the beanie hat – and David pounced with a wordless shout, and they grappled together, each trying to wrest from the other something long with a triangular-shaped end.

A gun.

It was an airgun or a shotgun.

It was like watching a fight from a science fiction film, the two un-human-like, glowing figures merging and separating as they struggled, grunting and growling. A third figure – Max – darted in, but David said, 'Stay back, Max!' and Max backed away. David eventually got the gun from Finn and lashed out with it, lashed out at his head, and Finn staggered back, the top of his head glowing brighter as, Bram assumed, the beanie hat fell off.

'*You fucker!*' David's tinny, disembodied voice filled the room as he hit him again, and again, holding the gun like a club. Finn stumbled away, disappearing and reappearing as he moved into the trees, and David strode after him.

'Oh God,' Kirsty breathed.

'Oh God,' a voice repeated. Max, on the video. '*Grandad!*'

'*Stay there, Max!*' came David's voice.

The two glowing shapes had now disappeared, and

Max's legs came into shot as Bertie turned to him.

'Okay, Bertie, okay,' Max whispered, bending over him. Then: *'Grandad!'* he shouted again, and began to move off, the picture shaking as Bertie followed him.

But now David was back, the alien infrared version of him, his heavy breathing audible on the soundtrack. 'Bastard got away,' he puffed, bending over to get his breath. In one hand he still held the gun. Then he straightened, and took hold of Max, and the shot became a close-up as Bertie moved in too, pushing his nose at them, ignored by them both.

'You need to keep your mouth shut about this, right, lad? I've already got a suspended sentence for assault. If the law finds out about this, I'm going to jail.'

'But *he* might go to the police. Whoever it was – He might accuse you of assault!'

'No way. How would he explain how it happened? "That's right, officer, I was off out terrorising the Hendriksens as usual...?" That bastard knows he's got to keep his trap shut about this, and so must you. Okay, Max?'

'Okay.' Max sounded so young, so scared but so trusting. Bram wanted to reach into the screen and hug him. 'Who was it? Who do you think it was?'

'No idea. But that's quite a whack I gave him. Anyone seen sporting a head wound in the next few days, we'll have our man.'

'And then what?'

'Let's cross that bridge when we come to it.'

Kirsty stopped the footage, and they stared at each other for a long moment. From the landing above, Phoebe called out: *'Daaad?* Where's my blue and white top?'

'In the drawer, Phoebe,' he called back. 'Second one down, I think.'

He looked at the screen of his laptop, at David's glowing image. 'This explains why Finn was weaving around when I first saw him, that night. David had already hit him. Concussed him…'

'It could have been the injuries *Dad* inflicted that were the fatal ones,' Kirsty said numbly. 'He hit him hard. You can see from the video that he hit him hard. Bram…' She grabbed his arm. 'You know what you're like – you literally wouldn't hurt a fly, normally. You *thought* you hit Finn's head hard against that bracket, but you might not have! You might be exaggerating it, in your head. The real damage…'

'… Could have been caused by David,' Bram finished, looking back at the screen where the glowing shape of David was frozen, an arm slung across Max's shoulders. He tapped 'play', and the two figures moved off across the grass, Bertie trotting after them.

Kirsty jumped up from her chair. 'For all he knows, *he* killed Finn. He probably *did*! And he's letting Max take the rap?'

'Isn't that what we're doing?' Bram had to say, in fairness.

'No, of course it isn't! We *know* what happened, so we *know* there can't be enough evidence against Max to charge him! But Dad doesn't. For all Dad knows, Max went back out there once he and Fraser had gone, and found Finn's body, and took it off in his car to dispose of it, leaving forensic evidence all over the car and Finn. For all he knows, Max is in this mess because of him, and he's sitting on his hands *doing nothing*!' She was sobbing hysterically.

Bram put an arm around her. 'In fairness, he's getting him a lawyer.'

'Oh, big deal!' She turned her tear-stained face up to Bram. 'He's a monster! My dad's a *monster*!'

24

After Phoebe had had breakfast, they sat her
down and told her that Max had gone to the
police station to answer some questions, but it
was nothing to worry about.

'What questions?' she demanded, lower lip
trembling.

'Well, about what happened the night Finn disappeared,' said Bram.

'But *Max* didn't *kill* him!'

'No, no, of course not. They just have to ask people
what they were doing that night.'

'How long will it take?'

God. 'Not sure, *kleintje.*'

'Dad and I are going to the police station now to sort
it all out,' said Kirsty. *They were?* 'How would you like
to spend the day with the Millers?'

'Okay,' said Phoebe uncertainly.

'I'll give Mrs Miller a call while you get ready. Go
and brush your teeth.'

When Phoebe had disappeared off upstairs, Kirsty
said, 'We can stitch Dad up for this. All we need to do is

take this footage to the police. Get Max to open up. With Dad's record–'

'Whoa! Kirsty! We can't do that! I can't believe you're suggesting... I know he's – I know he can be difficult, but he's your dad! You love him! I know you do.'

What the hell? Bram knew there was nothing as formidable as a mother protecting her child, but throwing David to the wolves... Did Kirsty really want to do that?

'This is all Dad's fault, and he should be the one who pays the price, not us and the kids.'

'Okay, so he grappled with Finn and whacked him, but Finn *walked away*.' He lowered his voice. 'We're kidding ourselves if we're trying to find a version of events in which David killed him. *I* did it. *I did it*, Kirsty. Not David.'

'Well, even if that's true, he's the reason you were out there in the first place. We were worried about what he'd get Max into on that stupid patrol, so you went after them. And he's been in your head, hasn't he, on and on at you to "man up"? So when you encountered Finn–'

Bram shook his head, and went on shaking it. 'The only person to blame for this is me.'

'No!' Kirsty almost shouted at him. 'You have to stop thinking like that! It's Dad. It's always been Dad, at the bottom of every bad thing that happens in our lives!'

Whoa. 'Isn't that... isn't that going a bit far?'

'I'm going to call Carrie Miller and ask if they can take Phoebe. If not, I suppose we'll have to leave her with Mum and Dad. Then we can talk about it.'

· · ·

THE MILLER GIRLS WERE SUPER-EXCITED, as their mum put it, to have Phoebe spend the whole day with them. Fortunately, their driveway wasn't directly opposite Linda and David's house, so Bram was hopeful they wouldn't have been spotted dropping her off. They declined Carrie Miller's offer of coffee and cake and headed out of Grantown on the A95 towards Aviemore.

'You want to know the reason I hardly ever came back here, when we were at uni?' Kirsty said after she'd negotiated the roundabout.

Bram felt a shiver go up his spine. 'Because of what happened to Owen. And – well, you were trying to be strong, weren't you? Trying to make out to your family that you were fine, having a great time?'

'No.' She looked in the mirror, indicated, and pulled over into a lay-by. Then she turned to look at him. 'It was because of Dad. It's always been because of Dad, Bram.'

KIRSTY KNEW she shouldn't sleep. She needed to get home. It was past two o'clock and she needed to get back to her bedroom window under the cover of darkness. But it was so cosy, lying here with Owen. In the daytime she didn't really like being in his bedsit – it was horribly grotty and he was such a slob – but in the dark she could forget about the dirty sink and the piles of boxes and the festering plates and mugs and the discarded clothes and the overflowing laundry bag that stank of man.

She was tucked into the crook of his arm, which meant more man smells, but she liked the smell of his sweat when it was fresh. Pheromones, she guessed. Designed to bring males and females together to propagate.

Not that any propagation would be happening. They were careful.

That was one of the many good things about going out with an older man. He was experienced. He wasn't going to make stupid mistakes and let her get pregnant.

She closed her eyes, drifting down into a dream in which she had a miniature baby Owen on her lap and was trying desperately to interest it in a Mars Bar.

Then the door banged open, and light exploded from the bare bulb that dangled from the ceiling, and there were men everywhere.

'Get him,' barked one of them.

'Dad!'

'Get your clothes on and get home, Kirsty,' Dad growled.

'No!' *She grabbed at Fraser's arm as he hauled Owen, naked, out of the bed.* 'What are you doing? Leave him alone!'

There weren't men everywhere, there were only two of them, Dad and Fraser, but they seemed to fill the room.

'She's fifteen!' *Dad roared into Owen's face, and Owen, still half asleep, cowered away but Fraser had a hold of him, he was wrenching Owen's arm up behind his back and Owen was howling in pain.*

'Oh, no, no,' *Kirsty sobbed.* 'Don't hurt him! Please, Dad, please!'

'We're not going to hurt him. Just teach him a well-earned lesson.' *Dad looked away from her.* 'Put on some clothes, for God's sake, Kirsty!'

As if that was important!

And now they each had one of Owen's arms, marching him across the room to the door. She ran at them, naked, like a mad woman, clutching at their clothes, at their hands, and then she put her arms around Owen's waist and tried to pull him away from them, screaming at them, but still they hauled him towards the door.

She jumped on Fraser's back.

She tugged at his hair.

But Fraser shook her off as if she weighed nothing and she landed on her back on the floor, all the breath knocked out of her, and she couldn't get a breath, all she could do was double up on the floor trying to heave air into her collapsed lungs.

When she could stand, they were gone.

She pulled on her jeans and sweatshirt and trainers and ran out of the room after them, ran down the stairs and out into the night, and she could see them, thank God, their van was parked across the street and they were bundling Owen inside. They had tied his wrists and ankles together behind his back.

She was pulling open the gate but she was too late, they were jumping into the cab and the van was moving off...

Her bike.

She'd left it propped against the wall of the house.

She jumped onto it and pedalled like mad up the street after the van's tail lights. The van was swerving all over the road, and at one point did a three-sixty, wheels spinning as it turned in a tight circle, and she could hear them whooping, Dad and Fraser, in the cab, and oh Christ, Owen was in there, in the back of the van, being thrown about!

But at least all the swerving around meant she was able to keep up on her bike.

She was panting, though, by the time the van's tail lights slowed, far in front of her, on the dead-end road through the woods that led to the Old Bridge of Spey. Why were they taking him here?

Her thighs ached, her leg muscles screaming at her to stop, but she pushed on, sobbing with the effort, forcing the wheels of her bike to keep turning, standing on the pedals and then sitting and then standing.

When she reached the bridge she could see them in the moonlight, Dad's shaved head a pale disc, Owen's naked body – Oh God, he was over the bridge! Dad was dangling him over the edge!

. . .

'I SHOUTED,' Kirsty whispered. 'I shouted his name. Owen's name. Dad said I distracted him, that Owen suddenly wriggled when I shouted and Dad let go of his feet by accident. He said they were just putting the frighteners on him. He hadn't meant to let him go. But *I saw him*, Bram. I saw him fling Owen away like he was something to be discarded, a piece of rubbish he was chucking in the river. It wasn't an accident. *It wasn't.*'

Bram couldn't find words. He just reached over and grabbed Kirsty's hand and the two of them sat there together, staring out of the windscreen at the cars and lorries whizzing past.

This was horrendous.

But somehow he wasn't having a hard time believing it. It certainly explained the rage against David that had been simmering in Kirsty, just under the surface, ever since they'd moved up here and she'd been forced to spend day after day in her father's company. And then when Max had arrived and been pulled into David's orbit... No wonder she had been freaking out. No wonder she had been so dead set against David taking action against whoever was harassing them. No wonder she didn't want Max and Phoebe to live with her parents.

'Why on earth did you want to move back?'

She sighed. 'For Mum's sake, mainly. And this is my home, Bram, it's always been my home – why should I be exiled from it because of what Dad did? And I thought... I thought I could get past it. Come to terms with it. Tell myself, as a parent, that he was only protecting his daughter from a sexual predator. I can see, now, how much of a shock it would have been for him to find out that this man, this twenty-three-year-old man, had seduced his fifteen-year-old daughter, or so he thought.' She stared into Bram's eyes. 'But it wasn't Owen. That's the awful thing. *It was me. I* was the one who went after *him.* I was obsessed with him, I used to follow him about town–'

'You were a child, and he was an adult. No matter how "obsessed" with him you were, he shouldn't have had a relationship with you. A sexual relationship. Any sort of relationship.'

'If I hadn't pressured Owen to be my boyfriend, to have sex with me… I was a wild child back then, Bram. I first had sex when I was thirteen.'

'With Scott?'

She shook her head. 'Other boys. *I* went after *Owen.* If I hadn't – if I hadn't done that, *he wouldn't have died.*' She choked on a sob.

No wonder Kirsty had been so broken at uni. No wonder she hadn't wanted another relationship. There was the trauma of what her own father and brother had done to Owen, but also her own feelings of guilt.

Bram took her in his arms. 'You were only a child. None of it was your fault.'

'I hated him so much,' she wailed. 'I hated Dad *so much.* The only thing that kept me going, after that night, through the years of school I had left, the years I had to stay here living in the same house as him, was the thought of escaping to university.'

'Which was why you chose UCL. As far away from here as possible.'

She nodded.

'Why didn't you tell me?' he said, holding her against him.

She hugged him back so tight it hurt. 'I couldn't. I couldn't tell anyone. Dad made me promise not to tell Mum, and I never have – it would *destroy* her if she knew. And… Oh, Bram, I was so ashamed! It was my fault Dad did it!'

'No,' he said fiercely.

'It was too hard,' she choked. 'Living with it, with what we'd done but also the lie, having to make out I had no idea how Owen had died. It was too hard, pretending, with Mum – I couldn't do it. When I went to uni in London it was the perfect excuse to spend the minimum time possible at home – it was so far away, I could reasonably limit my trips home to a few times a year, and I pretended I was caught up in this mad social whirl and was busy with studying so couldn't stay long when I did go back… But it was awful, Bram! Mum was so hurt. She thought I had… had left them behind, had more interesting people to spend time with. Then when you and I got together, I used that as an excuse too… I'll never forget what Mum said to me when she first met you. She said, "I'm so glad you've found such a lovely boy to be happy with." She knew I wasn't happy at home. She knew something was wrong. But I couldn't tell her, Bram. I couldn't tell her it was nothing to do with her.'

'So when I suggested you go freelance, and Phoebe ran with the idea of moving back here…'

'I felt I had to try.' She made a choked sound halfway between a laugh and a sob. 'And look how well that's turned out. For a while I thought it was maybe going to be okay, that I could cope with him, but then when Max joined us… The way Dad got his claws into him… And Max being here seemed to make Dad turn on *you*, pressure you *to be a man* and set an example.' She gulped. 'He's sick, Bram. He's *dangerous* and I *knew* that but I didn't do anything, I should have packed us all up and got us out of here when I saw what he was doing to Max, to you, but I didn't. And now Max…'

'Everything that's happened – it's not your fault.'

She took a deep breath. 'I left that boy in the shed to die. All I could think of was how we were going to cover it up. I was – when Finn was lying there on the ground, all I could think about was Owen, and how Dad got away with it. It's as if… as if he's poisoned us all.'

'We didn't know Finn was still alive.'

'But I should have checked him properly! We should have called an ambulance!'

For a long time they just sat there, watching the traffic, a bird flitting about in the branches of a big conifer, the clouds scudding past.

'Does Scott know?' Bram said at last. 'About Owen?'

Kirsty sighed. 'I'm pretty sure he suspects, but he's never asked me about it. We don't talk about Owen. Which is telling in itself, I suppose.'

'I'm just thinking, when he sees the Bertie-cam footage…'

'Oh, he'll buy into the theory it was Dad. No question.'

Another long silence, in which Bram just held her.

'He isn't sorry, you know,' she said eventually. 'For murdering Owen. He has no remorse about it. Owen got his just desserts, that's what he thinks. And you can bet he has no remorse about Finn, either. You think he's beating himself up about it, like we are? Oh no. No. For all he knows, he killed Finn, but he doesn't give a toss, Bram.' She took a big breath. 'He'll never face justice for Owen. And that's my fault. I should have gone to the police and told them what happened, but I couldn't do it. I couldn't do it to my own dad! But I can now. He can face justice for what he did to Finn. To us. To all of us.'

25

A t Aviemore Police Station, Scott left them in a small room containing a table and some chairs while he took the SD card away to hand over to the DI in charge of Finn's case. Bram could feel his heart hammering, his skin slicking with sweat, sitting there in the airless little room.

'DI Moira Cromer,' said the grey-haired, business-like woman who eventually came to speak to them, taking a seat at the table opposite them with another, younger woman with wispy blonde hair, whom she introduced as DC Rachel Henderson.

DC Henderson switched on the tape recorder. 'We're recording this, okay?'

It wasn't really a question, but Bram and Kirsty nodded.

DI Cromer gave all their names for the tape. Then: 'You found this footage on the camera attached to your dog's collar?'

'My mum's dog,' Kirsty corrected. 'Our daughter must have put the camera on him just before my dad and brother went out to check around the property.'

'And they were later joined by your son, Maxwell?'

'Yes.'

'Why didn't you come forward with this straight away?'

'We've only just found it,' Bram was able to say truthfully. 'Kirsty didn't know that Phoebe had attached the petcam to Bertie that night, and I just remembered after Max… after he was arrested.'

'Okay.' She consulted her notes. 'I'm going to ask the two of you to stay here in the station, and surrender your phones, while we arrest your father and apply for a warrant to search your parents' property. DI Sinclair will look after you. I understand you're old friends.'

Kirsty nodded. 'Max–'

'What we're going to do now is show your son this footage – which leaves no room for doubt about what your father did, Mrs Hendriksen. Maxwell seems like an intelligent lad. I'm sure he'll see the sense in telling the truth.'

'He was only keeping quiet out of – loyalty,' Kirsty whispered, and Bram grabbed her hand. He wasn't entirely confident, no matter what she said, that Kirsty would be able to go through with this. 'Loyalty to his grandad.'

'Yes, I appreciate that. Theoretically he could be charged with perverting the course of justice, but I don't think the procurator fiscal is going to consider that to be in the public interest. It's an understandable omission, to keep quiet about this, particularly as your father explicitly told him to do so.'

'What will happen to Dad?' Kirsty choked.

DI Cromer pursed her lips. 'Regardless of what we find on his property, we have enough here with the footage, your testimony and, it is to be hoped, that of Maxwell, to charge him with Finn Taylor's murder.'

Kirsty nodded wordlessly.

Bram squeezed her hand.

SCOTT KEPT them supplied with sandwiches and water and coffee, and updated on what was going on. For an hour or so, the updates consisted merely of the fact that Max was still being questioned. Then David had been arrested, but not yet charged. Scott reassured them that Amy had been hot on the heels of the officers who had arrested David – she'd picked up Linda and Bertie, and Phoebe from the Millers, and whisked them off to Scott and Amy's place before the team executing the search warrant had arrived.

Scott was showing the stress of the last few hours, as they all were, but in Scott's case this manifested as a boyish dishevelment and a slackening of his tie, rather than, as in Bram's, sweat marks under the arms and lingering body odour.

'Max will be released imminently,' Scott said finally, coming into the room and dropping onto a chair by the door. 'I think it's best you all come back to our place, for now.'

'Can't we go home?' asked Kirsty. 'To Woodside?'

'Not just yet. In light of this new evidence, the SOCOs will be going back there. But in the next few days, you should be able to return.'

'What about the Taylors?' said Bram. 'Have they been told about David's arrest?'

'Yes. I told them myself. I don't think you'll have any more trouble with them. David... He's well known for having a short fuse. I don't think any blame will attach by proxy to any of you.' Scott sighed. 'What a bloody mess. I should have... God. I know what David's like. When you were being harassed, one thing after another, and David was building up a head of steam… I should have seen the signs. I should have stepped in.'

So Scott probably did know about Owen?

'What could you have done?' Bram said mechanically. 'You couldn't have locked him up because you suspected he *might* commit a crime some time in the future.'

Scott grimaced. 'No, but…'

'It's not your fault,' Kirsty said, almost impatiently. 'When can we see Max?'

Scott's wife, Amy, was kindness itself, moving their little boy into their own bedroom so that Max could have a room of his own and not have to share with Phoebe. The little boy, five-year-old Stuart, was a perfect gentleman, solemnly offering Phoebe a range of toys which he thought she might like as she didn't have any of her own with her.

The gesture made Phoebe cry, sitting on Linda's lap in the conservatory as Stuart set a large drawing pad and crayons down on the table in front of her.

'Mummy says you like drawing,' he said uncertainly.

'Thank you,' sniffed Phoebe.

Scott and Amy lived in a grand Victorian house on Woodlands Terrace, set back from the road and screened from it by a huge garden filled with mature trees. It was wall-to-wall original features and amazing old fireplaces.

When Scott came home that afternoon, he asked to speak to Kirsty, Bram and Linda privately, and showed them into a panelled study overlooking the lawn at the back of the house. Scott sat in the swivel chair behind the desk, Linda and Kirsty in leather tub chairs by the fireplace, and Bram perched on the arm of Kirsty's chair.

'David has been charged with assault and perverting the course of justice, and released,' Scott said, smiling uncertainly, as if not sure what kind of reaction was appropriate to this news.

Kirsty had gone pale. 'But DI Cromer – she said he'd be charged with *murder*.'

'That was before we realised that the rest of the petcam footage gives him a watertight alibi for the remainder of the night and the next day, so there's no way he could have gone back and disposed of the body before the search began in the woods.'

Linda made a little sound. 'Oh, thank God!'

'That's great,' said Kirsty hollowly.

'But *I* gave him an alibi for the rest of the night and the next day,' Linda added.

Scott nodded. 'But your evidence – I'm sorry, Linda, but the evidence of a spouse isn't seen to be impartial. That of Bertie-cam, however… Bertie slept in your room with the two of you, and the petcam footage proves that David didn't leave the room until you both got up in the morning. And it shows David getting his breakfast, pottering about the kitchen and so on. Taking Bertie for a walk.'

'Well, thank goodness for the petcam,' Bram managed.

'Where is Dad?' said Kirsty.

'He's in the car outside. I thought it might be better if I, uh, broke the good news first.'

Bram felt his heart start to pound. David must be furious with him and Kirsty for taking that petcam footage to the police.

Linda got to her feet.

'I'll go and get him,' said Scott, also rising. 'I just

have to tell you that we're not out of the woods yet, so to speak.' He grimaced at the unintended pun. 'David's admitted to the charge of perverting the course of justice. An airgun was found in your garage, Linda. A .22 Winchester 55 RS. Wrapped in a towel and shoved under a pile of logs.'

'Finn's?' said Bram.

'David admits as much, and it's the same make and model as the air rifle owned by Andrew Taylor, the one the Taylors say Finn took with him that night. Finn's idea, apparently, was to take potshots at the security lights on your verandah. The rifle is currently under-going forensic examination.'

'Surely that's not necessary, if David admits to the altercation and – hiding the rifle?' Linda said in a low voice. 'And surely the assault charge won't stick? Finn was terrorising the family. For David to suddenly come upon a masked man in the wood, a man with a *gun*… He must have reacted instinctively. It was surely self-defence.'

'They were grappling,' Bram added. 'David got the gun off him and hit out with it. It was a natural reaction.'

Kirsty said nothing.

Scott got up from his chair and walked to the window, and then turned to face them. The bright light behind him made it impossible to read his expression. 'It's not just the assault charge he has to worry about. I have to tell you that DI Cromer still likes David for the murder.'

'*What?*' Bram's heart leapt.

'It's those couple of minutes when David went back into the wood, off camera, that are proving the stumbling block. The post mortem on Finn has revealed that he was struck multiple times with at least two different objects, one blunt, presumably the stock of the air rifle, and the other weapon or weapons possibly metal, with a flat surface two or three centimetres across. The best guess is a hammer.'

God. That would be the hose bracket, which was about the same width as a hammer, although it wasn't round, it was a sort of scroll shape, which would surely give more of a rectangular impression where it – where it smashed into Finn's skull. But maybe there was so much damage that it was impossible to isolate individual impressions?

'David is saying he only hit him a couple of times with the air rifle – although the footage shows it was three times – and that, although he did go after him into the wood, he didn't find him. But if this goes to trial, the prosecution will maintain that David went after him, found him, hit him with another weapon and killed him.'

Linda shook her head. 'But you've just said there's no way David could have disposed of the body.'

'DI Cromer's theory is that he had help.' He flicked a look at Kirsty. 'Probably from Fraser. Fraser has no alibi for the rest of the night. But she's also going to be looking at you and Bram. You're going to have to give DNA samples for forensic testing.'

'Okay,' said Kirsty numbly.

Scott left the room, and as soon as he'd gone, Linda burst into tears. Kirsty was still holding her when the door opened again and David barrelled in, grabbed Linda and crushed her to him. 'It's okay, love, it's okay. Everything's going to be okay.'

Bram backed away until he was standing in the bay window, his heart knocking against his chest, his mouth dry. Phoebe and Stuart were out there in the garden, incompetently kicking a ball about and trying in vain to interest Bertie in it, while Max sat slumped on a bench under an apple tree.

'Hey, Bram, relax!' David chuckled, patting Linda's back and looking over her shoulder at Bram and Kirsty. 'The two of you are like kids with their hands caught in the sweetie jar! I get it, that you had to offer up the Bertie-cam footage to clear Max. Don't worry, I get it.'

'Uh–' Bram couldn't think what the hell to say.

He supposed that David could understand, if anyone could, what a parent might be prepared to do for their child, but nevertheless, it was very generous of him to be so forgiving. Was he really such a bad guy? Look at how loving he was with Linda, with Kirsty, with Phoebe. He wasn't, surely, the monster Kirsty thought him. Maybe the Owen thing *had* been just an accident? He had just been giving the guy a scare, but had dropped him over the bridge by mistake?

'We had to,' Kirsty croaked.

David nodded reassuringly at her. 'And yeah, I know, I should have come clean about what happened, but how was it going to look, eh? How *does* it look? The theory the police seem wedded to is that I killed Finn and Fraser disposed of the body – with a mind-boggling incompetence I'd hope would rule him out from the get-go, but apparently not. That bitch Cromer is determined to pin this on me.'

'Really?' Bram got out.

David took a tissue from his pocket and gently wiped Linda's face. 'Okay, love?'

Linda nodded. 'But surely the police are clutching at straws, trying to bring Fraser into it?'

'Aye, but Cromer doesn't want to hear any other theories. Mine in particular.'

God. 'Which is?' Bram had to know.

'Someone else must have had a set-to with Finn,

right? The boffins have found other wounds on his
head, not just a dunt with the butt of a rifle. Someone
had a good go at the lad. Here's what I'm thinking. Finn
toddles off back home whining to Daddy about having
been jumped, his rifle taken off him and used as a
weapon against him. Andrew's incandescent. Finn was
bested by a bloody pensioner who got the rifle off him,
and now it's maybe going to be traced back to the
Taylors? He goes for the lad.'

'Oh, now, David.' Linda rubbed his arm. 'I don't
think that's likely.'

'He goes for the lad,' David went on as if she hadn't
spoken. 'Realises he's killed him, panics, dumps the
body.' He looked from one to another of them as if
expecting a prize.

'I suppose it's possible,' muttered Bram.

He escaped as soon as he could to the garden,
lowering himself onto the bench next to Max, and, when
Phoebe came running over to wriggle between them,
Bram gave her a hug.

'Well, kids, Grandad's back!' He tried to sound
upbeat about it. 'He's been released because Bertie-cam
shows he can't have, um, done what they thought he'd
done. Well, he's been charged with some other things,
but hopefully he's not going to be in too much trouble.'

Phoebe's face lit up and she raced off inside,
shouting at the top of her voice: '*Grandad!*'

Max stood to go after her, then turned back to Bram.
'Bertie-cam?' He frowned. 'I thought it was Bertie-cam
that put Grandad in the frame in the first place?'

Bram explained what had happened. 'Although it
seems the police still think David killed Finn. And
maybe Fraser disposed of the body.'

'Of course he didn't kill Finn!' Max rapped out. 'I
was there. Grandad didn't hit him hard enough. Finn

wasn't even badly hurt. He ran off into the wood afterwards. If the police are saying Grandad went after him and hit him again – there's no way that happened. Yeah, he went after him, but he didn't have any other weapon, a hammer or whatever – and if there'd been a second set-to I'd have heard it. And he was only gone like a couple of minutes.'

'The acoustics in woods can be strange – the trees have a damping effect on sound. That's why people who live on busy roads plant hedges and trees, to cut out the noise.'

'So you actually think Grandad did this?'

Bram stood and put an arm round him. 'He has a history of violence,' was all he could bring himself to say.

Max shrugged out from under Bram's arm and strode away towards the house.

26

B ram stood in the rain on the banks of the stream and looked down at the churning water. It had been raining for three days straight, and as soon as you opened the front door or a window you could hear the stream roiling. There was no need to lug pails back and forth any more – the water supply had been miraculously restored. Right after the For Sale notice had appeared at the end of the drive to Benlervie. Their own sign would be joining it soon.

Slowly, he turned and looked at the house.

Woodside. Their dream home.

He hated it now, although he knew that was irrational. The house, this place wasn't to blame. Bram had lost himself here, but that wasn't anything to do with Woodside. *He* was to blame. And, he supposed, David. *It's all Dad's fault* was Kirsty's constant refrain. He supposed she was right in that it was David's insidious, malign influence that had precipitated the horrendous chain of events that had led to that boy dying in their shed.

He made himself look at the shed.

He made himself think of Finn, crashing around, falling over, getting up again, trying to get to the window –

And all the time, the head wound Bram – no, David, and then Bram – had inflicted had been bleeding, bleeding away his lifeblood.

Just how hard had David hit him?

The police had questioned Fraser, Kirsty and Bram exhaustively. Small amounts of Finn's DNA had been found on the air rifle hidden in David's garage. The post mortem results had shown that Finn had originally been buried in the same type of soil as that around Woodside, soil with traces of weedkiller in it, and the vegetable patch had yielded an exact match. The theory DI Cromer seemed to be pursuing was that Fraser had buried Finn in the veg patch, then changed his mind, dug him back up, and taken Max's car to dump the body in the forest by the quarry. There were traces of Finn's DNA, somehow, in the car boot. But the witnesses in the forest hadn't been able to see who was in the car – it had been too far away.

Bram jumped as something wet nudged at his hand.

Bertie. He hadn't even noticed him approaching.

And now here was Max, slouching across the grass from the house in just a T-shirt and long shorts. He was going to get soaked, but Bram knew better than to say so.

Max was spending almost all his time in his room now. Overnight, he'd changed from a mature, personable young man into the sulky teenager he'd never been, avoiding his parents' company and vanishing, when he did venture outside, for hours at a time without explanation. Phoebe was also struggling. She would no longer watch 'scary' things on TV, and getting her to sleep in her own room was a nightly challenge.

And she had become completely paranoid about the Taylors.

Here she was now, running after Max. 'You forgot Bertie-cam!' She dropped to her knees on the wet grass to attach it to Bertie's collar, then stood, looking past Bram to the wood. 'Dad, could you come with me back to the house? Grannie's made flapjacks and she wants to do a taste test. And Max, as soon as Bertie's done his business, maybe you could come back too?'

'Right,' Max sneered, 'because *Oh no, look, there's Andrew Taylor, swinging an axe! And Cara with a shotgun! And Sylvia with a bazooka!*'

'Max!' Bram rapped out. 'That's *not funny!*'

'Yeah, tell me about it!'

Phoebe's lips trembled.

Bram put his hand on Phoebe's shoulder. 'Don't worry, *kleintje,*' he said for the umpteenth time. 'The Taylors know Grandad didn't kill Finn.'

Phoebe looked up at him with her big blue eyes. No matter how often they told her that the Taylors had moved out of Benlervie and would never be coming back, Phoebe was convinced that they were going to *come for revenge.*

'Yeah, everyone knows that except the stupid police and, it seems, his own stupid granddaughter,' Max spat, and Phoebe lifted up her head and howled.

AFTER BRAM HAD READ Max the riot act, he sulked in his room, refusing to come out for lunch with Linda. When it was time for Linda to leave – Kirsty was running her back into Grantown – Bram knocked on Max's door and, when there was no response, opened it and went in.

Max was sitting on his bed hunched over his laptop. He didn't look up.

'Grannie's leaving now, Max. Can you come down to say goodbye, please?'

Nothing.

'Max?'

'Piss off, Dad.'

Bram blinked. 'What?'

'You heard me.'

Who are you and what have you done with my son? Bram had no idea how to communicate with this new Max. 'Uh.' What on earth should he say? 'Well, Max, I don't imagine Grannie wants to see you if you're going to behave like this.'

Max finally looked up at him, and Bram's blood ran cold. Max was staring at him as if... yes, as if he *hated* him. The silence stretched on.

'Right. Come down when you've cooled off,' Bram ended up saying, pulling the door shut behind him.

BRAM MADE Max's favourite dinner of tacos with refried beans and a big salad. He set it out on the table and took off his apron. Phoebe plomped herself down on her chair and put a tomato into her mouth. Kirsty started filling glasses with water.

'No, I'll get him,' she said when Bram made for the stairs.

They tended to use a tag-team approach when it came to disciplining the kids. Not exactly good cop/bad cop – more a case of moving up the reserves to give the battle-weary front-line troops a break.

She was back down in thirty seconds. 'He's not in his room.'

A search of the house established that Max wasn't there. Bram had a quick look around outside – the rain had finally stopped, so it was likely Max had gone for a walk.

'Let's just start without him,' Kirsty said. 'He'll be back when he's hungry, which won't be long, knowing him.'

About an hour after they'd finished eating, when they were gathered round the TV, Kirsty's phone buzzed.

'Hi, Mum.' Her eyes widened as she listened. 'Right. Okay. Well, tell him we're not happy that he didn't tell us where he was going.'

She mouthed, 'Max is with them' at Bram.

'How... Oh, no, you mean he *hitch-hiked*? Can I speak to him?' A long pause. Phoebe was gazing at Kirsty with that virtuous look she assumed whenever Max was in trouble. 'Max. Are you okay?... What?... *What?* Don't you dare speak to me like – Max. Max!' She shook her head grimly at Bram.

Bram held out his hand for the phone. But when he put it to his ear and said, 'Max?', it was David's voice that replied.

'Bram. Listen, he's fine. He just wants to stay with us for a while.'

'To *stay* with you?'

Kirsty telegraphed to him frantically.

'I don't think that's a good idea, David. Can you put Max on?'

'He's not wanting to talk to you, Bram.' A sigh. 'Hold on.' Sounds of footsteps and a door opening and closing. 'Right. Truth is, Bram, we've got a problem. We need to talk. Man to man.'

'What sort of problem?'

'I'll come over – or no. Let's meet up somewhere. I would suggest the Inverluie Hotel bar, but I know it's not your favourite place in the world. How about Anagach? You know Anagach Wood, just outside the town?'

'Uh, yes, where you take Bertie?'

'That's the place. See you in the car park at the end of Forest Road in half an hour? At the start of the woodland walks? We can go for a ramble, have a bit of a chat.'

'Yes, okay then.'

He ended the call and told Kirsty what David had said.

'What does he mean by "a problem"?' Kirsty frowned.

'No idea.'

Phoebe sighed. 'Max is really going off the rails. Is he on drugs?'

Kirsty and Bram gaped at each other.

'What makes you say that?' said Kirsty weakly.

Phoebe shrugged. 'When teenagers go all weird, they're usually on drugs.'

What on earth had she been watching? As she skipped off to the kitchen, Kirsty urged, 'Go, Bram. Find out what's going on with Max and make him come back with you. Don't leave him with Dad. What if he decides he wants to stay with Mum and Dad permanently?'

'That's not going to happen.' Bram put a confidence into his voice he didn't feel.

Just what *was* going on with Max?

27

D avid appeared from the trees as Bram parked the Discovery in the tiny car park at the end of the tarmacked road, where the Speyside Way footpath met the woodland walks through Anagach Wood. Good – he hadn't brought Bertie. This was going to be traumatic enough without having to keep track of the dog. There was only one other vehicle, but it wasn't David's Subaru – presumably he had come on foot.

'Where's Max?' Bram asked as he pulled on his walking boots.

'Back at the house.' David was jigging from one foot to the other impatiently. 'Let's go, Bram.'

'Okay, okay.' Bram quickly tied his laces and they set off along the wide, well-maintained path into the wood. Despite all the rain, it wasn't too muddy, at this point anyway. 'Which walk shall we do?'

'The one that goes to Mid Anagach.' It wasn't a suggestion.

Bram wasn't sure where that was, but he nodded. 'David, do we have to do this? Can't we just go back to the house and talk with Max?'

David didn't respond, just marched off under the overhanging boughs of the trees.

Bram trotted after him.

For a while they walked in silence. It was a beautiful, wild place, the air heavy with pine resin. The sky had cleared and the sun was low in the sky, casting a warm evening glow over the tops of the trees. Soon they had left the deciduous trees behind and were in the pinewood proper, the path meandering through the heathery undergrowth, the massive old pine trees towering above them seeming to shelter the smaller ones, their offspring, that grew naturally, self-seeded, all around. Great for wildlife. If Max had been here he would have been on the look-out for capercaillie, the big turkey-like bird that was the largest member of the grouse family and critically endangered in the UK, although this was one of its strongholds.

Or would he?

He'd probably just have shambled along with his head down.

'David,' Bram said at last. 'Are we going to talk or not?'

'Oh, we're going to talk, all right.'

David marched on ahead, as if he was alone, never looking back to check that Bram was still following. Embarrassingly, Bram was soon puffing. David set quite a pace. Bram made an effort to catch up, and, where the path widened as it came out into a heathery clearing, he came alongside David.

'What's this "problem" with Max?'

David shook his head, his mouth a thin line. Then he suddenly stopped, rounding on Bram and getting right in his face. 'I hope you're proud of yourself. You've really messed that boy up.'

Bram stepped back. 'What do you mean?'

For a moment David just stared into Bram's eyes, his chest visibly rising and falling. Then his face contorted in a sneer, and he marched on ahead, leaving Bram to trot after him. God almighty. What on earth did he mean by that? In what way was Max 'messed up'? Was he talking about the whole Finn trauma, the police interrogation? But how could David know that Bram had anything to do with Finn's death? No, he must be talking about something else.

They'd been walking in silence for about quarter of an hour when David suddenly struck off the main path onto a much smaller, muddier one – was it in fact a proper path, or just a deer track? – and Bram's boots slipped around on the slick surface.

'Uh, aren't we supposed to stick to the paths so as not to disturb the capercaillies?'

'This *is* a path,' David snapped, not looking round.

As well as the mud, there were heather roots to negotiate, black, slippery trip hazards crossing the path, but David didn't break stride.

'David,' said Bram in the end, exasperated. 'I thought you wanted to talk?'

He turned. 'Aye, but not where any bastard could hear us.'

Bram gestured at their surroundings. There wasn't a sound except for the wind in the tops of the tall pines. Not a soul around. 'Isn't this private enough for you?'

David, hands on hips in Henry VIII pose, scanned the path behind and in front of them, and nodded. 'Okay.' He took his phone from his pocket. 'Max wanted to help me out. See if he could find something that would exonerate me. You'd said the cameras were stolen a couple of days before the night Finn was killed, although, weirdly, you didn't report this to the police. Max decided to see if they'd picked anything up. Maybe someone suspicious hanging around. Maybe one of Finn's dodgy mates. The real killer. Something that might get DI Cromer off my back.'

Bram had gone cold. 'But – with the cameras gone, how could Max check any footage that might have been on them?'

'The cloud.' David's unwavering gaze seemed to bore into Bram's head. 'He looked on the cloud.'

Bram couldn't speak.

He and Kirsty weren't tech-savvy. They tended to leave any IT stuff to Max who, like most of his generation, seemed to have absorbed his knowledge of it through osmosis. Bram hadn't even thought about cloud storage. He remembered, now, Max burbling on, when Bram had moved the cameras from the wood to the house, about how this meant they were now in range of the Wi-Fi, but Bram hadn't thought through what that meant.

It meant that all the footage taken near the house had been stored, through the Wi-Fi, on the cloud.

Wordlessly, David handed him his phone.

On the screen were infrared images of two figures, one holding the other, moving in a sort of macabre dance, the shorter of the two shaking the other, whose floppy head was flung back, again and again, to bounce –

To bounce off the wall of the shed.

It was Bram, bashing Finn's head against the hose bracket.

As he watched, Finn flopped to the ground and Bram stood looking down at him, then stooped and put his hands to Finn's head. Not to try to help him, not to try to staunch the blood, but to roughly pull off the mask. Finn's face immediately glowed brighter as the mask was removed, and the residual heat gave the mask in Bram's hand form, briefly, a dull orange face with dark circles for eyes and a dark leering mouth, before the heat dissipated in the night air and only a ghostly imprint of it remained.

Bram watched as the glowing alien version of himself moved off screen, and all that was left was the glowing shape of Finn lying on the ground. Glowing as brightly as ever.

Then Bram was back with another person.

Kirsty.

The two figures dragged the third into the shed.

Bram continued to stare at the screen as the glowing white and yellow shapes of himself and Kirsty – glowing brighter now, for some reason – left the shed and disappeared.

It was the end of the clip.

David snatched back the phone and switched it off.

'I – we–' Bram swallowed. 'I didn't mean to kill him!'

'Keep your bloody voice down!'

'He came for me. You must have seen, on the footage just before the bit where – where I'm pushing him back against the shed – he came for me. And then… I lost it. But I didn't mean to kill him.'

Max had seen this. He'd gone onto the cloud hoping to see some random thug prowling about, and been confronted with *this*. His own father battering the boy to death, and then both his parents concealing the body in the shed… He must have found the footage today and fled the house, gone to his grandad.

Oh, Max!

'You killed him,' spat David. 'And then you dragged Kirsty into it, you made her an *accessory*, you made her help you hide that lad's dead body in the shed and then – what? You buried him in the veg patch? Then decided to dump him further afield?' He snorted. 'Talk about bloody incompetence! And then you let Max be arrested! You let *me* be arrested! No – you *engineered* my arrest!'

'All we did was show the police the petcam footage,' Bram got out.

With a look of disgust, David turned on his heel and marched off down the path.

Bram ran after him. 'What are you going to do? Are you going to the police? Is Max – Is he all right?'

'Of course he's not *all right*!' David flung over his shoulder, not stopping, not slowing down.

Oh *God*.

Bram followed him. The path wound into a thicket of trees where it was difficult to see the path, the trees blocking out the low evening light, and Bram slipped and fell onto his side. By the time he'd picked himself up, David had disappeared.

Oh God, oh God!

He had to persuade David not to go to the police. And he'd have to talk to Max, explain what had happened.

He scrambled down the path where it headed off downhill, and then he was coming out of the trees onto a narrow tarmacked road. He could see David ahead, striding off into the gloom cast by tall pines. He hurried after him, but as they came in sight of a house, David turned to snarl: 'Keep your mouth shut!'

So they kept walking along the road in tense silence. On one side was a band of trees beyond which Bram got glimpses of fields. Where were they? Did this road lead back to the car park? In one way he wanted this nightmare of a walk to end, but in another he wanted it to go on forever because what was waiting at the end of it? An excruciating talk with Max. With Linda, he supposed. And then the police...

What the hell was going to happen?

There were more houses strung along the road, and then they were at a junction with another road, where David turned left and went on a few paces before stopping and wheeling round to face him. 'Of course I'm not going to the police,' he hissed, his face contorted with rage. 'How can I, when you've got Kirsty mixed up in it? I dob you in, that's my wee girl going down for what she did. What *you made her do!*'

Bram took a step back.

But David just shook his head in disgust and marched off.

Bram watched him disappearing into the dusk.

He had to make David understand. Surely, after what had happened with Owen, David could understand what it was like to be caught up in a moment of madness? But it was hopeless trying to reason with him when he was in this mood.

Coward.

As if his mood was going to get any better any time soon.

Unless Bram could explain.

He made himself start walking again, after David. Into the gloom of the trees and then out again. The sun was setting now, all the colours of the rainbow streaking the sky, making David's bald head glow a weird orange. He had stopped and seemed to be waiting for him. Bram could hear the roar of traffic – they must be near the A95. He passed between a pair of bollards and up an incline in the road, which had become less of a road and more of a track at this point, grass encroaching on either side. And then he realised where they were.

That wasn't traffic he could hear. It was water, roaring under them.

There were on a bridge.

Oh Christ! Was this the Old Bridge of Spey? Where David had killed Owen?

David was shaking his head. 'You say Finn came at you.'

'He did!' Bram looked around them, but there was no one else in sight. Should he make a run for it? But David, despite the age difference, was much fitter than Bram. He would catch him. And anyway, why would David intend him any harm? Okay so he was angry, but surely not homicidally so?

'And so you killed him.'

'I keep trying to tell you: I didn't mean to! The same thing happened as when you encountered him, and hit him with the rifle. It wasn't like I even meant to... to *assault* him. There was a fight. In the heat of the moment... I suppose I went too far. Obviously I went too far... bashing his... his head off the shed like that.'

'Until he was dead.'

It wouldn't help matters to bring up the whole he-wasn't-actually-dead thing. The clip had ended after Bram and Kirsty had dragged Finn's body – what they'd thought at the time was his dead body – into the shed. Presumably Max had stopped watching at that point.

Bram nodded.

'Until he was dead?' David repeated.

'Yes.' The word came out as a groan.

David's expression seemed to change.

In the low light, Bram thought he was smiling – but surely not?

'Thanks, Bram.' He held something up in his hand. His phone. David's voice came from it, tinny and distorted:

'*You say Finn came at you.*'

And then Bram's own voice:

'*He did!*'

'And so you killed him.'

'I keep trying to tell you: I didn't mean to!'

David stabbed a finger at the phone to cut the recording and pocketed it. 'That should do the trick. We don't want the police seeing that footage, after all, do we? Not with Kirsty on there. Now they won't have to.'

Bram felt his legs weaken, and backed up against one of the bollards. 'Okay.' He took a huge breath. 'But please, David… Let me go to the police myself, and tell them what happened. I'll leave Kirsty out of it.'

David took three steps to close the distance between them, and Bram shrank back, but David put an arm round his shoulders, giving him a shake. 'Good man.'

Bram let out the breath he'd been holding.

And then he was staggering in David's arms, trying to break free as David hauled him across the bridge.

'No! Oh, God, no! David! David?'

David half-lifted him.

Slammed him down on the parapet.

His back exploded in pain.

Bram was shrieking, he was clawing ineffectually at David's jacket, he was shouting something, he was trying to rip his arms free of David's grip. The sound of the water below was so loud it seemed to be inside Bram's head, and David was yelling over it, yelling into his face:

'You'd never withstand a police interrogation, would you? Once they started asking about your movements?' He screwed up his face, putting on a high voice. *'And didn't your wife realise you were gone half the night, Mr Hendriksen, disposing of an inconvenient corpse?* You'd land Kirsty right in it, guaranteed, whether you meant to or not. You fucking useless *twat!'*

'No! No, I wouldn't!' Bram babbled desperately, twisting in David's grip.

'This way's better. Poor Bram lost it after I'd got the confession out of him. Broke down and ran off. No idea what happened to him after that.'

'But they'll know!' The words came out as a whimper. 'After what happened to Owen, they'll know!'

'But they *don't* know what happened to Owen, do they?'

'Kirsty will tell them!'

'Yeah, grief does weird things to people, eh? Poor Kirsty's out of her mind. But she'll get over it. She'll soon see she's better off without a useless wee parasite latched on her back, sucking the lifeblood out of her.'

His mouth widened in a grin as he heaved at Bram, and Bram felt his feet leave the ground, the solid stone parapet under him slip away as the top half of his body was pushed out into space, nothing under it, and when he tried to throw himself forwards, back onto the bridge, David flung his whole bodyweight at him, and there was nothing for Bram to hold on to but David himself.

His only hope now was David, that solid, muscled body, and he clung to it.

He locked his fingers round the hard biceps.

But still he was falling, still he was falling backwards.

Out into space.

But he didn't let go.

So as he fell, David fell with him.

Then there was another explosion of pain as his body smacked down on the water, as it closed over his head, as it flooded into his nose and mouth. And now it was David who clung to Bram, the two of them tumbling over and over in the churning river, and he felt another blow, to his shoulder, and kicked desperately with his legs, desperately pushed his head above the surface as they were dragged by the current under one of the arches of the bridge and spat out at the other side.

Cold.

So cold.

All the warmth had been sucked from his body and he was shaking, his teeth knocking together, his chest cramping so whenever his head broke the surface he could only manage tiny gulps of air.

He was going to drown!

But into Bram's head came the words of the instructor on the wild swimming course:

If you fall into a fast-flowing river…

Don't fight the current. Go with it.

But David was pulling at him in panic, and his head went under again.

Flip onto your back.

Get your feet pointing downstream.

He managed to roll, in the churning water, onto his back, but David hauled him so he kept on rolling, buffeted and sucked under by the current.

'Can't… swim!' David's voice rasped in his ear as they resurfaced before they both went back under, David pulling him around and down so both their bodies were tipped over and over in the dark water until Bram didn't know which way was up, and there was freezing water in his nose and mouth, and the blackness was coming.

With the last vestiges of his strength, he pushed David away. Kicked out at him.

And now he was free, and as he flailed his frozen limbs, as he forced his body up to the surface, his nose and mouth up into the air, as he gasped it, *air*, he saw David's head in the water in front of him, just out of reach, bobbing away from him, the smooth, pale baldness of it standing out in the dark water. He flipped onto his back and pointed his feet downstream, his head lifted by the force of the current so, finally, he could breathe.

He tried to angle himself to follow David, to let the current sweep him in the same direction, but the pale bald head was gone. He couldn't see it any more.

Fill your lungs with as much air as possible for buoyancy.

He gulped in more air, spluttering as he inhaled water with it.

Look around you for calm water.

There were often eddies by the banks of a river where the water turned back on itself and cancelled out the force of the current, creating little pockets of safety. He got a hand up to his face to swipe the water from his eyes, squinting through the film distorting his vision, trying to keep his head still as his body was shaken and jarred by the current swirling around him.

There wasn't enough light. He couldn't see anything but the roiling water and the indistinct bank of the river, to his left, flashing past.

He would just have to take a chance and head for the bank.

Get onto your front and swim diagonally across the current, not at right angles to it.

Bram hadn't been in a pool for weeks. Months.

But he was a strong swimmer.

He could do this.

The instructor on that course in Wales had said Bram had an excellent technique, one of the best he'd seen.

He was a bloody good swimmer!

He pushed his head up out of the water and took a long breath before flipping onto his front and starting to swim, powering himself through the water, still going downstream but easing himself across the current towards the bank. His muscles protested, his limbs weak and so cold he could hardly feel them, could hardly tell where they were in the water.

But the muscle memory was there. His body knew what to do.

And then, before it seemed possible, he was scrabbling with his hands at the earthy bank, at the vegetation; he was hauling himself out of the water and flopping on the ground, lungs heaving, limbs shaking, coughing water up onto the wet grass.

28

'I'm glad he's dead!' sobbed Kirsty again, as if trying to convince herself that this was true.

Bram said nothing.

He was sitting naked on the edge of the bed while Kirsty gently towelled his bruised chest and back. She hadn't let him out of her sight since he'd got back, bathing him like a child, insisting he stay in the hot bath until he was warm.

He barely remembered how he'd found his way back to the car in the dim light of dusk. He must somehow have managed to retrace his steps along the road and up the path into Anagach Wood. He could only remember meeting one person, a woman walking a little dog near the car park, who had looked at him curiously, but he hadn't felt up to offering an explanation for why he was trudging along in soaking wet clothes.

He'd been trembling so much, by the time he'd got back to the car, that he had had great difficulty extracting the car key from his pocket, and God knew how he'd managed to drive home. That was a blur too.

When he'd got back to Woodside he'd found he

couldn't move, he couldn't get out of the car, and eventually Kirsty had come down the verandah steps and opened the driver's door and said something, but he hadn't been able to speak. She'd somehow got him upstairs and into the bath without Phoebe seeing him. And when the shaking had stopped, when his brain had started to unfreeze itself, he had been able to tell her what had happened.

And now she dressed him, like a child, talking to him firmly but gently, telling him to lift his arms, guiding them into the sleeves of his T-shirt, his warm cashmere jumper. As she tied the laces of his trainers, she asked him, 'Did anyone see you and Dad together?'

It was an effort to speak. 'I don't know. I don't think so.'

'Okay.' Kirsty took his hands in hers. 'Everything's going to be okay. You went to meet Dad at Anagach, but he wasn't there. You came home and tried calling him. We should do that now. Where's your phone?'

'In the car.'

She came back with the phone and made Bram call David and leave a message.

'And Mum called before, wondering if I'd heard from you. I said the pair of you had probably gone for a drink… I'll have to call her back. Oh *God*! I'll have to say you wandered about for ages looking for him… You forgot your phone so you couldn't call him…' She fell silent, staring off. Obviously thinking about Linda.

Bram sobbed: 'I'm sorry. I'm so sorry.'

'He tried to kill you! *You've* nothing to be sorry for!'

'What are we going to say to Max? What are we going to do? Should we go and get him?'

'Mum will need to report Dad missing. And then – Bram, I'd like her to come and live with us. Wherever we move to.'

Linda! *Oh, poor Linda!*

'Of course.'

'We'll need to tell Max about Finn. That you didn't mean to kill him. We can delete the footage from the cloud. Dad's phone... The footage was on Dad's phone, and there's your confession on there too, but maybe his body will never be found. Or if it is, the phone will be too waterlogged to work.' A silence. 'If it does work...' She caught herself up. 'But we can only deal with the things we can control. And hope for the best.' She nodded, and repeated quietly, as if to herself: 'Hope for the best.'

FOR TWO DAYS they lived in a terrible kind of limbo while the police searched for David in Anagach Wood. The sniffer dogs seemed to pick up a trail but then lost it again. Fraser and his mates assisted with the search, as did Bram, Kirsty, Max and Linda. Linda walked the paths through the wood with Bertie and Kirsty, and Kirsty said it was one of the hardest things she'd ever done, pretending to Linda that there was still hope.

When she wasn't helping with the search, Linda moved about the house like a ghost, hardly speaking, her sightless eyes seeming to accuse Bram whenever she turned to him. Phoebe was unnaturally quiet too, bursting into tears at random moments.

Max, presumably in deference to Linda, was behaving impeccably.

It was like living with a polite stranger.

Bram longed to be able to talk to him about that cloud footage, but if he had supposedly not met David at Anagach Wood, there was no way he could know about it. They had decided that it would be too suspicious to suddenly confess to Max about Finn's death

right after David had gone to meet Bram to show him
the cloud footage, so were waiting for Max to bring it up
himself. If he didn't do so soon, though, they would
have to broach the subject, regardless.

And then Scott called round to tell them that David's
body had been found, several miles downriver from
Grantown. The theory was that David had arrived early
for his meeting with Bram, gone off to look at the river
in spate, and somehow fallen in.

They needed someone to look at the body and identify it.

'I'll do it,' said Bram at once.

'I'll come with you,' said Linda dazedly.

He had prepared himself for David's face to be a
mess after being bashed about in the water, but, apart
from a pasty, doughy appearance and some bruises, it
was remarkably unchanged, so much so that Bram
could almost imagine his eyes opening, his mouth
moving as it framed an accusation, the muscly body
propelling itself off the gurney, hands reaching for
Bram's throat –

Linda stood quietly until Bram said, 'Yes, it's him,'
and then she asked if she could touch his face. Bram had
to turn away at that point. It took all he had to master
his emotions, to put his arm around Linda, when she
was ready to leave, and speak hollow words of comfort.

That evening, after Linda, numb with shock, had
gone early to bed, Max asked if he could speak to Kirsty
and Bram, and they all sat down at the kitchen table.
Bram's heart was pounding, but he managed to offer
coffee without his voice sounding too strange.

'No, thanks,' said Max politely. 'Dad, could you
come and sit down?'

Bram obediently subsided onto a kitchen chair.

'Did you kill Grandad?'

Time seemed to slow right down. Bram was aware of the fridge chuntering; a weird buzzing in his ears; his own breath filling his lungs.

'No,' he said at last.

'But you did meet him, didn't you?' Max's tone was flat. 'You know about the cloud footage. You know – you know that *I* know about Finn. That you killed him.'

Bram nodded. Expelled the air he'd been holding in his lungs.

He tried to explain, and Max heard Bram's halting recitation in silence, just saying, at the end, 'I know you wouldn't have meant to kill Finn, Dad. And I get that you only let them arrest me because you knew they could have no evidence against me. But Grandad... You were going to stitch up Grandad?'

'Yes, we were,' said Kirsty. 'He hit Finn too, Max. It could have been those blows that killed him. And Grandad – he'd killed before and got away with it.' Her mouth twisted. 'He killed Owen. My boyfriend when I was at school.'

Kirsty told Max about Owen, and suddenly it was obviously too much. Max jumped up from his chair, sending it crashing back onto the slate floor, and then he was striding across the Walton Room to the front door.

'Max!' called Bram.

At the door, Max stopped and turned. His chest was heaving.

Bram ran to him, but when he reached him Max stepped back. 'Don't worry. I've deleted the footage from the cloud and my phone. And Scott says Grandad's phone is knackered – been in the water too long. So you're good. It's all good.'

'Max–' But what could he say?

Max was looking at him coldly. 'Seems the police are thinking Grandad killed Finn, and Fraser covered it up.

Now Grandad's dead, the investigation will probably fizzle out eventually. It won't be a priority for them, with the probable culprit dead.'

Kirsty had joined them at the door. She reached out a hand, tentatively, to touch Max's arm, and he let her but didn't respond in any way.

'It will all be okay,' Kirsty got out. 'All we need to do is say nothing.'

'Yeah,' said Max, looking from her to Bram with an awful little smile. 'Yeah. I get it.'

29

B ram didn't want to let go of Kirsty's hand. They were standing in the car park, the two of them, holding tight to each other's hands like scared children. Bram had never really liked Aviemore. It was a tourist village, and the long, modern, ugly main street stretching to either side was full of outdoor clothing shops and cafés and gift shops against the incongruously spectacular backdrop of the Cairngorms. This morning, though, it was a happy confusion of tourist coaches and cars and people in brightly coloured jackets. He wished he could stay standing here forever.

'But think of the kids,' Kirsty burst out, squeezing his hand even tighter.

'I *am* thinking of the kids.' Bram had to go. He had to let go of her hand and turn and walk away across this car park. 'What kind of message would I be giving Max, if I let this go on any longer? That it's okay to – to do what I did, and let someone else take the blame? If we make him cover this up for us, he'll come to hate us, as you hated David. And for good reason.'

Kirsty shook her head. 'He doesn't want you to do this!'

But the only thing stopping Bram from running back to the car with her and jumping in and roaring out of here was the thought of Max's face, the way Max had looked at him, when he had explained what he was going to do now.

'No, Dad!' he had sobbed, but his face...

There had been devastation there, desolation, but also relief, a dropping away of a burden no boy of eighteen should have to bear. It had been the way Max used to look at Bram when he was little, when something had frightened or upset him and he'd run to his dad, his face contorted, but his eyes... his eyes so full of trust, so full of certainty that Bram would know what to say and what to do to make it right.

He let go of Kirsty's hand. Gently, he kissed her, he pulled her close, as on the street someone laughed, a coach full of tourists chugged by, the world kept turning.

And then he left her there.

He walked into the police station.

He asked to speak to DI Scott Sinclair.

And when Scott had shown him into a boxy little room and gestured for him to sit on the other side of the table, Bram didn't sit, he remained standing, he looked Scott in the eye, and he spoke the words that had been fighting, every second of every day since that terrible night, to be released.

'I killed him. I killed Finn Taylor.'

EPILOGUE

This was Kirsty's night-time ritual, now: going round the house pulling the curtains across the windows. They were deep-set little windows, with the original Victorian sash-and-case frames – each one a picture, showing dusk gathering in the old orchard that surrounded the house. A late dusk, of course, this far north in summer. Mum and Phoebe were already in bed and the light had only just begun to fade. The walls were thick, so the windowsills were deep, and on each one she had arranged a collection of pretty things – tiny blue and green glass bottles, an old stoneware jug, a vase with roses from the garden, a papier-mâché elephant Phoebe had made at school.

Little Knowes Croft couldn't have been more different from Woodside.

Built in 1802, it was on a miniature scale, with small, cosy rooms and low ceilings. Perfect for hunkering down over the winter, when the four of them, Max, Phoebe, Mum and Kirsty, had seemed to want nothing more than to light the fire and put the TV on and sit here together, Phoebe cuddled between Kirsty and Mum on the sofa, Max in the chair or stretched on the hearth rug.

Kirsty had sold most of their old furniture and bought new stuff, mainly antiques to suit the cottage, at auctions and on eBay. She was particularly fond of the grandfather clock which just fitted into the low-ceilinged living room, ticking away now companionably.

The sale of Woodside had funded the purchase of Little Knowes Croft with plenty to spare, although they'd got much less for Woodside than it was worth because of its associations with Finn Taylor's death. But they had enough money in the bank to allow Kirsty to work only part time, to pick and choose the less stressful clients, the work that interested her, and let her spend more time with Mum and the kids.

Bram was so pleased about that.

He'd decorated his cell with the photographs Max had taken of Little Knowes, usually photobombed by Phoebe or Bertie or both. When Kirsty, sitting across the table from him in that awful prison visiting room, had sobbed that she felt so bad that he had never even seen Little Knowes, that it couldn't seem like home to him, he had smiled. 'Of course it does. My home is wherever you are. You and the kids.'

This would be another good photograph for Max to take for Bram, she decided: the view through the tiny window next to the fireplace, from which you could see an old apple tree and the hedge, and the slate roof of Sebastopol, the tiny neighbouring croft house. Bram loved that name, and the fact that it dated the cottage so precisely to the Crimean War, to the 1850s. A veteran from that war, Bram speculated, had come home and built himself a little croft, and settled down to hoe vegetables and keep hens and a cow and a pig, and

never have to fight again. Had the name Sebastopol
been a sort of boast, a reminder to his neighbours that
here in their midst was a war hero? Or had the name
been a reminder of what was now behind him, a
reminder to be thankful, every waking hour, that he was
here and not there?

Bram had been sentenced to eight years but had
already served one and would be home in another three,
all being well. He was in Porterfield Prison in Inverness,
just an hour's drive away.

The conviction had been for manslaughter, not
murder, given that Finn had been terrorising the family
for weeks and Bram had, at least initially, been in fear of
his life. He'd got the higher end of the sentencing range,
though, because he'd left Finn for dead in the shed and
failed to call an ambulance, and then perverted the
course of justice by disposing of the body and trying to
cover up what had happened.

He had kept Kirsty out of it completely. Kirsty had
no idea, he claimed, what he had done. Because Bram
had pled guilty there had been no trial, only a
sentencing hearing, and it had felt so wrong, sitting
there in court listening to Bram take everything on
himself. He had stood there so bravely in the dark grey
suit she had pressed for him, the new white shirt, the
blue tie he had worn at their wedding. Her Bram. Her
wonderful Bram. There was no one in the world
like him.

She had thought, when she'd first met him in those
bleak early days in the halls of residence, that he was
like Scott – a good person, a person with integrity – but
she'd had no idea just *how* good Bram Hendriksen was,
how selfless and modest and funny and kind and
loving.

She had wanted to jump up and tell the sheriff all

that, tell him what a good man Bram was, how he had always looked after her and the kids, and that was what he was doing now.

But of course she hadn't.

Bram had told the police the truth about what had happened to Dad, not expecting to be believed, but after Dad's body had been found, a witness had come forward who had seen Dad attacking Bram on the bridge. This witness had been a couple of years below Dad at school, been bullied by him, and gone in terror of him ever since. There was no way he was going to try to intervene – or even tell the police what he'd seen, until it had been confirmed that David McKechnie was dead.

Kirsty felt herself tensing up whenever she thought about Dad and what he had done. What he had been. She had loved him, of course she had, and he had loved her – but his love had been a fierce thing, his need to protect her so all-consuming that it had come close to destroying her life, not once but twice.

After Owen's murder, Kirsty had been terrified to start another relationship in case Dad turned against her new boyfriend too. When she and Bram had married, though, and started their lives together in London, it had seemed possible that it would be okay. Once Dad got to know Bram, surely everything would be fine?

She still couldn't believe that Dad had *tried to kill Bram*!

Her stomach plummeted.

But she'd promised Bram she wouldn't dwell on that.

Onwards and upwards was his new motto. Against all her expectations, Bram seemed to be adjusting well to life behind bars. All her fears that he wouldn't cope had proved groundless, and really, she should have antici-pated that he'd be fine. He was so much stronger than his easy-going personality suggested. And people liked Bram. Even those scary criminals liked him, and Kirsty had helped the process along by chatting to other prisoners' partners and parents in the waiting room, laying it on thick about how their kids, one only nine years old, had been threatened by the yob Bram had accidentally killed. And he had a lovely cellmate, an older man who was in for fraud, whom Bram was teaching to play the guitar.

Kirsty made herself a cup of cocoa and one for Max, and opened the back door to call him in. He was in the tiny garage that faced the side of the cottage across the gravel drive. The garage was a wooden 1920s original, far too small for the Discovery, so they'd had it insulated and Max and Phoebe shared it as a 'studio'. Max had partitioned part of it off as a dark room, and the walls of the rest of it were covered in his photos and Phoebe's artwork. Max had got a taste for photography after he'd started documenting their lives in pictures for his dad, and was now experimenting with old-fashioned film as well as digital.

The double doors were standing open, and there were moths fluttering in the light cast by the bare bulb hanging from the ceiling. Max was hunched over his laptop adjusting the light in a photograph of a sparrow. He straightened when Kirsty came into the garage, and smiled, and took the mug of cocoa from her.

'Thanks, Mum.'

She was going to miss him so much!

His gap year was happening, although it had been a struggle to persuade him to go ahead with it; a struggle to persuade him that she and Phoebe would be fine without him.

'Looks like Phoebe's burning the midnight oil again,' he said, nodding up at the window of his sister's bedroom, which was glowing yellow. 'Or the ten o'clock oil, at least.'

Phoebe, never a good sleeper, had been particularly restless in the last week or two. Kirsty knew she was dreading Max's departure in September as much as she was.

While Max returned to his photograph, Kirsty went over to the table against the wall where Phoebe created her artwork. There was a big pile of completed drawings, and Kirsty smiled as she saw that the top one was an ambitious attempt to capture Grannie and Bertie in motion. Bertie looked like a small cow, and Grannie's right leg, stretched out in front of her to take a step, was twice as long as her left one. This would bring a smile to Bram's face. She'd ask Phoebe if she could give it to him next time she visited the prison.

She started to look through the rest of the pile. Phoebe's medium of choice was usually felt-tips, but she had been experimenting with the vividly coloured oil crayons Mum had bought her. There was one of the cottage, with Mum, Kirsty, Max, Phoebe and Bertie each at a window. Bram would like this one too. Then a stormy scene with a shipwreck and two pirate ships which seemed to be rescuing the casualties. Then a rather scary clown. Then –

Oh God, it was the 'psychopath'. The same leering face as Phoebe had drawn on her notice, where she'd depicted him shooting at Bertie. This time, his face was framed in a window.

As she flipped to the next picture, she was aware of Max speaking. Of a moth landing on the sleeve of her top. Of a car engine, faintly, somewhere far in the distance, moving away on a descending note.

She muttered something about going to check on Phoebe and snatched up the pile of drawings. She ran back inside, the sheets of paper clutched to her chest, and up the steep little stairs to Phoebe's bedroom in the eaves. Phoebe was standing by the window in her Snoopy pyjamas, bare feet cold-looking on the wooden floor. Kirsty set the drawings down on top of the chest of drawers and ushered Phoebe back to bed. Then she went to the window and pulled the curtains across it.

'Phoebe,' she said, sitting down on the bed. 'I was looking at your drawings in the garage and – I found this.'

Phoebe took the drawing from her and frowned at it.

It showed the 'psychopath' lying on the ground in a pool of blood, his mouth turned down in a sad face. Behind him was a shed, and two figures had each lifted one of his feet and seemed to be dragging him towards it. One of the figures' hair was shoulder-length and black, the other's short and brown.

Kirsty and Bram.

Dragging Finn to the shed.

'What's this?' Kirsty got out.

Phoebe bit her lip. 'It's – Finn.'

'And me and Dad?'

A nod.

Kirsty struggled to control her breathing. Struggled to ask, levelly: 'You saw us?'

'Yeah. I was woken up by a noise from outside and I went to the window and I saw...' She looked up at Kirsty, her blue eyes wide. 'I saw the psychopath. Then I saw Dad fighting him.'

'Oh, Phoebe!' Kirsty took her hand.

The small fingers squeezed Kirsty's. 'I was so scared that the psychopath was going to kill Dad, but I couldn't do anything, all I did was stand there and watch. I didn't even shout for help.'

'You must have been in shock. That's what happens – you sort of freeze.'

'Then Dad went away and the psychopath was lying on the ground. I hoped he was dead.' Her voice wobbled. 'Then I saw you and Dad pull him into the shed and then leave again. You shut the shed door *but you didn't lock it*. The key had fallen onto the grass – I saw Dad drop it.' A sob escaped. 'I was watching the shed and then – and then – *his face was there*! At the window! And you hadn't locked the door and he was going to get out!'

'Oh, Phoebe, darling!' Kirsty gathered her in her arms and rocked her as she sobbed. 'It's all right now. Everything's all right now.' The drawings must have been Phoebe's way of telling them what she'd seen. What she knew.

Phoebe cried for a long time, and then subsided back on the bed. Kirsty got a washcloth to wipe her face, and a towel to dry it. Then she sat by the bed, stroking Phoebe's hot head and murmuring reassurances.

'I went outside,' Phoebe whispered. 'I got my torch and ran out and found the key on the grass. I was going to padlock the door but I needed to check he was still in there so I very very carefully opened the door and looked in. I shone my torch in the gap in the door and I saw him. The psychopath. He was lying on the boxes next to the window. There was blood on the back of his head. I got Dad's hammer from the wall of the shed and I hit him. Maybe five times. Where the blood was on his head. Where he was already hurt.' She reached up to touch the back of her own head to indicate the place. 'Grandad said you have to hit them where they're already hurt.'

For a long moment, Kirsty couldn't speak. Then:

'When did Grandad tell you that?' she found herself saying.

'He didn't tell *me* – he told Max, when he was showing him what to do if someone was fighting him. So that's what I did. I hit him on his head where it was already all blood. His arms and legs were going like this.' She pushed down the covers and twitched her arms and legs about. 'Then I hit him two more times, really hard, and he didn't move any more after that. He was dead then, wasn't he, Mum?'

Kirsty had a sudden memory of the shed, of the blood spatters all over the walls, on the ceiling... Of course. That couldn't have been caused by Finn himself, stumbling about. That had been caused by an attack. By a weapon connecting with a bloodied wound.

'Then I locked the door and put the key under the stone. Was it...' Phoebe blinked. 'Was it *manslaughter*, what I did, like Dad's in jail for? If the police find out, will I go to jail too? I hid the hammer. I hid it in my bag and then when I was at Grannie and Grandad's I took it to a bin on the street. And my pyjamas. They had blood on them.'

Kirsty shook her head, and pulled the covers back up round Phoebe gently, as if to cocoon her from it, from this terrible truth that seemed to press in on them from all sides. 'Listen, darling. You must never, *ever* tell anyone else about this. Not even Dad or Max or Grannie. This has to be something only you and me know about.'

'So I won't get in trouble?' Phoebe whispered.

'That's right. You won't get in any trouble if it's just our secret. You have to forget about it, as if it never happened. As if it was a bad dream.' Her fingers stroking Phoebe's hair were trembling.

'Okay, Mum,' said Phoebe, with a little smile. 'It was just a bad dream.'

Kirsty, numbly, took her hand. 'You were only nine years old. You didn't understand what was happening. You didn't mean to hurt him.'

'Yes, I did. I'm glad Finn's dead so he can't hurt Dad or Bertie or Max or the crows again. He was a psychopath. He had it coming.'

Kirsty made a wordless sound and stood, but still she clung on to Phoebe's hand, still she squeezed it, offering a reassurance that, it seemed, her daughter did not need.

He had it coming.

It was what Dad had said about Owen.

It was what he'd said about Finn. And, in the days leading up to Finn's death: 'He's got it coming,' she could remember him saying about the intruder, in Phoebe's hearing. Not once, but several times.

Oh no.

Oh God.

It was as if he was in the room with them, an unseen, triumphant presence.

Dad.

THE CHILD WHO NEVER WAS

Her child has been taken. But no-one believes her.
Sarah's beautiful baby son Oliver has gone missing.
And she will do anything – anything – to get him back.
But there's a problem. Everyone around Sarah, even her
beloved identical twin, Evie, tells her she never had a
son, that he's a figment of her imagination, that she's not
well, she needs help.

And on one level, they're right, Sarah does need support. She has suffered massive trauma in the past and now she's severely agoraphobic, very rarely leaves the house, avoids all contact with people.
But fragile though she is, Sarah knows deep in her heart that Oliver is real, that the love she feels for him is true. And that can only mean one thing – someone has been planning this. And now they've taken her baby.

GET THE BOOK NOW

Please continue reading for a special preview of The Child Who Never Was.

PROLOGUE

The biggest risk, of course, was that some busybody would see the smoke and in due course mention it to the police. In fact, she wouldn't put it past the village busy-body-in-chief, Mrs Bowles across the lane at The Laurels, to see the smoke and decide to investigate, to come and see what was burning, to 'pop over just to check everything was okay' – because autumn or winter was the proper time for a bonfire, not the middle of June. Not the middle of the breeding season. Only a barbarian would cut back and burn vegetation while birds might still be nesting in it.

But it had to be a bonfire.

She could hardly dump a binbag of blood-soaked clothing in the charity recycling bank at the village hall. Or in their own or a neighbour's wheelie bin. The police were unlikely to devote much in the way of resources to the investigation, but she couldn't count on them being slack enough to neglect the basics.

If she'd had a bit more time she could have jumped

in the car and driven thirty miles and left the bag in a random bin no one was going to search.

But she had no time.

And complete incineration was the safest option.

She wanted to know that it was gone. That all trace of what she had done was gone. Maybe then she could get into the mindset of the person she needed to be when the police got here, like an actor, a method actor inhabiting her role so completely that she almost believed it herself, almost believed that she was just a poor traumatised soul who was as bewildered by the whole thing as anyone else.

The traumatised bit was going to be easy enough.

Her hands were shaking so much that she dropped the matchbox into the tangle of sticks and logs that she'd built up and had to rootle around in them to retrieve it. Striking a match was the next challenge, but she managed it, she managed to hold the wavering flame to the scrunched-up newspaper until it caught and flared.

Only when the fire was roaring away, the centre glowing orange with a heat so fierce that she had to stand back from it, did she throw on the first of the garments.

The saturated T-shirt.

It smouldered for a while, damping down the flames under it, sending streams of billowy white smoke up over the yew hedge that screened this workaday part of the garden from the lawns and the house. Then, when the moisture had evaporated off, the material caught and started to char, permeating the air with the aroma –

She staggered away from the fire, bile rising as, in a vain attempt to dislodge the smoke trapped there, she forced a long breath out through her nose.

But then she had to breathe in again and *oh God*.

Yes.

What she was breathing, what she was tasting at the back of her throat, was the savoury aroma of a summer barbeque.

She couldn't do this.

She just couldn't.

She had to get away from the smoke so she ran, she ran down the shadowed path between the woodshed and the hedge, feet pounding on the damp, moss-slick packed earth –

And straight into the person standing there, quite still, in the gloom.

The person standing there, silent and wide-eyed.

CHAPTER 1

Oliver Oliver Oliver.

Her feet seemed to beat out his name on the road as a sort of invocation, a prayer, an entreaty to whatever gods there may be, whatever forces for good there may be that had the power to keep him safe.

Oliver Oliver Oliver as she ran through the dark, through the funnels of light under the streetlamps that illuminated, briefly, the rain that stung her face and hands, as she ran through the foaming sea that crashed onto the road, flung against her by a wind so strong it was like a solid thing, a thing she had to push through, breathe against, somehow.

Let him be safe.

Let him be there.

Let him be safe as she ran past all the empty blank windows of the empty cottages to the one she needed, the one where he must be.

Oh please.

Oliver.

It was so narrow, the pend between the fisherfolk's cottages, that she could almost have reached out and touched the wall of Evie's house and the wall of the house opposite at the same time. In the shelter of the buildings, in this shelter from the storm – *please let this be his shelter from the storm* – it was possible, finally, to breathe.

She filled her lungs and she shouted:

'*Evie!*'

She tried to put her finger on the doorbell but her hand was shaking so much it slipped off the little plastic nub and she had to hold that hand with the other one, she had to *focus focus* on pressing that white plastic nub and she was still shouting and why was it so dark in there? And *please please Oliver.*

Why weren't there any lights in the windows?

She banged on the door and she kept shouting her sister's name.

'*Evieeeee!*'

Where was Evie?

Why would she have taken Oliver? Without even *telling her*?

A widening triangle of yellow light shone on the rain as a door opened but not Evie's, it was the door of the next cottage and it wasn't her own face looking back at her, it wasn't her own twin's face, it was an old woman, it was Margaret who lived next door and

'*Where's Evie?*' Sarah shouted into her saggy face and Margaret just stared at her, she stared and then she shook her head and said something but Sarah didn't know what she was saying, there was too much noise from the wind and the crashing sea and Margaret was standing back inside her house and

'*Oliver!*' she shouted and '*Oliver's missing!*' and

'Who?' said Margaret with a funny pursed-up face and

'*Oliver!*' and

'Who's Oliver?' said Margaret and

Oh God and 'My son, my *son!*' and please let Margaret not have dementia, surely Evie would have said if she had, but Sarah hadn't seen Margaret for months – no, *years* – so this was possible, this could be, because sometimes Evie didn't tell her things she thought might upset her but

The stupid old bitch!

It wasn't her fault, she knew it wasn't poor Margaret's fault, with her staring eyes, her frightened eyes but

'My son!' She pushed the words out. 'You know – my son – you know – *Oliver!* He's *missing!* I just – checked. His cot. *He's gone* – someone's *taken* –' She dived at the closing door but she was too late, the old woman had slammed it and when Sarah tried the door handle and pushed she met the resistance of a lock, the bitch, didn't she *care*, didn't she *care* that *a little boy was missing*? That Oliver was *gone*? He was out here somewhere –

And suddenly she couldn't move, she couldn't do anything but stare at the locked door. There was a tightness in her chest, as if her lungs were shrinking and shrinking and every time she breathed out they shrank a little bit more. Soon she could only get sips of air, tiny sips, before her tiny shrunken lungs pushed it back out again.

Oliver.

She shut her eyes and made herself *not* breathe. Made her lungs be still, as Evie had taught her.

Oliver loved being outside.

He wasn't afraid.

It wouldn't even occur to him to be afraid.

She heaved in a breath.

The sun is coming out to play...

When he was born, when Evie had seen him for the first time, she'd whispered, 'Rah-Bee!' – the twins' childhood codename for Sarah, Sarah Booth, Sarah B., Rah-Bee – 'Rah-Bee, he looks exactly like the sun in Teletubbies! You know, the sun with the baby's face in it!' Evie had started watching children's TV, even before Oliver was born, to select the programmes she thought would be suitable for a child prodigy, which of course he was going to be. Oliver's red little newborn scrunched-up face didn't really look like that Teletubbies baby, or, indeed, any kind of prodigy, but that was where it had started, with Evie saying that.

'The sun is coming out to play,' Sarah would warble at him whenever they were going outside to the garden. '*Hello* Mr Sun, how are you *today*!' And she'd pop a sunhat on Ollie's head or, in cold weather, bundle him up in lots of cosy layers and a woolly hat and a hood until he looked like an adorable little maggot.

And as he'd got bigger, as soon as she started to hum it, Oliver would stop whatever he was doing and start squirming in time, his head rocking comically from side to side, his arms held out with his little palms turned upwards as if he was holding a giant invisible ball. Sometimes he would smile like the Teletubby baby, but mostly it was a serious business, his sun dance. Lately he'd begun trying to sing along –

Oliver.

Where are you?

He couldn't have somehow wandered off himself, could he? She couldn't have somehow left the doors unlocked and he'd managed to get out of his cot and stomped down the corridor and into the hall and through the atrium and out on his little sturdy legs, out into the dark and the storm, his high voice happily burbling:

'Sun as cowin *ow* an pay!'

His tiny chubby palms lifted to the storm –

No no no, she had locked both doors, of course she had, she always locked them, she'd had to *un*lock them to leave the house –

And she could feel herself, now, slipping inside her head, slipping down, like she hadn't since the night Oliver had been conceived. And she wanted to squat there on the streaming wet concrete where a brave winter weed was peeping from a crack and she wanted to put her arms over her soaking hair and push her face into her knees –

No.

She had to find him.

She had to be stronger for him now than she'd ever been.

Oh, *Evie!* She needed *Evie*, or *someone* at least, but in the winter there was no one here, all the holiday people had gone and there was only Evie and stupid old bitch Margaret and

Lewis!

There was *Lewis*, he was a *doctor* and he was kind, he'd know what to do, he'd know how to find Oliver!

Sarah ran.

She ran back down the pend to the road and the harbour and she remembered that Lewis's house was the last one of all, the one right at the end of the road where it stopped because there was just the long line of the rocky shore and the sea after that.

'*I'm coming!*' she sobbed aloud. '*Mummin's coming!*'

She ran into the wind, into the storm.

Lewis. Lewis would help her.

The little harbour was invisible in the dark beyond the streetlamps, but she could hear the sea sucking and crashing, she could taste it on her lips, she could feel it on her head, like a big cold wet blanket someone kept throwing over her, pressing down her hair, pressing her soaked sweatshirt down onto her shoulders and her back.

'*Lewis!*' she shouted, stupidly, because how could he hear her, inside his house?

Lewis's cottage faced the sea, not like the others, the others that had their shoulders to the weather, as Evie put it. Lewis's house had its garden in front of it – sea, road, garden, house – and Sarah had to open the little gate, hands stupid and fumbling, to get in.

There were lights on inside, the windows a welcoming orange glow.

Lewis must be here!

She banged on the door, she banged the iron knocker until the door opened and Lewis was standing there saying, 'My God! Sarah!' and 'Come in, come in!' and she was shaking so much she couldn't speak, she could hardly move, she moved like an old woman into his narrow hallway and then she was able to say it:

'Oliver is missing.'

'You're soaked to the skin!' He led her down the hall, guiding her into his sitting room, where the wood-burning stove was roaring and big round copper table lamps glowed.

The warmth enveloped her but she couldn't sink down into it, she had to tell him:

'I think – Evie's – taken him. But I can't – find her either. Not answering her phone.' She felt so tired she could hardly think, she could hardly get the words from her brain to her lips. 'We need to call the police.'

He was very tall, Lewis. Very good-looking, very

alpha. She remembered boys like him at school who had had everything, who were handsome and funny and nice and clever, who were destined for careers in medicine or law, who were almost like a different species from the rest of them –

'Police,' she managed.

'Okay. I'll call the police. You get warm. I'll get you a towel and some dry clothes –'

'No, *now*. Call them! *Please!* He's... He's not even two years old!' Her jaw spasmed. 'Evie... Maybe it's not – Evie... Why would she take him without telling me? He was in his cot. Sleeping. When – I went to check – after supper – *he wasn't there!*'

Lewis frowned. 'I'm sure there's a simple explanation, but yes, okay, I'll call the police right now.' He shook his head at her, his handsome face full of concern. 'Come here.'

He folded her into his arms, rubbing her back, murmuring, 'It'll be all right.' His voice was a little bit nasal, like he permanently had a cold. 'We'll sort this out. Don't worry, Sarah. Don't worry.'

As she slumped against him, against the solid warmth of him, she felt the spinning in her brain slow, the feeling of vertigo, of falling down and down to a place she couldn't get back up from for anything, not even her own child... she felt it all recede until she was able to take a deep breath, and pull away, and thank him quietly.

And then he was gone, and Sarah stood in front of the stove, mesmerised by the dancing flames and dripping onto the colourful ethnic rug, all oranges and browns and greens and yellows, that he'd probably bought in Kathmandu on a trip that was more like an ordeal than a holiday.

He was back more quickly than seemed possible.

'Did you call them?'

'Yes. They'll be here soon.' He dropped a large towel and bundle of clothes onto the sofa. 'A bit big for you, but you can roll up the sleeves and the legs.'

'Thank you,' was all she could say.

He left the room while she dried herself off and changed into the soft grey joggers, black T-shirt and multicoloured, slightly oily-smelling woolly jumper, which had probably been knitted from yak wool in a hill village in Mongolia. They were all much too big.

And suddenly she wanted to pull off these warm dry clothes and wriggle back into her cold wet ones, because how could she be nice and safe and warm while Oliver –

Oliver was out there –

Maybe alone –

Maybe freezing cold and wet and terrified –

And not understanding why Mummin didn't come.

'Are you decent?' said Lewis from behind the door.

'Yes.'

He came in and made her sit down on the sofa with him, and he put his arm round her and rubbed at her shoulder.

'The police –' she got out.

'On their way.'

They would search for him, wouldn't they?

A little boy missing would be their very top priority.

They could probably use Evie's phone to find her. They could track people's locations using their phones, couldn't they? Maybe Lewis was right and there was a simple explanation – maybe Evie had taken him for some reason and left Sarah a note but Sarah had been too panicked to see it –

But why would Evie do that? Why leave a note, when she knew that Sarah was *right there in the house*?

'Someone – I've been thinking... Someone could have

got a la-ladder...' She stuttered on the word – 'They could have used a *ladder* to get onto the roof, and pulled it up, and lowered it down into one of the courtyards, and climbed down and got in that way – I often don't lock the sliding glass doors into the courtyards, which is so stupid, I know, but they're secure, they're safe, that's what I thought. The house is *safe*...'

It had always felt safe, with its blank outer walls and its internal courtyard gardens, onto which all the rooms faced. A modern take on a Roman villa; that had been her 'vision', as Evie called it.

'I think that's pretty unlikely, don't you?' said Lewis gently.

He was rubbing comforting circles on her shoulder with his thumb, and it felt so nice, but she didn't want to be comforted. She pulled away from him, and in the same moment the doorbell jangled.

Lewis stood. 'They've made good time. You wait here in the warm, Sarah, and I'll bring them through.' He left the room and closed the door behind him.

She sat on the sofa for three seconds.

She couldn't sit.

She went to the door and opened it and she could hear their voices and smell the drift of wet salty air, and she could hear Lewis saying, '....remitting/relapsing delusional disorder. She's also severely agoraphobic. She's very confused.'

'You're her GP, sir, is that right?' It was a woman's brisk voice.

'Yes. Dr Lewis Gibson – here's my photocard ID. I'm going to have to authorise an emergency detention, I'm afraid, under Section Two of the Mental Health Act. I'll come with you to the hospital – to Marnoch Brae. We can do the paperwork there.'

'And social services?' This was a man's voice, deep and calm.

'Yes, I've called them. An AMHP – an approved mental health professional – will meet us there.'

'Will she require restraint?'

Sarah barrelled into the hall, she barrelled past Lewis, she grabbed the woman in her bulky black uniform and she screamed at her: 'My eighteen-month-old son is *missing*! I don't need you to take me to a *hospital*! I need you to *find my son*! My *child* who's *missing*! Who's been *taken*!'

From behind her: 'She doesn't have a child,' said Lewis.

Sarah stared into the policewoman's carefully blank face.

Had she heard that right?

Or had she imagined it?

When she turned, when she rounded on him, when she said 'What?' he repeated it, over her head:

'She doesn't have a child.'

And now he looked down at her, his handsome face full of sympathy and understanding and pity.

Why was he saying that?

'Of course I have a child! Lewis! What –'

'Sarah.' He reached for her arm but she pulled away, she backed away, she turned to the policewoman.

'I have an eighteen-month-old son and his name's Oliver, Oliver Booth, and he's disappeared! I don't know why he would say –'

'All right, Sarah,' said the woman, finally, looking at Lewis. 'Does she have shoes?'

Sarah ran.

She ran the other way, into the kitchen, making for the back door, but she could hear them behind her, the policeman saying, 'This isn't helping anyone, is it?' and she felt herself grabbed from behind and then she was *smack* down on the floor, her face pressed to the wood-effect vinyl, her arms yanked up behind her back, cold metal handcuffs snapping on her wrists.

DOWNLOAD The Child Who Never Was TO
CONTINUE READING

WE HOPE YOU ENJOYED THIS BOOK

If you could spend a moment to write an honest review, no matter how short, we would be extremely grateful. They really do help readers discover new authors.

Leave a Review

And feel free to connect with Jane at the following places…she'd love to hear from you!

www.janerenshaw.co.uk

FROM JANE

Thank you very much for reading *No Place Like Home*.

It was a new challenge for me to write a whole story from a male point of view, but I loved spending time in Bram's head – he was in touch with his feminine side, which made it a bit easier! This one was tricky for me, though, in terms of plotting, and would never have seen the light of day if it hadn't been for Brian Lynch's expert guidance and help with all aspects of the plot.

I must also thank Brian's colleagues at Inkubator Books for all their work in preparing the book for publication and giving it the best chance of being read out there in the world. Thanks in particular to Sara J. Henry and Shirley Khan for their detailed editing of the manuscript and to Garret Ryan for working his magic on the marketing side.

For encouragement and support of my writing efforts generally, many thanks to my mum Grace and sister Anne, Auntie Witty, cousins Barbara, Catherine, Mary and Morag, and friends Adam and Ali Campbell, Maria Davie, Jocelyn Foster, Abi Grist and Helen Ure. As ever, my writing friends Lesley McLaren and Lucy Lawrie were always at the end of an email to provide any help needed as well as the welcome distractions of non-writing-related chat and fun. Thank you all!

ALSO BY JANE RENSHAW

INKUBATOR TITLES

THE CHILD WHO NEVER WAS

WATCH OVER ME

JANE'S OTHER TITLES

THE TIME AND PLACE

THE SWEETEST POISON

Published by Inkubator Books
www.inkubatorbooks.com

Printed in Great Britain
by Amazon